A Thousand Salt Kisses

A Thousand Salt Kisses

Josie Demuth

Wise Ink Creative
Publishing
Minneapolis

ISBN 13: 978-1-63489-919-2

eISBN 13: 978-1-63489-918-5

Library of Congress Catalog Number: 2016937787

First Printing: 2016

Wise Ink Creative Publishing

837 Glenwood Ave.

Minneapolis, MN 55405

www.wiseinkpub.com

My mother used to dream about gemstones every night when she was pregnant with me. Pink ones, blue ones, purple, green, and white. That's why I was called Crystal. Crystal Sarah White.

Chapter One

The party was in full swing, and I sat beside Rosie, roasting by a giant bonfire on the beach. We had taken off our shoes and sunk our bare feet into the hot sand, warmed by the flames that licked at it.

There were a surprisingly large number of people for tiny, remote Coney Bay. There were also a lot of interesting people that I'd never seen before, not here on the mainland and certainly not on Starfish, the isle on which I lived.

Three young guys with dreads were banging on drums while a troupe of fire jugglers spread out amongst the party-goers. They chucked flames to one another over peoples' heads before quickly sweeping them up into the orange circles, which rotated around their upper bodies.

I had watched on transfixed for the first half an hour as I sipped my beer. The smell of paraffin had been intense, but I kind of liked it.

I had not felt the slightest tinge of excitement since my move to Starfish a couple of months ago. It had been filled with long, lonely days spent roaming aimlessly around the island, wishing I could return to London, my hometown. I was grateful to my school friend Rosie for taking me under her wing this past month. It had truly helped in brightening up my new life.

Now Rosie leaned in, pushing her glossy dark hair back behind her ear. She had such a pretty face—big, brown doe eyes and hundreds of freckles. "You see Crystal, all the hot surfers come out of the woodwork this time of year."

"Yes," I agreed, looking around.

"I bet they fancy you," said Rosie, her eyes sparkling. "All the guys at school do." I smiled awkwardly, but she continued. "They all think you're so cool, with your long hair and nose-ring."

My fingers trailed over the little ring in my nose. My friend Jess had done it last summer with a drawing pin and a can of athlete's foot freeze spray. I bit my lip as I remembered the whole experience. It had not been pretty, and my parents had gone totally ballistic. "I'm lucky to still have a nose," I said to Rosie, remembering the aftermath.

She laughed. I had told her all about the botched up job at the pub last week. "You city people are so much more fun than us," she said.

"Hmm, I don't know about that," I said, looking around. "This is a pretty good party."

"Yes," sighed Rosie, "It is." She nodded subtly to her right, where Will Destouches sat. "By the way, I have been in love with him since I was thirteen, and he was like, nineteen," she said in a hushed voice. I strained closer towards her so that I could hear over the noise. "Obviously, he didn't look twice at me back then—because that would be weird, but he just said we should go for a drink ... I think he meant just the two of us, but I'm not sure."

I looked at her with surprise, more preoccupied with the maths than anything. "He's that old?" I hissed. "Twenty-three?"

"Yes," said Rosie. "Well, I always wanted an older man. I'm so tired of these school boys. And now that I've come into fruit ..."

I exploded into giggles. "Come into fruit?" I said eventually, looking at her in disbelief. Rosie had always come across as so prim and proper; I was really quite surprised by the way she was talking. In fact, I wondered if it was her in there, or the beer.

"Yes, I'm not quite as straight-laced as you think," she said as though she had read my mind.

"So I see," I said, biting my cheek and leaning forwards to steal a glance at Will. I had to admit, he was very good-looking with his tall, broad build and scruffy blonde hair. In the flickers of the firelight, I could see that he too had a face full of brown freckles—just like Rosie.

As I looked around, I realized, that at seventeen, we

were younger than a lot of these guys. I leaned back again and took a big gulp of my beer. There was definitely something interesting about the idea of an older, more experienced man.

Rosie had turned her attentions to Will, and I looked down towards the sea, tugging my short, tie-dye dress over my thighs. One woman blew flames from her mouth as she paddled. She cut an intriguing figure wading through the shallow waters in hot pants while exhaling huge flames. A small crowd surrounded her on the shore, cheering her on as she united the four elements.

It wasn't long before Rosie was entrenched in a deep conversation with Will. I noticed he kept putting his hand on her back as he spoke and leaned in close for her replies. I was now pretty sure he had meant the drink to be for just the two of them. I felt happy for her, even though I was now officially a third wheel. All I could see now was the back of Rosie's head, but I could tell she was gazing adoringly at him. I felt a small pinch of envy; she had liked Will for so long and now here they were, about to get it on.

I looked away, turning my attention back to the sea when I suddenly became aware that Will's friend Allan now beside me.

"Um, have you been allocated to me for the next hour?" I asked with an awkward laugh, glancing up at him. I could only assume Will had sent him to babysit while he chatted up my friend.

Allan looked at me with disbelief.

"Er, no!" he said before laughing. I smiled, relieved. "Completely the opposite actually."

Oh no, did he like me? I felt uneasy again. *As nice as Allan seemed, I was not remotely interested in him.*

"I take it you're not at school?" I said, in a lame attempt to keep the conversation running.

He looked at me stunned for a second before he threw back his head and laughed. "I know I'm not that big but ... school?"

I warmed to him right there and then. He had scruffy hair and these twinkly slanted eyes. He was indeed a little small, but he had this ... nice aura.

We began talking and the next hour shot by, in what seemed like minutes. He was twenty-five and owned a surf shop up the coast. By the time we had swapped life stories, I had drained two more beers and was feeling really quite merry.

"I like your ankle-thing," said Allan suddenly, putting his finger on the string of seashells that was tied loosely around my ankle. I looked down.

"Thanks, I got it here," I replied. It had been my first day in Coney Bay, and I had wandered up to one of the stalls that aligned the sea front. I had felt so lost that day, so far away from everything I knew. The anklet had been expensive—around twenty quid—but I had handed over the money in a daze.

I realized Allan's finger was lingering on my ankle and decided to change the subject rapidly.

"So, do you ever see anything strange when you're out surfing?" I asked crossing my legs and removing myself from his touch.

Allan laughed raucously again. I seemed to have this effect on him, but I was not trying to be funny. I had been warned of some "off-beat things" in the ocean by a fisherman from Starfish. The old man had mentioned it as we queued in the corner shop the other day, and it had been playing on my mind ever since.

"Well, I have seen some cod and mackerel out there in my time, a few boats—that was odd," said Allan, in answer to my question. "Oh yeah—oh, my God, once I saw a fisherman!"

I opened my mouth to protest, but it quickly spread into a smile. "Come on!" I laughed.

"Okay, like what?" he said, smirking.

"I don't know, this old guy on my island said that you can see some strange stuff around here," I said, my tone becoming serious again.

"Was he pissed?" asked Allan.

"Huh, no," I protested. "He wasn't drunk. I'm a little bit, though."

"Oh good, I've been waiting to take advantage of you," said Allan, raising an eyebrow at me.

"Eugh!" I shrieked, moving away.

Allan doubled over again. He had a deep, booming laugh for a man of his size.

"I was joking. I'm not that sleazy," he said leaning back onto the sand and holding up his hands.

"Good!" I said, relaxing again.

"You are gorgeous, though," said Allan, in a more sincere tone. "You know that, don't you?"

I felt uncomfortable all over again. Maybe I was weird, but I didn't like it when people mentioned my looks. At around fifteen years old, I had shocked everybody with an almost overnight transformation. My blonde hair had changed from a frizzy bush to silky waves, while my face went from round to shapely as all my puppy fat somehow disappeared.

I knew I should have been grateful, but the reaction had been quite hard to take. I hated all the prepubescent boys and their lame, pervy jokes, and I hated even more how this had alienated me from the other girls at school. I had become accustomed to exclusion, albeit at times subtle. The girls in my class would not laugh at my jokes or react to my attempts to make conversation with them so that I almost began to fear I was somehow inadequate, unfunny. I didn't know what it was, at first, but the few loyal friends I had kept insisted that it was envy. I felt depressed but then guilty. I had been blessed with these good looks, but yet I here I was near resenting them.

I felt that dizziness of awkwardness, as Alan waited for my answer. *What to do, what to say ...?*

Fortunately, Will cut in.

"Hey guys, how's it going?"

"We're good," I replied brightly, looking over at them.

"I just realized we've been—" Will began.

"All over each other?" Allan cut in.

We both laughed, and Will looked at us sheepishly.

"Let me give you your friend back," Will said to me, getting up. He put a hand on Rosie's shoulder as he passed her and then sprang into action jumping on top of Allan, wrestling him to the ground. A couple of their other friends now joined in, and I turned to Rosie, glad to be reunited.

I handed her another can of lager.

"How's it going?" I whispered, eager to know all about her budding romance.

"I'm going to marry him," slurred Rosie.

I looked at her face and could see her eyes were completely glazed over.

"Babes, you're wasted!" I hissed, snatching the beer back. "What the hell?"

Rosie suddenly threw her arms around me.

"I love you!" she said, hanging from my shoulders. I hunched forward from the weight and somehow managed to turn my head to the left. The men had not seen. They were too busy joking with each other. I stuck my hand in my bag and rummaged around for some water for Rosie.

Suddenly I heard thumping in the sand and people started running towards the sea, tearing off their clothes as they went.

As I watched on my heart began to race. Had someone drowned?

Suddenly Allan got up and howled out into the night like a wolf. I jumped, my beer sloshing everywhere. *What the frig was he doing?*

His friends laughed too before standing up one by one and joining in. The next thing I knew they had ripped off their t-shirts and were racing alongside the others towards the sea.

Will came up behind us and scooped Rosie in his arms. "Huh, what are you doing?" I squeaked, looking up at her limp body.

But Will had not heard, and before I could stop them, they too sped off towards the waters.

"Swim time!" I heard him holler.

Chapter Two

"Rosie!" I shouted running to the water's edge.

People were jumping into the sea in their underwear. It was carnage.

I was in a panic. *Will obviously didn't realize how drunk Rosie was. What if he dragged her out deep and lost her?*

I charged into the water until I was waist-deep and then I felt how cold it was.

"Bloody hell," I yelped.

I looked around me. I could not see her anywhere. I searched for Will and Allan, but all I could see were strangers.

"Oi sexy, I'd like to see that dress a little wetter," a man shouted at me from a group to my left while emptying a bottle of wine down his throat.

There a big splash as the lady next to him, presumably his girlfriend, lifted her arm and slapped him.

I shuddered. These older men were turning out to be just as gross as my peers.

I could not even dignify the comment with a response—I had to find Rosie. I threw myself to the right just before a wave came rolling in. It pinned me down for a minute as it travelled over me and then I was able to surface. I swam past the partygoers looking desperately for my friend's face in the moonlight.

As I swam further, I realized the water must be getting quite deep, but the party had spread so far out that I had no choice but to keep going and keep searching.

Eventually, the crowd began to thin, and just a few figures bounced ahead in the waves. I strained my eyes to see if any of them were Rosie, but a wave rose every time, splashing me in the face. I swam a little further, but an uneasy feeling was beginning to wash over me. I was too far out.

I was sobering up, and logic was beginning to get a grip on me. Rosie would never have made it out this far in her state, I realized.

I turned and gasped. As I looked back to shore, everything appeared so dark, so far away. I could see the bonfire, but it looked tiny from here, like the flame from a lighter. I saw some little orange flickers around it—the fire jugglers. The current must have pulled me out further than I could swim.

I started to swim towards the lights, but there was a

force pulling me back out and away. It was as if I was on a treadmill; I was going nowhere.

"Oh, God," I gasped, paddling desperately. *What had I done?*

Ideas began to race through my mind. *I could get swept out into open water and die. What if a shark got me? There were basking sharks out here on the southwest coast—the ones with the big gaping vacuum mouths. I could get sucked up easily. Maybe that was even what was pulling me!*

I began to cry. All I could think of was my mum and dad. I was an only child, and they would be devastated if anything happened to me. I couldn't bear the thought. I had to get back to shore.

"Help!" I quivered into the night.

Maybe the other guys out ahead would help me. I strained my neck over the waves. I made a real effort, this time, gave it all I had. I arched my back and peered as high as my body would allow me.

This time I saw clearly two spherical plastic shapes glinting under the moon. Buoys.

That was what I had chased out here!

I cursed myself. I was an idiot.

"Hey," said a voice softly behind me. I immediately felt relief. I was not alone in my peril. I could at least share my last moments with another person.

I felt gentle hands on my shoulders, and I slowly turned around.

I could not see too much of the man, except for the

lower parts of his face the moon illuminated. He had a strong jaw and shoulder-length dark hair, which appeared to stop around broad shoulders.

"Are you okay?" he asked. His voice was so calm; he was clearly fine with being dragged out to sea.

"We're stuck!" I cried. *What was wrong with him?*

He reached out and placed his hands on the outside of my upper arms, steadying me in the waves.

"No, we're not," he said. "You just got a bit nervous."

"Nervous?" I yelped. We were about to die.

And then I was hit by another stroke of paranoia.

"You were watching me?" I whispered. *He was a psycho, waiting in the waves. Now I was going to be killed by him instead of a current or shark.*

"For a little while," he said soothingly, wrapping his right arm around my waist and extending the left out into the water. "Let's go back," he said.

I allowed him to pull me along, now rendered speechless. I had felt so helpless out here, but the stranger carried me swiftly over the waves that I had been unable to conquer, his arm sliced confidently through the waters I thought would take my life. I looked up at the sky as we travelled. It was a clear night, and every star was out. The moon was near full, and watched over us, giving us light in our moment of need.

Soon we were close to the beach again. The fire, no longer a little flame, cast an orange glow onto our faces. We were now amongst the only few people left in the sea.

I looked at my rescuer properly as we stopped, still deep enough to tread water. He was watching my face too. I immediately looked away again.

Oh, my days, he was handsome!

He had these thick arched eyebrows and lively sparkling eyes. The color I could not make out, but they were friendly and intriguing. I instantly felt that these eyes had seen many things, stuff that I couldn't even imagine. Underneath his eyes were high cheekbones and then perfect big lips—the type you would just love to kiss.

I felt so embarrassed. *Could he feel me ogling over him? And who was this heroic stranger, anyway? How was I ever going to regain my cool after my crazed panic attack?*

"You were very far out," he reassured me. It was as though he sensed my humiliation. I bit my lip and nodded. I noticed he had tattoos on his chest and arms. I could not make out the details, but it appeared to be symbols and letterings. I squinted, peering closer. Perhaps they were words in another language. I could not be sure in this light.

"Yeah, well, so were you thank goodness," I replied finally.

He smiled. "You were at the party?" he asked, in that tranquil voice. He swam close to me; we were a couple of inches apart.

"Yes," I said staring to the right at the waves that lapped at my arm. "Yep, I was here."

"You were having fun?" he asked, an eyebrow raised.

"Yeah, until my friend's boyfriend took her into the sea.

She was so drunk. I was trying to find her," I said remembering Rosie and beginning to worry all over again.

"I think I saw her if she is the girl with long dark hair. Her mate took her back."

"Oh thank heavens for that," I breathed. I felt so relieved that I did not question his peculiar reference to Will.

His fingers touched my cheek and lifted up my face so that his gaze met mine. At first, I blinked taken aback, but when I looked into his eyes, I was overcome by intrigue.

Again, I got the sense that he was very wise. He had experienced all kinds of things—beautiful things, heart-breaking things, incredible things.

Why the hell was I thinking all this stuff? This was weird.

"You are quite curious, aren't you?" said my stranger. His hand now trailed down to my shoulder.

"Well, I've never been rescued before," I explained guiltily, looking away. "I'm from London. I think the closest thing was when this kid mugged me down an alley, and then his friend came to find me with the SIM card from my phone ... and so you know, I got all my numbers back."

He frowned, looking lost for a moment.

"Oh, don't worry," I said dismissively. "You're probably too country for all of that ..."

"Country?" he replied. I saw again, a flicker of confusion.

"Well, are you?" I said, confused that he was confused. *Was he foreign, maybe?*

"What's your name?" he asked, not answering my question.

"Crystal," I replied, looking up at him again.

"Wow, that's a really wonderful name," he said. He seemed genuinely impressed. "It suits you."

"Thank you," I replied. I was grateful that it was dark, and he could not see me blush, but as I looked up, I saw he was smiling at me.

I relaxed a little, and this time, our eyes stayed locked.

"What's your name?" I asked.

"Llyr," he replied.

I frowned. I had never heard that name before.

"Yeah?" I asked skeptically. "Where is that from?"

"Oh, it's an old, old name," he replied smiling.

He reached into the water and took my hands, and I watched dumbstruck as he moved in closer, so that our bodies almost pressed together. A million butterflies danced in my stomach, as I felt an intense attraction sweep through me. I swear the whole world simply melted around us.

"Crystal," a voice boomed over the waters.

I looked backward, now a little dazed, and could see one of Will's friends waving at me from the shore.

Rosie.

"I should probably go see him," I said looking at Llyr.

He nodded, and I eased my hands away from his gentle hold, turning and beginning to swim back to the beach.

"Hey!" I shouted at Will's friend. I tried to remember his name as I swam.

I lowered my legs and felt the sand beneath. I was now knee-deep and began to wade towards him—my dress now drenched and heavy as a rock. I squeezed out the water as I walked.

"Is Rosie okay?" I asked.

"She's pretty drunk. She's thrown up a few times."

"Oh no," I cried, cringing for her. *She would be so embarrassed tomorrow.* "I need to call a cab and get her home."

"Uh-huh," he said, looking at me strangely. "What were you doing anyway?"

"Oh," I laughed, remembering my escapades. "I swam out too far. I seriously thought I was going to die, and then Llyr here brought me back ..."

I trailed off as I turned and saw only the black sea behind me. He had gone.

I walked quickly up the beach behind Will's friend whose name, it turned out, was Frank.

Frank led me up to a car park where the party now seemed to have relocated. We walked across the black tarmac floor, weaving between hundreds of caravans.

Someone had set up a sound system somewhere between the vans because music was pumping and people were dancing. The vans were lit up from within, and as I passed, I could see people drinking around the little tables inside.

We finally came to the end of the car park, and I began to hear a retching. *Oh dear Lord, was that Rosie? If it was, then how could she possibly get that drunk on a few beers?*

Sadly enough, I saw a little figure on all fours behind a van. And then I saw Will crouching next to her, holding back her hair.

"Oh Rosie," I cried dropping to my knees next to her. "What on earth happened?"

Will looked panicked. "I gave her some tequila just before I went to talk to Allan. I made her do five shots; I'm such a fucking idiot. She was fine and then ..." he trailed off as Rosie came up onto her knees.

"Hi, love," I said reassuringly.

She looked at me. Her usually radiant face was pale and clammy. I peeled away some hair that had become stuck to her face. She looked like the girl from the horror movie *The Ring*.

"Home," she managed to croak.

I nodded, "I will call a taxi. You can stay at mine."

I got up, and then I remembered. My shoes and bag were on the beach.

"Looking for these?" I spun around and saw Allan, holding my stuff in his hands.

"Amazing!" I cried, grabbing my bag and rummaging around for my phone.

I called the sea taxi, and as we stood there waiting, I thought about Llyr.

"So, I was out in the sea looking for you all, and I bumped into this guy ..." I began. "I was getting swept out, and he ... you know ... he rescued me." Allan raised his eyebrows at me, questioning, but from the way his lips pressed together, I could tell that he was jealous. I hesitated, but I had to find out more. "Do you guys know him? He had longish hair and he was called Llyr?"

"Er right, a long-haired person called Leah?" snorted Allan. "Are you sure it was a bloke?"

"Yes, I'm sure," I replied coolly. "It's LLYR," I said rolling the 'R,' just like he had done. "Not Leah."

Did he think he owned me or something?

"Anyway, anyone know of him?" I checked.

Will shook his head, "No, sorry Crystal."

All of their other friends shook their heads. I was baffled. *Where had he gone, and who was he?*

Chapter Three

The following morning I watched a very hungover Rosie sit at my breakfast table wearing my diamanté sunglasses. She brought the spoon of Coco Pops closer to her mouth and then gagged.

"I can't."

She pushed the bowl away and rested her head in her arms.

"My life is over," she said miserably.

"No!" I cried. "It was just one night. Who cares?"

"Will cares. I care," she sniffed.

"Well, Will only cares because he likes you and he was worried about you. He seemed devastated," I reassured Rosie, reaching across the table and putting a hand on her arm.

"Yeah, so why hasn't he written back?" she mumbled.

Rosie had sent an embarrassed, apologetic text as soon as she woke up.

"It's ten a.m.," I offered.

"Yeah. Okay."

We sat silently for five seconds before she erupted all over again.

"Oh my God!"

I felt so bad for Rosie. I could see and feel her pain.

"Look, you threw up, Rose. Do you think you're the first person in the world to do that?"

"On a first date, yes."

"No, babes. I bet it happens all the time. In fact, I bet right now, this very second, someone is vomiting on a first date."

Rosie looked up at me hopefully, and the sunglasses slipped down her nose. She scrunched up her face at the bright June light, which flooded into the room.

I giggled and reached out, propping the sunglasses back up over her eyes.

"Now turn that frown upside down," I urged. Rosie smiled. "If he doesn't call again, we'll hatch a plan to make him really jealous," I continued.

Rosie looked at me hopefully, "Like what?"

"Like ..." I paused, scanning my brain for ideas. "Instagram loads of pictures of you and gorgeous men!

Rosie was smiling now, "We will make him sweat!"

I grinned, "Yes! Operation Sweat."

Rosie clapped her hands. "I love it!"

"Trust me, they do not like another man on their

territory," I continued, knowledgably. "Just look at Allan, and he only knew me an hour."

"I can't believe him!" screamed Rosie. "He got all jealous because you simply met another guy."

Now my mood took a dive as I thought of my bizarre sea-romance last night. "I had a real connection with that guy," I said.

"Yeah but you only met him for a little while," laughed Rosie, "less than Allan knew you!"

"That's what was so weird about it," I replied staring dreamily ahead. "It was like ..."

I bit my lip before I said the most nauseating thing in the world.

"What?" asked Rosie curiously, leaning her head to the side.

I sighed. "Oh, it doesn't matter. I'm still drunk."

The truth was I had never felt like this before about a man, and I felt like a complete fool. It was true what Rosie said—I barely knew him, or, coming to think of it, barely knew if he existed.

Rosie's phone beeped. She pounced on it like a famished cheetah upon its prey.

I looked at her, hopeful.

"It's my dad," she said glumly.

———

I had walked a distraught Rosie home across the island,

and now I stepped out of her house and into the warm sea air. Rosie had begged me to stay but it was a hot day and my Labrador, Maurice, was gagging to get back out again. Rosie lived on the east side of Starfish, which was the most populated area, namely as it was flatter and more habitable.

I let my chocolate-brown pet pull me past the seven vibrant houses that made up Rosie's street. Each one was a different color, and according to our neighbor Mrs. Hart, every house on the island was painted to stand out so that the fishermen could see their home when they sailed in. It was a nice thought.

Starfish was not far from the mainland at all, and on a clear day, you could see people wandering around the shore like colorful ants. It had a population of about two hundred and was shaped like the creature it was named after—a big round center with five slithers of land that jutted out into the ocean.

As far as I could make out, there was a bakery, fishmongers, church and corner shop. For everything else, you needed to go to the mainland, including school. My dad had bought a little red speedboat, and he dropped me off in Coney Bay every morning. He was happy as a sand-boy here while my mother had not been able to wrench herself away from the city yet.

As I made my way through the cobbled streets, I felt the inquisitive stare of the locals; they were still adjusting to a new face on the isle, it appeared. It was times like this I missed the anonymity of London.

A woman with a hunchback stood bent over her stick, looking up at me as I passed by. I smiled awkwardly and said "hello," trying not to shudder at her fierce widow's peak and beady little eyes.

"See anything out there yet?" came a voice from behind. He sat on a bench outside the fishmongers. I had been so perturbed by the woman that I had not noticed him.

"Hi," I smiled distractedly. It was the same fisherman I had met last week in the shop—the one who had mentioned the strange things in the sea. He was clearly quite preoccupied with the whole thing, I thought, as I paused and looked down at him. He had dark gray hair and a kindly but well-weathered face, like many of the fisher folk out here.

I wondered if he had dementia or something. Maurice tugged at the lead, and I bent down and unclipped him, letting him bound off onto the little beach below.

"Come on," he persisted. "You must have seen something by now."

"Do you mean strange like her?" I whispered, rolling my eyes in the direction of the woman with the hunchback. She was still watching me like a hawk.

He smiled. "Well, we locals can be quite unnerving, that's for sure."

"Tell me about it," I muttered as she shuffled past.

"I'm Crystal, by the way," I said, realizing we had not yet

done formal introductions. "Crystal White. I just moved here last month."

"Yes, I know your father," replied the man in his thick Westcountry twang.

"Oh," I said, raising my eyebrows. "Well, yes, I suppose the whole island must know Dad by now." He had been going around feverishly introducing himself to everybody. He was just so excited to be here.

The old man chuckled and pulled out a packet of cigarettes from his pocket. He held them out to me, and I giggled and shook my head firmly.

"He joined us just yesterday at the seamen's meeting," he continued, lighting up and exhaling a thick cloud of smoke.

I couldn't help but burst into laughter. "He spends a couple of weeks in a speed boat, and now he thinks he's a fisherman?" I giggled.

The old man smiled. "Well, he was very passionate about the issues we raised, especially with regards to the sea pollution. He even volunteered to go and represent us at the council."

"Ah yes, well he's your man for that," I said. "If you want anyone to represent you, it's Dad."

"Seems like a very smart man," he agreed.

"He was a top lawyer before he retired last month," I continued, proudly. "He took on a lot of cases to do with the environment."

"Yes, so he told us, kid," said the man, standing up

slowly. "It must be fate, you folk moving here. They're dumping more and more toxic around Coney."

I sighed. I never understood why some people were so intent on obliterating the planet. As my father's daughter, I had grown up hearing all about the dreadful things man did to nature.

"I'd better get going, but I forgot to ask your name?" I said.

"George," he said, stopping again and extending his hand.

"It's nice to meet you, George," I shook his hand.

"It was a pleasure. Now remember if you see anything funny, it's normal around here."

I frowned and waved goodbye, calling to Maurice, who was bouncing about in the waves. As we continued our walk home, I became curious again about the 'strange things' George spoke of. He didn't seem particularly batty during the last five minutes of our conversation. Maybe he was referring to the sea life. Well, as long as he didn't mean Great Whites. ... The papers were always going on about sightings off the southwest coast, but Dad had assured me that this was many miles out at sea. I really didn't know what else George could possibly mean. I needed to know more before my foghorn of an imagination began to fill in the blanks.

We crossed a little bridge to the west side of the isle—my side. It was much greener on the west, bearing luscious grass and trees, which thrived being so close to the water. However, the land was very hilly, which meant that there were just twenty houses over this side nestled into the level patches of land.

I lived on Lighthouse Lane, the reason being that astonishingly, it led to a lighthouse. It was annoying living so close to the tower as huge blinding flashes would keep me awake at night, even though the curtains. Dad said that when he bought the house, there was a big tree blocking its glare from the back of the house, but then they discovered it had a disease and had to cut it down, just before we moved.

Asides from the lighthouse, our new home was just gorgeous. We had a big beautiful garden with roses of every color. Inside we had three bedrooms and a big dome glass conservatory where we would eat dinner every night. Oh, but the best thing of all was the view from the back of the house that looked straight out onto the endless blue sea.

Chapter Four

I leaped in front of the door, blocking Maurice from coming into the house.

"No!" I squealed as I felt the wet bulk push against my legs. "Bad dog!"

I stood by the door exasperated, but suddenly he turned and then I felt his soaking tail pound against me as he stood wagging, ears cocked. The sound of an engine hummed from the back of the house.

Maurice barked and together we sprang into action, racing around the side of the house and across the back garden. When we came to the stone staircase at the bottom of the lawn, we saw a familiar little red boat pulling in.

Maurice leaped down the staircase in one big jump and bounded onto the jetty.

"Dad!" I shouted, laughing.

My dad was beaming from ear-to-ear, and I could see an

enormous mountain of shopping sitting inside the boat. He rigged it up and clambered onto the jetty.

Maurice promptly leaped all over his front, and Dad shouted as wet paw prints decorated the front of his cream linen trousers. I couldn't help but giggle.

"Hungry, Dad?" I said nodding at the shopping.

"Oh no, I'm having the Seal Society round for dinner," Dad replied chirpily. "Can you help me, darling?"

The Seal Society? He really was getting down with the whole sea life crew.

I hopped onto the boat.

"Er, Dad. If you're having the Seal Society round for dinner, does that mean you can't take me to the mainland later?"

I passed some bags up to him from the boat, and from below I noted that his tummy was getting larger by the day.

"Mainland? Why are you going there again?" said Dad, in his very British accent.

"Oh, I just wanted to go to the pub," I said, casually.

The truth of the matter was I wanted to take a stroll along the surfer's beach and see if I could find Llyr. I wanted to thank him for helping me but of course, I was also hoping we could hang out again.

"You have school tomorrow," he said, firmly.

"Yes," I said, "but I won't be late."

"Your mother is coming Friday. She will hit the roof if she knows I've been letting you out on a Sunday night."

"Yes, Dad, that's the whole point," I argued from the

boat. "We only have four more days left of freedom. Where I can go out ... and you can eat chocolate croissants!" I exclaimed, pulling out the giant bag of pastries from one of his bags. "Oh, Dad!" I cried. He was borderline diabetic, not to mention overweight.

Dad looked away sheepishly. "It's for the fellows tonight," he said.

"Who eats croissants in the evening?" I said.

Dad sighed. "I will pay for a sea taxi then," he said. "Just this once."

"Oh yay!" I cried, jumping up in the air and then tumbling backward as the boat rocked. I scrambled back to my feet unhurt, using the edge of the boat to push up against.

Dad frowned. "Are you alright?" he asked.

"Yes," I said. "Why?"

"You just seem very excited for a trip to the pub," he said.

Now it was my turn to be sheepish. "Oh, I'm just making some friends finally," I said, searching desperately for an exit point from this conversation. "By the way, Dad, you'd better do some sit-ups before Friday, you know?" I said, pointing to his tummy as I climbed out of the boat.

Dad squeezed my cheek with his fingers. "I've had enough of your cheek young woman!" he said with mock sternness.

"But I'm serious!" I protested linking his arm and

gesticulating out to the ocean. "If you lay on your back in the sea you could start your very own island!"

Dad raised an eyebrow and looked down at me. I could see he was semi-amused. "I'm going to have both of you on my back soon, I suppose."

I frowned, my mood dipping a little. Mum and Dad had not been getting on so well the past six months. It had all started around the time of Dad's retirement. She had become short and snappy with him, accusing him of being a layabout all the time. We had decided to move here a long time before then, but as the move neared, she had become more and more upset about it. I don't think she much liked the idea of growing old and leaving behind her glamorous city life.

"Well, more sit-ups, fewer croissants then, Dad," I said, covering up my concern.

The water sparkled emerald under the clear blue sky, and I leaned my head on Dad's shoulder, gazing at its beauty.

Dad laughed. "What am I thinking, anyway? She will be so mesmerized by the sea that she won't even notice anything else," he said.

———

The heavens had opened yesterday evening, crushing all my hopes of going back to the beach. I had initially cursed the skies as they turned black but today I decided it was probably for the best. I would have just ended up looking like a desperate stalker showing up on that beach on my own.

The bad weather had continued all through today, meaning Dad had not been able to take me to the mainland for school.

Of course, when Dad came into my bedroom in the morning to tell me that we would not be able to travel on the seas I had reclined back into bed triumphantly, believing that I was going to have a lovely lazy day off.

Unfortunately, it was no such luck. All Coney School pupils from Starfish Island were summoned to special classes in the church, led by one of the teachers who lived here—Mrs. Vendercum. I had been gutted. Mrs. Vendercum, the Maths teacher, was straight out of boot camp and cut us no slack what so ever.

It was now three p.m., and we were still in class. The only okay thing about it was that the age group was mixed, mainly with much younger kids, and so the lessons were a piece of piss. I had done the exercises in no time, and now I sat passing notes back and forth with Rosie.

HE STILL HASN'T CALLED

Rosie despaired in block capitals.

OP SWEAT

I replied, with a smiley face.

LMFAO

Rosie smiled gratefully and returned to her work.

I watched for a moment as she tapped slowly at her

calculator. The poor girl was so disturbed by her behavior on Saturday night that she had not even completed the first few tasks.

But she wasn't the only person in the room distracted by a man. Although I was slightly more compos mentis than Rosie today, I would almost immediately find myself daydreaming about Llyr at any opportunity.

I fantasized about finding him again. Maybe I would bump into him at another party. He might be juggling some fire or hanging out by a van playing guitar. Maybe he was a surfer too; it seemed to be that kind of party. Perhaps that was why he had been such a good swimmer.

Maybe one day I would walk into a beach bar in another town, and he would be sitting at a table having a drink. He would probably be wearing just shorts and would look super gorgeous with his tattooed muscles. We would stare across the room not quite believing that we had found each other again ...

And then I remembered. He could have seen me again. He could easily have followed me onto the beach and asked for my number. *So why didn't he? Was he was annoyed I just left him like that, after he rescued me? No, he seemed decent, and he had understood that I was worried about my friend. Did I say something to offend him? No, he had seemed into me right up to the end, taking my hands and looking deep into my eyes. So what the hell?*

It was all a total mystery.

I sighed and flicked through a local paper that had been left on the desk.

BLAZE AT OFFICE KILLS FOUR

I read the headline slowly, my frown deepening as I continued through the article. A father of four had been amongst the victims, trapped in the building with the fire. I shuddered. I would die if anything like that happened to my dad.

"Crystal, are you bored with Maths?" barked Mrs. Vendercum. "There's some rather complex trigonometry I could teach you? You could even stay behind after class, for some extra tuition."

I dropped the paper on the floor and smiled sweetly. "That's alright," I said, picking up my pen and pretending to frown at my notebook.

But it wasn't long before my thoughts returned to my night in the sea.

Chapter Five

The thunderstorms had continued for a couple of days. It was the end of May, but they had been relentless and very intense.

On Thursday evening, I went to the Seaman's Lodge. The weather appeared to have settled slightly, and the lodge was just around the corner from the church. I had been able to walk over in the rain when we had finally been dismissed from class.

There was some kind of meeting which Dad had called. I thought I would go and watch him in action, seeing as I had nothing else to do.

It was a small wooden building just down by the fishing sheds. These sheds were nestled between the two lower limbs of the starfish-shaped isle, furthest away from the mainland. It was the 'gateway to the ocean.'

I lowered my little red umbrella and stepped inside, immediately greeted by the smell of dry wood. I imagined the waves must have thrashed over the hut during the storms, but the interior appeared nice and waterless—a safe house.

I saw Dad in the corner of the crowded room. He appeared deep in conversation, and so I left him to it.

I circled the room instead. It was a cozy little hut, brightly lit and decorated with maps and lots of black and white photographs of the fisher folk with their catches. I examined one of the pictures.

"Found me?" said a cheery voice from behind.

I turned and found George standing behind me with a mug in his hand.

I laughed and pointed towards the jolly face in the forefront of a picture. Here, he had a cigarette in one hand and a humongous fish in the other.

"That was Sylvester," he said pointing at the catch.

"Well, Sylvester was a biggun!" I joked.

"Sylvester nearly broke the scales."

I laughed. *I really liked George, I decided. There was something so fun and relaxing about his company.* "Oh, where'd you get that cuppa?" I asked, nodding at his mug. "I could murder a tea right now."

"Ain't no brew, my darling."

I peered into the mug, and a strong smell of liquor shot up my nostrils. George offered me the mug—which was full to the brim—but I shook my head. I was not too fond of spirits, especially after seeing Rosie the other night.

"Okay, let's get down to business," I heard Dad shout out. He saw me from across the room. "Hello, darling."

Everybody turned and looked at me with curiosity. I had to stop myself from grimacing. They all looked so haggard, and their skin thick and rough. These faces were well-weathered from decades out at sea.

"Hi, Dad," I said awkwardly, lifting my hand.

I made a mental note to moisturize more regularly, as I too would be spending a lot of time in the foreseeable future whizzing about on Dad's boat. I did not want to end up with skin that I could file my nails on.

We all settled around a long table.

"Now," began Dad, putting on his glasses and passing around pieces of paper, "I've been speaking with the council with regards to SKANX."

The fishermen all leaned in. I could sense that this was a topic of great interest.

What the hell was SKANX?

I looked at the piece of paper in my hands.

SKANX: *The Facts So Far* read the bold letters.

"Now, they have clarified to me, under the Freedom of Information Act that the containers being dumped out at sea by SKANX, have indeed been leaking."

One fisherman banged his tattooed arm angrily on the table. I jumped.

The room became awash with noise. The fishermen were up in arms, it appeared.

"They promised us that this wouldn't happen," shouted one man, his eyes bulged with outrage.

"I know, I know," said Dad calmly, capturing everybody's attention again. "But really, this is confirmation of what we already knew. Something had to be amiss, with all those fish and seals washing up dead in recent months. Seemed like too big a coincidence with SKANX opening their factory down the road."

I felt myself getting upset now. *Dead seals?* Seals were like sea versions of Maurice. Dad had not told me about this.

"The good news is, we know—for certain—what the cause is now, don't we?" said Dad.

The fishermen all grumbled.

"Call me thick, but what's so great about that?" said one man with straggly blonde hair.

"Yeah?" another shouted out.

"It means we can take action!" said my dad, with a great assertiveness. I was impressed with my old man, but the fisherfolk still didn't seem convinced.

"We will lobby!" explained Dad, tapping the table with his finger.

There were a few grunts of approval.

"We will protest!" Dad declared, again tapping the table.

This time, there were some murmurs of agreement.

"We will campaign!" shouted Dad.

"Aye!" came a shout.

"We will write to the press!" shouted Dad.

The fisher folk clapped.

"We will fight!"

"YEAH!" a collective shout.

"And we will win!"

The room exploded into cheers and Dad was suddenly swamped by the locals, taking it in turns to slap him on the back as I smiled on proudly.

Somewhere in the furore, I resumed conversation with George, who had sat down next to me.

"Your dad's a very good man," he said as we stood up.

"Yes, he's amazing!" I beamed, feeling a swelling of pride as I saw my dear dad standing across the room, surrounded by his fans.

"This company is very corrupt," said George. "They will destroy Coney and all its seas if we let them."

I bit my lip and nodded. My summer holidays were just around the corner; maybe I could do something to help.

"We have been campaigning a while ... but no one pays much attention to us. They just see us as a bunch of grumpy old men. Hey, maybe we should have you in the forefront if we are ever going to get the local press drawn in. We'd get right on the front pages with a pretty girl like you."

I screwed up my face. Maybe not ...

"Hey, see anything strange yet?" said George suddenly.

I hit him playfully on the arm. "Oh stop it!" I cried.

"Nothing?" he said.

I sighed. "I saw a couple of cods, a couple of trout ..." I began, reciting Allan's joke.

"Yeah, that's what they all say," said George, rolling his eyes. "How about someone then?

My heart skipped a beat. "Okay, there was this one thing ..." I began.

Dad cut in.

"Good evening George," said Dad putting his arm around me.

"Hello, Keith," said George. "Nice work."

"Thank you," said Dad. "Now, sorry to drag my girl away but I have to take her home. Her mother's coming tomorrow and we need to have one last clean, don't we dear?"

I groaned. *One last clean?* He hadn't cleaned in months. Well, aside from this one time when I saw him stroke the mantelpiece with a dish cloth.

"Well, it's going to be a long night," I grumbled, doing up the zip on my coat and picking up my soggy umbrella.

"Come back anytime, Crystal," said George. I nodded and smiled, but as I looked into his twinkly blue eyes, I could not help but feel they carried a message. I suddenly wished I did not have to leave.

Chapter Six

The entire house was bathed in the aroma of roses, and every set of curtains was thrown open so that sunlight poured in. The storm had well and truly passed, and everything about our house was heavenly.

Dad had spent the last couple of hours picking roses from our garden and arranging them in vases, so they looked like little clusters of rubies dotted around the house. Dad was determined that everything would be perfect for Mum when she arrived, and this was the finishing touch.

I think we were both aware that today was going to be difficult for Mum, and we wanted to make this move as pleasant as possible for her. Not only would she arrive with all her insecurities of growing old, but this was actually going to be a big change for her. She had had a lot of reservations about moving somewhere this remote, but like me, when she saw the way Dad fell in love with

Starfish she had eventually buckled. I just hoped she was going to be okay today. When Mum was on edge, she was a little scary.

Rosie stopped by just before we left at midday. She was as bright as a button and had brought us some jam from her auntie's local business.

"A housewarming present." She smiled as she handed over the basket to my dad.

"How very kind of you Rosie!" he chirped. "I'm so delighted Crystal has made such a nice friend."

We giggled as Dad bustled off to the kitchen.

"So ..." began Rosie. She was beaming.

"So ...?" I repeated. I was intrigued as to what had made her smile like this, given how gloomy she had been all week.

"I just bumped into Frank, you know, Will's friend?"

"Oh God, yes. The one who found me in the sea that night."

"Yes," said Rosie brightly. "Anyway, he told me that very night, after we left, Will fell down a hole and broke his leg."

I gasped.

"And this is good news ... why?" I squeaked.

"Because that's why he hasn't called!" she exploded. "He crushed his phone. Everything. He's been in hospital all week, desperate to contact me."

I looked at her in disbelief. "Okay, that's a plus, I guess."

"Obviously, like, poor Will and everything but I've been in hell."

I sighed, as I began to empathize. "I know the feeling."

Rosie's grin faded slightly. "Babe, Frank mentioned you. I don't mean to upset you or anything, but he said that when he found you ..."

She stopped.

"When he found me what?" I asked, my stomach fluttering.

Rosie looked down. "He said that you were swimming by yourself."

I laughed with outrage. *What the hell?*

"But, it was dark, right?" Rosie offered. "I mean, he probably couldn't see."

"Yeah ... probably," I agreed, trying to sound upbeat. But the truth was, I felt like someone had slapped me.

Dad came out of the kitchen.

"Right, shall we hit the sea?" he asked.

Rosie giggled. "Hit the sea, Jack!" she sang.

"And don't you even consider coming back!" Dad warbled, pointing at Rosie in an embarrassing attempt to sing along.

"Come on, Dad," I snapped ashamedly. "You've got all the words wrong, anyway."

Rosie collapsed in giggles as we made our way down to the ocean stairway, and I slapped Dad on the back, as he continued his muddled version of the song.

"Stop it, Dad!"

"Bye, guys!" called Rosie still laughing and waving from the top of the stairs as we made our way along the jetty to the boat.

Dad, Maurice, and I boarded the speedboat and set off to the mainland. Maurice had on his best collar for Mum—a smart red, leather band with golden studs.

I hugged Maurice as we travelled. He was still very nervous on boats and trembled as the engine started up. I rested my head on his warm fluffy neck as the boat pulled out into the vast expanse of the sea ahead. Once we had passed the lighthouse, Dad arched to the left, so that the mainland came into view ahead.

I watched him driving the boat for a while. His red shirt and white hair were glowing brightly in the midday sun.

As we glided along, my mind travelled to Llyr, as it always did these days.

Some strange things had been said in the past twenty-four hours. I was perturbed by George's comments last night. It was almost starting to feel as though he knew about me meeting Llyr the other night. *How would George know though? He would have been tucked up in bed on Starfish at that hour, with a cup of hot cocoa—or quite probably whisky.*

I couldn't make sense of Frank's remarks either. Llyr had been visible enough for me to have seen all his features in the firelight, so unless he were a figment of my imagination, Frank would have seen him too. *Oh gosh, had I gone crazy? Or, was Frank trying to make me out to be crazy? Maybe it was to make Allan feel better or something. Yes, this must be it.*

Once I had satisfied myself that Llyr existed, my thoughts returned to wishing he was with me now.

I wondered where he was at this moment in time. Maybe with another girl ... he probably went to exciting beach parties every night and frolicked about in the sea with beautiful women. I sighed. He'd probably completely forgotten about me.

Suddenly Maurice barked. I jumped and looked out to sea.

My heart did about a million somersaults. *It was him!*

Llyr was in the sea a dozen yards away from the boat and was looking straight at me. I had absolutely no doubt that it was him. It was the same chiselled jaw, the same hair—I could even see the tattoos. I met his gaze for about one second, and my heart raced.

He disappeared beneath the surface.

"Dad, stop the boat!" I screamed.

Dad carried on oblivious.

He couldn't hear me over the engine.

"Dad!" I screamed.

I got up and tapped him on the shoulder, and he jumped.

"Stop the boat!" I shouted into his ear, pointing frantically out to sea.

Dad turned off the engine, and the boat bobbed.

"What the hell is going on?" he asked, worriedly.

"There was a man!" I shrieked. "I know him. He saved me once."

"Saved you from what?" Dad shouted, his brow folding into deep lines of concern.

"Oh, I just swam out deep once—there were currents and stuff. But Dad, he was back there in the sea. And then he disappeared."

We looked back. The sea was calm, placid even. We must have been exactly half way between Starfish and the mainland, and there was not another boat in sight.

"Crystal, how on earth would a man be out here alone?"

"Maybe he swam! He's a really good swimmer—I told you, he saved me!"

"Yes, but it would have taken about an hour to swim out here. No one would do that. And anyway, if he's such a great swimmer, then why would he just suddenly drown?"

"I don't know," I despaired. "He didn't look like he was in trouble."

"Well then!" said Dad, although he was looking at me with worry. *Great, he thinks I'm mad too now.*

"What if a shark got him?" I said.

"If we were in Cape Town, I could see your point, Crystal, but this is Coney Bay."

"It's still the Atlantic," I protested. "What about those sucky sharks. They might have sucked him down."

"This is silly. We're going to be late for your mother," I could see Dad was getting irritated, and I didn't know what else to do.

"Can we call the 'Search and Rescue' people?" I tried.

Dad returned to the front of the boat. "You can do what you like when we get to land, Crystal, but one thing we will certainly be doing is having a conversation about why you were swimming in currents."

Great.

He turned on the engine, and we zoomed away. I stared at the spot where Llyr had disappeared until it was so far away it became too difficult to locate anymore. Maurice, too, seemed transfixed by the sea behind us.

If he hadn't barked, I would have thought that I had hallucinated it, but somehow I knew that I hadn't. I was certain of it.

I hung up the phone and stared blankly at the gravel path outside the station. There were no reports of a missing man named Llyr, and the police assured me they would inform the Coastal Guards.

There was nothing else I could do. I came out of my trance and looked down at my outfit. I supposed I should try to make myself look a little smarter. I did not want Mum going off on one about my appearance. I tucked my daisy-patterned shirt into my shorts and pulled my oversized cardigan back up over my shoulders.

Suddenly Maurice yanked me in the direction of the

station, and I saw my mum emerging through the big wooden doors. She looked good.

Mum was fifty but had not appeared to have aged since she was thirty. She was tall and slim and wore a tailored white suit and sunglasses. Her blonde hair was cropped just below her chin. She looked so very city.

"Mum!" I cried, dropping Maurice's lead and throwing my arms around her.

We hugged for about a minute. I could smell her perfume; it was a distinctive smell called *Pas Regret*. She owned that scent.

I suddenly felt a huge surge of comfort and joy. *My mum was here!*

Dad followed closely behind, his arms loaded with suitcases.

"Darling, I'm so happy to see you," she said placing her arms on my shoulders and looking at my face. Tears streamed from beneath her sunglasses. "I missed you so much."

I smiled happily. She was in a great mood.

Dad dropped the suitcases onto the floor with a big thud, letting out a big sigh of relief.

Mum looked at him and frowned. "Have you been exercising much since you got here, Keith?" she asked disapprovingly.

"Well ... not really, Sheila. It's been very busy," he replied, wiping away beads of sweat from his brow.

"Oh, so there are things to do here?" said Mum sarcastically.

I cringed, as Dad looked at her forlorn. They were not getting off to a good start.

"Anyway," said Mum. "I've got some brilliant news. I just got a phone call as I was pulling into the station."

"Who was it?" I asked curiously.

My mum stood back so that she could look at my dad, too. Her fire-engine-red lips formed a huge smile, and she beamed at us.

"I had a telephone interview last week with this energy company in the next town. They have the most dreadful name. They're called SKANX—imagine! But anyway, I got the job."

Chapter Seven

My mother was grinning at us.

One word churned around in my head, and it thudded over and over like a big soggy bundle of clothes in a washing machine.

Shite!

I looked at Dad. He had been smiling at Mum, in anticipation of her happy news, but it had now frozen. It was as though somebody had pressed *Pause* while he processed this info.

Shite.

My mother looked at both of us confused. She took off her sunglasses, as though she couldn't quite believe what she was seeing.

Mum and I had identical blue-grey eyes, and I watched as her set scrutinized our faces.

If there was one thing I knew, it was that she was highly

observant. She read body language like text and was, therefore, able to cut straight to the point.

"So, what's wrong with SKANX then?"

Dad laughed. It was a high-pitched laugh, almost like a giggle. *Was it nerves or anger?* I couldn't quite tell.

"Well, Sheila, if you must know ... everything," he began. His voice was terse but defiant.

"Well, like what?" she answered reasonably, lifting her shoulders and holding out her hands in a gesture of inquisition.

"They kill seals!" I chipped in nervously.

"What, like actually slaughter them?" she said with mock outrage. "SKANX is secretly a slaughterhouse pretending to be an energy firm? Well, that is a scandal."

"Yes, actually, yes!" boomed Dad, in a tone that was way too assertive for Mum's liking.

She raised her eyebrows and inspected her nails. "I see," she said, with a tone of deep disdain.

Shite! I looked at my feet, as I began to dread the evening's "celebrations" at home.

———

I reclined into my big turquoise cushions and tried to focus on the sound of the waves gently cascading into the garden wall below.

"You made me give up my life—and for what? To stare at the sea all day, bake us all some cupcakes?"

I could still hear them. They had been at it for hours, ever since we got home from the station.

A door slammed.

The door was then opened. Presumably by Dad.

"You're completely over-the-top!" shouted Dad. "I want you to be happy here, but why do you have to work for my one and only nemesis? It's ... treachery!"

I turned on my side and gazed across the ocean at the light blue line on the horizon—the last streak of daylight. I managed to ponder momentarily how the day constantly travelled across the globe and thought about the Aussies who would be pounding the buttons on their alarm clocks right now, as sunlight began to seep into their time zone.

"Your one and only nemesis? You're a bloody lawyer; you've got about a million enemies. This is preposterous," Mum bellowed, disrupting my meanderings.

"This is different!" Dad despaired loudly. "This is personal!"

The argument continued. *Dammit, why did this have to happen? She would have to get another job ... I mean, she couldn't go with them, surely?*

They would sort it out, I reassured myself.

I remembered Llyr in the sea today. I had not thought of him since I hung up the phone to the police. This had to be the longest time he had been absent from my thoughts since we met. It clearly took a family crisis to strip him from my mind.

So, what the hell had he been doing out at sea again? I

searched my brain for answers, but it could not produce them.

I picked up my mobile and scrolled through my phone book. My finger hesitated over Rosie's name. I sighed and put the phone down. *Could I trust Rosie not to judge me?*

I pressed *Call.*

Rosie answered immediately.

"Hey!"

"Hi, Rosie, it's me."

"I know!"

We giggled for several moments. I loved this about our friendship. When we were both happy, we seemed to find practically everything amusing. It was like this static buzzed around us, making us erupt into giggles at the tiniest thing.

I told Rosie about my mother's latest career move.

"Oh shite!" said Rosie.

"Exactly!" I exclaimed. "Shite is the word."

I hesitated.

"Rosie ..." I began.

"Yeah ...?"

"Okay, this is really embarrassing, and you're never going to believe me ... but ..."

"What?" she cried, immediately.

"I saw Llyr today."

Rosie gasped. "Oh my God! Where?"

"Er, in the sea."

There was silence.

"This guy likes to swim, right ..." she began hesitantly. "Was he far out?"

"Erm, yeah you could say that. Dad and I were halfway between Starfish and Coney, and he just appeared, Rose."

More unbearable silence.

"Are you there?"

"Yes, babe, I'm here."

"Do you believe me?" I asked worriedly, dreading her response. *My only friend was going to think I was completely bonkers.*

"I believe you, Crystal."

There was a long pause, and I squirmed and picked at the skin on my fingers.

"Look," she said eventually. "There's something you need to know about the sea. Only Starfish Islanders know the truth."

Chapter Eight

MINE @ 2

I double checked the text again. I was restless. I wanted to see Rosie now. It was bad enough I had had to wait all night. I had tossed and turned for hours. *What was this big secret? What did it have to do with Llyr?*

I didn't want to have to wait until two p.m. to find out.

My imagination was running rampant in my skull right now. *Was Llyr some criminal on the run? Did he have to hide in the sea or something? Maybe he was a Starfish native, and only islanders knew of his hiding place. ... Maybe that was the big secret.*

I thought about George and all his ramblings about the sea. *George must be his side-kick. Maybe they wanted me to help them in some way, and that was why Llyr had been waiting for me out at sea? What had he done, anyway? I would have to turn him in if he had killed someone. Surely I couldn't let my insane crush on him get in the way of justice?*

I couldn't believe I was caught up in such madness—and where on earth did Llyr sleep? He must get awfully cold out there all the time ... Surely he would drown at some point or catch pneumonia. Maybe I wouldn't have to turn him in after all.

I did a Google search on my phone, typing in "Most Wanted" and "Coney Bay."

A jokey news article came up about a kid who had released his goldfish into the sea and now wanted it back.

I screamed with frustration and threw my phone on the sofa. I stormed out into the back garden and down the ocean stairway.

It was a blazing hot June Sunday, but I didn't care. I would search for answers. When I got to the jetty, I marched to the end of it, and I stood there gazing out to sea.

I must have looked a little strange to the neighbours standing so determined on the edge of the jetty, fists clenched at my sides, my hair yellow in the sun.

I was a woman on a mission, but with nowhere to mission to.

My eyes scanned the sea, begging for something, but asides from a fishing boat and a couple of gulls, the surface was barren.

"Darling!"

It was Mum. She was making her way down the stairs.

I sighed.

"Hi, Mum."

"Are you alright, standing around in the boiling heat like this?" she shouted.

"Yeah, I'm fine," I said distractedly.

She made her way down the jetty. She wore a big, floppy black sun hat and a black fitted strappy dress.

"Are you off to a funeral, Mum?" I asked, glancing at her as she neared. It was surely not normal to wear such dark colours in the summer.

"I suppose I'm mourning London, Crystal," she said putting her arm around my shoulders.

God, she was so melodramatic. She was probably trying to give Dad a guilt trip.

"It's nice here," I said reassuringly, as we looked out to sea. "I miss London, too, but I've not thought about it one bit in the past week or so."

I was still scouring the waters.

"That's great," she said watching my face carefully, "but you don't really seem yourself."

"Oh ... well. I'm fine," I pretended.

My mum was silent, and I knew she was waiting for me to explain myself.

"Oh, it's just this guy."

"Oh, well, say no more," she said, looking relieved. "Now, my motherly advice is to keep cool, kid."

I laughed, "Okay Mum."

"Let them do the chasing."

Well, I couldn't chase Llyr even if I wanted to.

"Crystal, you're absolutely beautiful ... even with that

thing in your face," she said, glancing at my nose-ring. "You could have any man you want, just remember that. Now, please let's not fry here a minute longer."

She pulled my arm in the direction of the house. I took one last glance at the sea and followed her.

"How's Dad?" I asked cautiously.

"Oh, he's coming around," she replied.

"Really?" I was surprised.

"Yes. I won."

"Wow," I said. Maybe I really should listen to my mum's man advice.

"Mm-hmm. I told him I would provide some insider info ..."

"Well, are you?" I asked, pausing on the step.

"I'll chuck him a harmless scrap here and there," she sighed.

This was all sounding extremely messy. I swiftly changed my mind about listening to my mum.

"Are you sure you want to work for SKANX?" I asked quietly, as we crossed the garden. "I mean, everyone here's against it."

"Maybe the people your father associates with," said Mum, with disdain. "I'm sure most people are grateful to have such a high-powered company in the region."

I turned up my nose. I wasn't too sure, but I didn't want to argue with her as well.

Mum paused before opening the back door, raising an

eyebrow over her sunglasses. "I'm sure your father will get bored of this whole eco-warrior thing anyway ..."

———

I walked slowly across the island. I now sported my mum's black sun hat, at her insistence.

It was only 1:30 p.m., and I even sat on a bench for a little while to prolong my arrival.

I reached Rosie's at 1:55 and was perplexed to see her father, Oliver, lugging a suitcase out of the front door.

"Hi, there!" I said brightly.

Oliver looked up, and I could see an expression of alarm on his face.

Rosie appeared behind him with a huge rucksack. She stopped dead in her tracks when she saw me, and then her sister suddenly appeared and crashed into her from behind. There was an unmistakable air of chaos.

"Crystal! Oh my God!" she shrieked. "I forgot to text you! I'm so sorry; we've got to go to a bloody family wedding!"

Oliver turned to her. "Language, Rosemarie!"

"Sorry, Dad." Rosie ran over and hugged me. "We had the wrong date in the diary. Fortunately, my auntie called this morning. We have to travel to St. Caroline's by four—it's a late ceremony, thank God!"

My heart sank. St. Caroline's was miles down the coast.

It didn't look like I was going to find out the big secret for a good day or two.

"Oh gosh, you'd better hurry," I said, trying not to let my disappointment show.

"We're all going to have to get changed on the boat," said Rosie, giggling. "Dad, when are we back, again?"

"Monday evening," said Oliver, locking up the house. Then his face filled up with more panic. He looked at his wife, Mandy, who was rummaging frantically through her handbag. "It's bank holiday, isn't it? No school? No work?"

Mandy looked up at him with exasperation. "Oh, for goodness sakes, Oliver, I thought you knew these things."

"It's bank holiday," I chipped in.

"Right, well I'm sorry to tear Rosemarie from you on the long weekend, but I'm sure you two can live without each other until then."

Rosie laughed and looked at me.

"We'll talk Monday," she whispered, hugging me again and racing down the garden path after her family.

I was left standing in the front garden by myself.

———

Later on that evening, Mum, Dad, and I took a sea taxi to Coney Bay. We were going for a family dinner on the mainland tonight at some posh seafood restaurant.

I had put in a little effort with my appearance, as it was a special occasion, and wore a short black velvet dress and black ballet pumps. My hair was plonked on top of my head, for the journey, so that it didn't wrap itself around my face.

My mum wore a perfectly fitted leopard-print trouser suit. She had not attempted to dress down this rather loud outfit and donned chunky, golden accessories and humongous wedge heels. She looked amazing, but I couldn't help but wonder what the locals would think of her.

Dad, too, wore one of his best suits, although I noted that Mum repeatedly frowned at the bulging buttons around the tummy area.

We strolled along the sea front, watching the huge golden sun lower itself further and further behind the sea. It was glorious.

Passers-by looked at Mum as she passed. I'm not sure they had ever seen anything like it in sleepy Coney, and I had to swallow a giggle on a few occasions.

When we reached the restaurant, I realized we were on the very same beach where the party had been. It was crazy to imagine a surfer's rave had taken over this pristine strip of cafes and restaurants, apparently known as "Pearl Boulevard."

My mother seemed impressed by Pearl Boulevard, and her mood lifted considerably.

"This is promising," she stated, with a little brightness to her voice as we neared the restaurant.

Inside, waiters glided over pink marble floors carrying

ginormous silver platters piled high with crabs, prawns, and mussels. The walls were a pale coral shade, decorated with golden art-deco patterns. It was swanky, for sure.

We were invited to sit at the bar while we waited for our table, and I excused myself, asking my parents if they would mind if I went for a quick walk along the beach.

"It's just so gorgeous outside," I told them, and they smiled and nodded.

Once on the sand, I kicked off my pumps. The sun still peeked over the horizon, and I walked in a mauve-coloured dusk towards the sea.

It had been one week exactly since the party.

I dipped my toe into a wave that crept up-shore, and I instantly remembered his strong arms wrapped around my waist carrying me protectively to land. I remembered those mystical eyes watching my face, reading my thoughts, my feelings, as though they were taped to my forehead.

"Come back to me," I whispered to the sea.

Chapter Nine

I woke up and groggily turned towards my clock. The glowing red letters informed me that it was 5:30 a.m. I sighed and rested my head back down on the pillow. It was warm and comfortable in bed, and my eyes still felt tired, like I could be lulled back into an inviting, deep sleep. But for some reason, it wasn't happening.

I was filled with an energy, and I had no idea why. It's probably just the total lack of life, I thought sitting up and rubbing my eyes. I had done nothing but lounge about yesterday.

Today was bank holiday Monday, and it was the first time I had ever been up so early since moving to the sea. In fact, I had been sleeping very deeply this past month, sedated by the sea air.

I sat up and looked out of my window and realized that there was a lot of activity in the sea at this hour.

Fishing boats dotted the water, which looked like

mercury in the early morning light. They were all returning from their morning fish, ready to take their catches to the market.

I realized the necessity of the lighthouse, as much as it annoyed me. In the darker winter months, these boats could easily crash into Starfish on their way back to the mainland.

I was still bleary-eyed but was enjoying the moment; it was all so new to me. I couldn't take my eyes of the boats. I had a sudden impulsive thought—I would go and watch the ships sail in outside.

I leaped out of bed, tiptoed carefully downstairs and quietly made myself a cup of coffee. Even Maurice was still asleep, and I did not want him to hear me and bark, waking up Mum and Dad.

As I quietly poured the water into the china cup, I pondered on how unusual this was for me, venturing out into the solitary dawn like this. I just had this urge to get outside as quickly as possible.

I quietly stirred my coffee and unlocked the back door, stepping into the garden. I wore just my nightie—a light floaty garment with tiny straps. It was light purple and cut off mid-thigh. It was a little over-revealing, but I couldn't imagine anybody would be up to see me at this hour.

I felt the morning dew on my bare feet as I walked across the lawn to the Ocean Staircase. I figured I'd perch on one of the steps.

The birds were singing in the trees, and the morning sea

air was crisp and fragrant. I placed a foot on the top stone step and descended a little, fixated by the yellow sunbeams now dancing over the sea surface.

"Crystal."

My gaze lowered to the jetty, and my cup smashed on the steps below me.

He sat with his legs dangling in the water; his hair was tied back to reveal the whole of his handsome face. I gaped at him for a moment, not quite believing that this could be.

I walked down the stairs and towards Llyr speechless, imagining he would disappear any second. When I got closer, he reached out slowly and wrapped a gentle hand around my leg, pulling me down to sit beside him.

When I felt his touch, I knew that he was really here this time. I sat down next to him in a trance.

I looked at his beautiful face, and then my eyes travelled over his body. He wore just shorts, and his top half was toned and tanned. Celtic-like patterns and strange lettering were inked over his flesh in places. It was hot. Mysterious.

I looked back into his eyes. In the light, I could see they were a wonderful deep green.

"Finally!" I heard myself say.

He laughed.

"Yes, finally!" he said calmly, leaning towards me.

He lifted a finger to my face and then ran it over my hair, following the blonde wavy strands all the way down to where it ended just below my shoulders. He let it rest there, in that area just between shoulder and breast.

I felt this fluttering inside me. I didn't know why or how he was here, but I didn't care at this point in time. I just wanted to enjoy this moment. It felt so precious, like it would only last a few minutes.

"I wanted to see you again," he said, never taking those eyes off me. "Properly."

"How did you find me?" I asked, even though I somehow didn't even care.

"I saw you," he murmured, "a couple of days ago ..."

My mind flashed back to when he appeared in the sea between Starfish and the mainland. I wondered if he had followed us out to sea.

He put a hand on one of the straps on my shoulder and all my questions vanished with his touch. I looked down, and then I remembered I was wearing my nightie.

I laughed giddily, slightly embarrassed.

"It's my nightie!" I explained.

I saw that confused look cross his eyes again.

"You know, like, I sleep in it ..." *Why was I having to explain this to him?*

"It's very nice," he replied.

"Where are you from?" I asked.

He looked out to sea, as though that was an answer.

"Another island or something?" I asked, trying to fill in the blanks.

"Something like that," he turned back and smiled at me.

"I've got a boat today," he said, nodding to a small motor boat that was tied to our jetty. It had an orangey-brown base, and the interior was wooden. I could see two little planks to sit on. "What are you doing?" he asked.

I thought of the endless, empty day ahead on the isle with no school and no Rosie.

"Nothing," I replied honestly.

"Come with me?" he asked, an eyebrow raised, hinting at fun and adventure.

I couldn't think of a single thing I'd prefer more.

———

We glided effortlessly past the fishing boats. I felt a rush of adrenaline.

I had to admit, part of me was a little scared heading out to sea like this on a teeny little boat, with absolutely no idea where we were going and without telling anybody.

But excitement overrode all of that. I was high with the rush of being with Llyr again. I wasn't for one second afraid that he was still practically a stranger—I trusted him for some reason.

I pulled Mum's black sun hat down over my face when we passed the boats, praying that no one aboard would recognize me and tell Mum and Dad.

After Llyr had asked me to come with, I had returned to my house and raced upstairs. I had thrown on some clothes and grabbed a pen and paper. *What on earth could I tell Mum and Dad?*

Gone to Coney, I had scrawled, before hesitating. I was going to have to be a bit more specific, or they would freak out. I had picked up the pen again.

With a friend from school—got my mob.

I had scribbled a big heart. A guilt heart.

I hoped they wouldn't be worried. I looked at my phone as we headed further out. It had zilch reception bars.

We had eventually passed all the fishing boats, and there was nothing around us except for the everlasting seascape. Llyr turned off the engine.

I looked at him and laughed. He smiled back.

"What the hell are we doing out here?" I exclaimed, giggling. I felt drunk from all the endorphins.

"I just like this part of the sea," he replied.

I giggled again. "But it looks exactly the same as the sea back where we came from!"

He frowned, and I wondered if I had offended him somehow.

"I guess it does," he said slowly, as though he'd never considered this before, "but underneath the surface, it all looks different."

"Well, I wouldn't know ..." I said.

"Have you ever used the, you know ..." he appeared at a loss for words and made circles with his fingers over his eyes.

"Goggles?" I asked.

"Mmm. Yeah, goggles," he said. He sounded strange when he repeated the word "goggles." It almost reminded me of how a foreigner pronounces an English word for the first time.

But he didn't sound particularly foreign.

"Erm, well yeah a bit, just in really shallow water, though," I said.

"The sea nourishes everything, Crystal. Flowers and plants never wilt underneath her, before their time. You know, sea gardens are so, so beautiful," said Llyr.

He sat on the floor of the boat, looking over the rim at the waters.

"Is there a sea garden here?" I asked slowly, wondering where this was all going.

He looked at me and grinned.

"Yes, there's a wonderful garden below us. I just wish I could show you," he replied. "You would look ... beautiful down there."

"Well, I'll bring my scuba kit next time," I said slowly. *What was with this guy and the sea?*

"It has a tree that grows five types of sea fruit, and they're all different shades of pink. Every branch bears a different colour," he continued.

"Oh come on, you don't get sea trees!" I cried. He was joking. Either that or delusional.

He reached out and took my arm and pulled me from my seat to him so that he held me in his arms.

71

I looked up at him from below. I was a little startled, but I liked the confident way he grabbed me like that.

"So you think I would lie to you?" he said, looking down at me.

"I don't know," I said, pulling my hat over my eyes to shield them from the sun. "I kind of trust you, strangely enough. I wouldn't be here if I didn't, right?"

"Well, that's good," he said with a tone of deep sincerity. "I would hate it if you didn't."

He pulled back my sun hat and leaned forward so that he blocked the sun for me. I saw he had a pendant round his neck.

I reached up and touched it. It was made from a hard white substance and was in the shape of some kind of symbol. It was almost like an "S" shape but back to front.

I suddenly realized something.

"I'm boiling," I said, sitting up and looking at the sky. The sun had risen and was beating down on the water around us.

Llyr stood up quickly. He put one foot on the edge of the boat.

"So we'll go swimming!" he declared brightly.

Before I could protest, he had dived backwards off the boat and into the water.

"No!" I screamed. *Was he insane?* We were WAY out. I looked back to land, and to my horror, realized that I could not even see it.

I peered nervously over the edge. The waters rippled where he had disappeared, and the boat rocked.

I waited for him to reappear, but there was nothing.

I became frightened.

"Llyr?" I wailed over the boat.

He resurfaced.

"You didn't come in!" he said, completely casually and with no symptoms of breathlessness.

"I'm not coming in!" I shrieked. "We're in the middle of the ocean."

"Yeah, but that's okay," he said flippantly, "you know I can save you from currents."

"Hello! Sharks!" I cried.

"I can sense them miles off," he said.

I looked at him incredulously.

"There are no sharks, Crystal, seriously. Not here, not now."

I wasn't entirely sure I believed him, but even so, there was one more problem.

"I don't have my swimming costume."

He raised his eyebrows. "You really need one?"

He wanted me to go in without a swimming costume. *Seriously?*

I shook my head.

"You're shy," he said gently.

"Okay, look I barely know you!" I cried.

He looked at me for a moment as though he was trying

to figure something out, and then suddenly he disappeared under the water again.

"Oh for fuck's sake. Now where are you going?" I cried. God, most men took girls to dinner or something on their first date. "Llyr! Come back!" I shouted.

An agonizing minute or so later he emerged and swam towards the boat. I could see he had something in his hand.

"Here," he said, holding out his hand.

I gasped when I saw what rested in his palm.

It was a perfectly spherical shape and a deep ruby pink. I took the fruit and examined it closer. It was soft; an almost leathery texture and pink leaves bloomed from its core. They were like rose petals. I was in awe of it.

"I just wanted to show you that you can trust what I'm saying," he said from the water.

I nodded. I knew I would want answers at some point, but for this very moment, I didn't care. I just wanted to live this magical moment and not ruin it with any further scrutiny.

My arms reached automatically for my shirt, and I started unbuttoning from the top. I must have unbuttoned two or three when suddenly I saw a look of alarm on his face. At first, I thought it was me, and I stopped, worried.

He reached for the edge of the boat and hauled himself aboard. Water splashed all over me.

"There's going to be a storm," he said, starting up the

engine. I looked behind, and sure enough, I could see a huge black cloud coming from the direction of Coney.

———————

We sped back to Starfish as fast as the boat would take us.

The sun still shone brightly over us, but the grumble of thunder could be heard in the distance.

I dreaded to think what would happen if the storm were to reach us before we did reach Starfish. We were in this flimsy tin can of a boat and would never be able to contest such a force.

I also had a very long standing fear of being struck by lightning. Out here at sea, we were the tallest point in our little boat; we may have easily attracted a bolt to us.

It was as though Llyr sensed my fear. He turned around.

"We're going to make it, don't worry," he shouted over the engine, and I felt a little reassurance.

"I know you still don't believe me," he shouted jovially. "Even though I brought you that fruit."

I wanted to talk back, but I was too scared. I nervously scanned the sea. True to Llyr's words, the luscious mound of Starfish came into view.

It grew larger and larger as we neared, as did my relief. Detail began to fill in, and I could soon see the fisher huts, steeple, and houses.

Llyr zoomed towards my side of the island, and I prayed

that Mum and Dad wouldn't see us. As we neared my house, I could see Dad's red motor boat was bobbing about, meaning that they were more than likely at home.

Soon we were positioned just inches away, and Llyr reached out and grabbed one of the legs of the jetty, pulling us nearer. Big raindrops began to splatter on us.

He laughed, carefree.

I too laughed, but more so with relief.

"You want to come indoors?" I asked.

Mum and Dad were bound to be peeved when I showed up with this rugged and topless, older-looking man, but I could hardly send him out to sea in this storm.

"Thank you, but I need to get going," he said.

Rain now splattered all over us. I shuffled on my knees towards him as the boat rocked and the waves grew larger.

"Come on, please, I'll worry about you," I begged.

"Why?" he said calmly.

"What do you mean, '*Why?*'" I cried, my hand was now on his knee as I steadied myself.

He put his free hand around my waist to support me, while the other still hugged the boat to the jetty. Here we were again, inches apart, yet moments of our togetherness remained.

The rain bucketed on us.

"I have to go!" I shouted, wishing so badly that the weather would ease so we could say goodbye properly.

He lifted my hand from his knee and brought it to his lips. I smiled through the rain. It was romantic.

"You promise me you'll be okay?" I said.

"I knew you still doubted me," he said.

"No, I don't," I said standing up. I had to acknowledge that everything he had told me so far turned out to be true.

I wanted to ask him when I'd see him again, but the rain was now thundering on the deck, and the boat looked like it was beginning to fill up with water. It was torrential.

He waited until I was safely on the jetty and then he pushed himself back out to sea. I watched as he started up the engine and then disappeared behind a thick wall of rain.

There was a flash of lightning, and I screamed.

"Llyr!" I shouted into the storm.

The thunder clapped, and I screamed again. I had no choice but to run up the stairs, through the garden and up to the house. I pulled open the back door.

Mum and Dad were sitting at the kitchen table.

"Crystal!" they exclaimed in unison as I slipped through the door, looking like a drowned rat.

"We just made it!" I said breathlessly.

"Let me get you a towel," said Mum, rushing out of the room.

Dad looked me up and down. "Didn't you have shoes on?" he said.

Oh, shoot. I hadn't bothered with shoes at all in my rush this morning.

"Erm, I left them in the boat," I said quickly. "They had holes in them."

"Hmm," he said, looking back at the paper, appearing to have accepted this. "Did you have a nice time?"

"Yeah, it was cool," I replied, taking a towel from Mum and wrapping it around me.

My mum appeared to do a double take at my chest, and I looked down and realized my front buttons were still undone.

I quickly covered myself with the towel.

Bugger.

"Why ever did you go so early?" asked Mum.

"Oh, erm ... just because my friend's dad wanted to go to the market and get the best fish," I managed to blurt out.

"Ah yes, well, it's probably not that he wanted the best fish. I imagine that he wanted to gut them ASAP and get them in the fridge," Dad said wisely. "Much better gutted early."

"Yeah, yeah okay!" said Mum holding out her hand at dad.

"Well, Dad's the expert!" I said laughing nervously. "Anyway, I'm going to have a bath; I'm really cold."

I raced out of the kitchen and up the stairs, before they could say another word. I went straight to the bathroom and shut the door behind me, realising now that I hadn't just been making excuses. I was freezing. My hands shivered as I turned on the taps, and I stripped off my wet clothes as quickly as I could. Once the bathtub was full, I climbed inside and let myself de-thaw before reclining back into the water. I began to process everything that had happened to me today.

Of course, there were so many questions, but I still couldn't really think straight. I was giddy with all the excitement.

All my mind wanted to think about was, quite simply, him. I lay there remembering his touch, his words, even his lips on my hand.

We had had all this chemistry but still hadn't even kissed. I started to think about what it would be like to kiss him. I imagined it would be soft and gentle to start with and then the passion would build and build, and he would grab me and pull me to him as close as possible.

The thought of it made me wish that it had never ended. *What would have happened if the storm hadn't come, if I had gone into the water with him?*

Throughout all my dreaming, there was one question that was very much thrashing about in my consciousness. *Would I ever see him again?*

Chapter Ten

I sat in History idly taking notes. This was my favourite class, and today we were learning about Spartacus, the former gladiator. I had been looking forward to this class for ages, but now I was struggling to concentrate.

Spartacus had led thousands of slaves into an uprising against the Romans, and I had always found the whole story fascinating. Mr. Cloones, our teacher, was showing us some pictures of the weapons they would have used, and I willed myself to focus, but I had all this other stuff swimming around in my head.

Of course, I was still processing every moment of my time yesterday with Llyr, but, also, I was worried about what was going on at home.

Mum and Dad had had an argument this morning. It was her first day at SKANX, and she had been on edge to say the very least. She had snapped at Dad over everything, even telling him that he was too slow pouring milk over the cereal—his own cereal!

What was wrong with her? First day jitters? Guilt?

Whatever the case, it had been a tense journey over to the mainland, as poor, abused Dad drove us in his red boat.

I thought about how ecstatic he had been when he first glided home in it; you could see his grin a mile away. He couldn't wait for Mum to see it. He thought she would think it was very glamorous—"just like her." But now he was using it to chauffeur her to the detestable SKANX while she glowered at his back from the passenger seat.

It was breaking my heart.

The buzzer went for lunch, and I looked down at my notes. I had written three words:

Glad

Presumably, I had started to write "Gladiator."

2 AC

A date, perhaps. I wasn't entirely sure.

Gaus

I had no idea what this meant.

Dammit, how would I ever be able to know what Mr. Cloones had said from this? I trudged down the corridor when I saw the unmistakable waif-like figure of Jemima Jones walking ahead. She took History.

I had not spoken to her much before, but I didn't think it would be too cheeky to ask for a one-off favour.

"Hey, Jemima!" I said catching up with her.

She turned around. She was a tall girl with slender limbs and long, thin, sandy brown hair.

"Hi?" she said with a cold inquisitiveness.

I laughed nervously, a little taken aback.

"How are you?" I asked.

Jemima answered this with a quick, tight smile—the type that really means, "fine until you came along."

"Okay, well sorry to pounce on you like this ..." I said, deliberating whether or not to just walk off. "I was just looking for someone from History. It's just that I made really rubbish notes, like I don't even know what planet I was on in there. I think there's a total of three words. Genius. Anyway, I'm uh, I'm rambling. I was just basically wondering if you wouldn't mind if I copied your notes ...?" I trailed off hopefully.

Jemima looked down her nose at me.

"Seriously?" she said, before turning on her heel and walking off.

I was left standing in the corridor in a state of confusion. *Was note-copying offensive here in Coney?*

Suddenly somebody jumped on my back, and I screamed. I was completely shocked, thinking I was being attacked, until I heard a familiar cackle in my ear.

"Oh my God, woman, what are you doing?" I screeched as Rosie fell to the ground laughing.

"Oh sorry!" she cried. "I couldn't help it. Why were you standing like that anyway, looking so gormless?"

I told her about Jemima, and Rosie's eyes widened.

"Sooo rude!" she exclaimed. "Eugh, it's because we've been really good friends since year 11, and she's peed off because you came along."

"Oh, I see," I said, relieved that there was a logical reason for her behaviour, albeit slightly petty.

"But I've told her, she has to accept that I'm going to make other friends in life," Rosie continued linking my arm as we walked. "I mean don't get me wrong, I love her to pieces, and we've been through e-e-e-everything together, but at the end of the day, I never signed a contract to be her only friend in the world. What will she do when we go to uni next year? Expect me not to talk to anybody? Norma-no-mates?"

I laughed at Rosie and her funny little quaint sayings—I didn't realize people actually said some of the things she came out with.

"I'm sure she'll get used to it, Norma," I said. "Maybe we should invite her out next time. She might like me, and I can get some history notes!"

Rosie wasn't convinced.

"I've tried," she explained. "She's always like 'you want me to be the third wheel now?' And I'm like 'No, Crystal's really nice, we would never exclude you.' And she's like 'Yeah, right.' Eugh, it's exhausting, I'm just letting her stew."

"Oh well, how was the wedding?" I asked, changing the subject.

"Oh it was nice," said Rosie. "Except Mum and Dad

got horrendously drunk and started doing all this sexy dancing. It was sooo embarrassing. Me and my sister were dying!"

I laughed. "Oh, no."

"Yeah ... oh yeah." Rosie groaned. "Mum was kind of doing this twerking up against Dad; I swear to God. Can you believe it? It was just the most mortifying thing in the world."

I was now laughing hysterically, and tears were building up in my eyes.

"It must run in the family," I managed to joke when I got a breath in.

Rosie stopped dead in her tracks. "Please don't tell me I danced that night?"

"No, I just meant with the drinking, don't worry!" I laughed.

"Thank GOD for that," Rosie relaxed. "Yes, it must be the Welsh in our blood ... but trust me Crystal, me and alcohol are over after that night."

I smiled, wondering how long this would last. "Heard from Will yet?" I asked while we were on the subject of that famous night.

"Yes," she breathed, her eyes going misty. "He called me this weekend."

"Oooh!" I squealed.

"He wants to go for a drink this week. His leg's getting better now, but he's still on crutches."

"Ah, so no twerks for a while!"

Rosie lifted her arm to hit me, and I laughed and shielded myself.

"What about you anyway?" she asked. "Any more sightings of your mystery man?"

"Well ... as a matter of fact, I went out on a boat with him yesterday."

Rosie's eyes widened. "You're joking!"

"I'm not actually," I said.

Upon eager request, I told Rosie every last detail of my weird and wonderful date, and she hung onto every word from the unexpected arrival, to the fruit picking, the touchy-feely-ness, and the sudden storm.

"I just can't believe he just rowed out into the frothing waves!" I exclaimed at the end, my frustration building up all over again. "What if he bloody died?"

"Oh, Crystal, he will be fine," said Rosie.

"How do you know?" I asked, and then I remembered that she still had something to tell me. "And what was this big secret that we were supposed to talk about before the wedding?"

Rosie looked around us. We were standing in a bustling school corridor, where groups of pupils stood in clusters by lockers. She steered me into a classroom.

It's fair to say I was bursting with curiosity, and yet a bundle of nerves also swelled in the pit of my stomach. *What was I about to discover?*

"Okay," Rosie began sitting down on top of a desk. She leaned forward and looked me in the eyes. I looked back into her warm, chocolate-brown eyes and saw a look of solemnness.

Whatever was coming, it was not a joke.

"So ... on the island we live on ... there's a myth," she began slowly.

"Okay ..." I said. George's hints of "strange things" echoing through my mind.

"Well, actually, it's more than a myth. We kind of all know it's actually true," said Rosie quickly.

"What is true?" I said my heart was drumming in my chest.

"I'm not crazy, Crystal, right. You know that," said Rosie.

"You're far from crazy," I replied. *Rosie was the most together person I'd ever met.*

"Okay, so there's like ... I'm just going to say it. There are these sea people that we sometimes see around Starfish."

Sea people? Huh?

"Like sailors?" I asked. *Was Llyr a sailor? Was that really the secret?*

"No, not sailors. They're like ..." I could see Rosie was trying to choose her words carefully.

"What?" I breathed.

"Mer ..."

My heart stopped. *I had been right all along.*

"Murderer," I finished for her. He was on the run after all, but I did not think he would have killed anybody. *I was going to have to contact the police.*

"No, Crystal. They're merfolk."

———

Maybe I had been sufficiently prepped for it ... all the talk of strange things succeeded by a series of bizarre happenings. I just wasn't feeling that jolt of disbelief that you would have thought inevitable.

Maybe I was just numb from the shock.

"Merfolk?" I clarified. My tone was calm. "As in, *Ariel*?"

Rosie, who had been staring down at her hands, looked up.

"Uh-huh." She reminded me of a deer caught in the headlamps, her brown eyes wide with worry, awaiting my response. "They live in the sea."

"But Llyr has legs," I said. My mind was actually logically processing this. "Merfolk have a fishtail, right?"

"Well, apparently they can morph into humans for a bit," Rosie explained, "when they come to the surface."

"So, he has a tail?" I asked inquisitively.

"If he is what I think he is then he will live deep below and have a tail," said Rosie. "They can swim better that way, I guess."

"Makes sense," I said slowly, not knowing if I quite believed the words as they came out of my mouth. I mean, it made sense, but at the same time, it made no sense at all.

"I can't believe you actually believe me!" cried Rosie.

"Why, are you joking?" I asked, suddenly unsure all over again.

"No!" said Rosie. "It's just you're handling it so well."

"I guess most people would call the doctor," I admitted.

"Er ... yeah!" said Rosie. "It's not every day someone tells you you're dating a merman!"

I put my hands to my head; I was suddenly feeling a little dizzy. Maybe it was starting to hit me. I mean, I knew something very unusual was going on—but *this?*

"Look, it's shocking, but once you accept that they exist, it just becomes part of everyday life," said Rosie, leaning forward over her knees and putting a reassuring hand on my arm.

"Do you know any of these mer-types?" I asked.

"Well, no not personally, but I saw some years ago," offered Rosie. "There was this one time when I was about eleven, and I had been out at sea. George, your friend the fisherman, had taken my sister and me out there because our parents had paid him, you know, for the whole fisher-type experience."

I nodded, my brow furrowed.

"We had such fun that day," sighed Rosie. "We saw seals with their babies and caught tons of fish with the big nets. Anyway, we were on our way back to Starfish ..."

The shrill ring of a mobile phone came from Rosie's big, purple bag, and she unzipped it. The ring grew louder.

"Oh come on!" I hissed. *Was she seriously going to answer her phone?*

"Okay, okay," she said putting the bag down and regaining focus. "So, we were coming back to Starfish, and this woman and man were just sitting on a rock in the middle of the ocean. It was so odd ... there was no boat, nothing. I always remember her hair; it was incredible. She had these auburn waves right down to her waist. It was a little wet at the ends but shiny and wavy at the top from where it had dried in the sun. It was just mesmerizing, Crystal. George told us that they were the sea people. We were amazed, and we looked around at the other fishermen, but they had not noticed a thing."

I remembered how Frank had said I was swimming by myself that night at the party when I was with Llyr.

"Only Islanders can see them, I'm not sure why that is ..." said Rosie, reading my mind, "but everybody on Starfish knows they exist; we kind of turn a blind eye to it, you know. It's like there's an understanding."

"Do they need us for something?" I asked, wondering why they chose to make themselves known to us.

Rose held up her hands. "I don't know anymore."

But I needed to know more. Because suddenly I was questioning whether or not Llyr needed me for some kind of purpose.

Chapter Eleven

Rosie's mum took us home from school that day. On the ride back to Starfish, Rosie and I sat silently next to each other. I imagined Rosie was letting me process our conversation. She looked a little upset. I wanted to talk to her, but a) the motor was really loud, and b) my head was swimming with thoughts.

"I feel guilty," said Rosie, when we said goodbye outside her house.

"No, don't!" I pleaded. "I'm so glad you told me. I mean, at least now I know what might be going on. It was driving me insane."

"I know, that's why I told you, but at the same time, it's such a shock for you to take in."

"I'll be okay," I said, forcing a smile.

"Do you want to come and stay over?" Rosie offered.

"No, thanks. I think I should be at home in case Mum and Dad kill each other," I said.

Rosie nodded and hugged me. "Call me," she said.

It was true; I did need to get home for mediation purposes, but I also had to pay somebody a visit before I returned to Lighthouse Lane.

I headed down the crooked cobbled streets.

It was the equivalent of rush-hour here on Starfish, with school children weaving mischievously through the streets, no doubt playing some kind of game on their way home. Ordinarily I would have stopped and smiled, maybe joined in for a little bit, but I was on a mission and in no mood for fun.

"Mermaids," I muttered as I stormed along.

I marched through the back streets, and when I reached the southern edge of the island, I headed to the fisher huts in search of George.

I knocked on the thick red door of Seaman's Lodge.

"Come in!" came a voice.

I stepped inside. Roger, one of the skippers, was sitting at the table with a cup of tea. He had big, grey, bushy sideburns and wore a bobbly, old, maroon jumper. He lifted a hand at me in what I believed to be a wave.

"Hi, Roger, have you seen George?" I asked.

"Mainland," Roger grunted in response.

"Any idea when he'll be back?" I asked.

Roger appeared to down his drink in a succession of gulps.

"Tomorrow," he replied, tea dribbling down his beard.

I thanked the monosyllabic Roger and made my way

back out, but something caught my eye. On the wall by the door was a poster.

MISSING BOAT

My eyes travelled from the writing to the picture and I gasped. It was the same orangey-brown boat that Llyr had driven that day.

"Whose boat was this?" I cried.

Roger looked at me suspiciously

"A kid I know. He got it for his birthday. Just turned eighteen."

"That's terrible," I winced uncomfortably.

"Seen it?"

"No," I said, a little too loudly. I was sure that the guilt was written all over my face, and I moved towards the door and pushed it open. "Sorry, no," I said again before stepping outside.

Not only was Llyr a merman, but now he was also a thief.

———————

Later on back at home, things were tense, to say the least. Mum talked about her first day of work brightly, as though she was completely unaware of how Dad felt about the company.

"Everybody was extremely professional!" she gushed, unbuttoning her black suit jacket. "I mean, we said our 'hellos' and our 'how-do-you-dos,' but then it was straight back to business."

"Hmm ... Business. Is that what they call it?" asked Dad sarcastically.

Mum continued, ignoring Dad. "My boss Mr. Geake is absolutely marvellous."

Dad glowered from behind his paper. "Nice name," he muttered.

"Tomorrow, I'll be down at Agatha's port, coordinating the waste disposal," Mum declared excitedly. "The ship goes out at night time, so I won't be home until around 10 p.m."

Dad appeared to snap at this point and threw down his paper. I cringed. "Waste disposal," basically meant the dumping of the toxic waste out at sea.

"Are you doing this deliberately to get to me?" he shouted.

Mum raised her eyebrows in a disapproving fashion. "Not everything's about you, you know, Keith."

"Oh, and what do you mean by that?" spat Dad angrily.

"Well," began Mum, "so far, everything in my life is designed to fit your needs. We live on this desolate island to suit your new-found dream of being a fisherman, or whatever it is you're so desperately obsessed with ... and now, now my job is supposed to revolve around your tastes too."

Was this what it was all about? Mum was so deeply resentful about leaving London that she was making a stand.

Dad didn't quite grasp this.

"I give you a wonderful fantasy home in the most beautiful part of the country, and you have to find something to moan and groan about, don't you?" he barked.

"I think you've had a bit too much wine, actually," said Mum.

This appeared to wind Dad up even more.

"I don't think I've had nearly enough!" he shouted, grabbing the remainder of the bottle and storming upstairs.

Mum, too, exited the kitchen with a big, dramatic sigh, leaving me sitting at the dining table alone in a horrified silence.

Chapter Twelve

I smiled for the first time in days as the school bell rang. It was the second from last day of school, and then a six-week summer break awaited.

I left the classroom and chatted to a boy from my English class called Lloyd. Lloyd was really nice and quite cute looking, although he was a little on the chubby side. He was off to France for a couple of weeks, I learned.

If I were to get away, I would need to spend most of my holiday working. I told Lloyd that I was starting to think about getting a job, and he suggested Pearl Boulevard.

"They're always hiring pretty girls," he said in what I sensed was a platonic tone, "and you get decent tips over there. It's where all the rich people go."

I thought about how Dad had taken us to Pearl Boulevard on Mum's first night and felt sad. If only that bloody job hadn't come up, things would not be so bad. She would probably have a few tantrums but would be focusing on getting settled here and not rubbing this job in Dad's face.

I turned the corner and slammed straight into Jemima. She wore a tight black dress and Converse high tops, and her expression transformed from neutral to disgust when she realized who she had made contact with.

"I'm so sorry!" I cried, jumping backwards.

Jemima's pasty skin flushed crimson with rage, and then her gaze shifted towards Lloyd.

"Whatever," she said and stormed off.

"Woah!" said Lloyd. "Time of the month, maybe?"

"Oh, she's just like that with me," I sighed, not even bothering to challenge Lloyd's derogatory comment. *Why should I defend her, when she was so rude to me? What did she expect me to do, hang around by myself?*

"She's usually really nice, she's like my mate," said Lloyd. "I've never seen her like that before."

"Ah well, it must just be me then," I sighed, not caring anymore. I was looking forward more and more to my summer break. And I was looking forward more than ever to this time next year when school would be out. Forever.

After school, I made my way through the hustle and bustle down to the fisher huts in search of George.

The door to Seaman's Lodge was open, and I poked my head in and was instantly overcome by the smell of fish.

There was George, standing in the middle of the hut. He was studying a big piece of paper that was unfolded in his hands.

He looked up and smiled. I smiled back, relieved that he was here and on his own. It was perfect.

"I was wondering when you would make an appearance," he said.

"I came by yesterday," I said, moving closer. The stench of fish became more and more profound as I neared George and I had to stop myself from grimacing. I was now close enough to peer over his shoulder at the paper, and I began to breathe through my mouth.

It appeared to be a map of some kind. I studied it closer. There were grid lines and names of places, but one thing was missing.

"Huh, where's the land?" I said, realizing the entire map was a light blue.

"Now, why would I need a map of the land, Miss White?"

I chewed this over.

"Well, I just thought all maps generally included land ..." I offered.

George laughed. "Not this one."

George was wearing a blue t-shirt, and I could see for the first time he had blue inkings on his wrinkly flesh.

"Now, I need to be heading out here ..." he mumbled, squinting at the far right of the map.

I looked at some of the names on the blue seascape.

I couldn't understand them; they were in a different language, but one name, in particular, caught my eye.

"Gaird-Gai—" I began.

"Gairdín bán-dearg," said George. "Gairdin means garden, and I think you can tell me what ban-dearg means, can't you?"

I was taken aback. *Why on earth would I know that?*

"I don't speak any of these funky languages!" I protested holding up my hands.

"Well, I thought you knew about sea gardens, that's all," he said looking back at the map, his eyes twinkling knowingly.

My mind flashed back to my day with Llyr above the pink sea garden. In my head, I saw him hand me the ruby colored fruit, and I felt a tingle as I remembered our time together. I looked back at George, my eyes wide. I now had no doubt that he knew of my meetings with Llyr.

"What are you doing later?" said George.

"Oh, the usual. Absolutely nothing," I replied flippantly, although inside I was drunk on a cocktail of curiosity, intrigue, and nerves.

What were these mermaids like? Were they really as nice as Llyr had appeared? Did they have dangerous powers? Did they like us normal people?

"Meet me here at eight."

When I got home at around four, I found Dad sitting on the bench in the back garden staring out to sea.

I sat down on the bench and put my arms around his neck.

"Are you okay, darling?" he asked, placing a hand on my arm.

"Oh not too bad, Dad," I said resting my head on his shoulder. "School was a bit stressful. This girl hates my guts but asides from that ... all is good."

"Ah well, you've always had a problem with other girls," said Dad, "and you probably always will."

"Oh great, thanks, Dad," I cried. *How reassuring.*

"It's the price you have to pay for being beautiful and wonderful," said Dad. "Trust me, a lot of girls will be very jealous of you."

I sighed. "I don't know if she's jealous of me. She's just annoyed that she doesn't have Rosie all to herself anymore."

"I bet she wouldn't be so annoyed if Rosie was friends with a door-mouse-type," said Dad knowledgeably.

I giggled. "Maybe, who knows? She just seems like a petty person."

"Well, you can always squash nastiness with niceness," said Dad wisely.

This was an interesting idea.

"Unless you're your mother, of course," continued Dad, "and then you squash nastiness with brutality. Or maybe death."

Dad laughed at the thought of Mum and her aggressive qualities. I could see how much he still loved her, even despite her recent behaviour.

"Well, you never know, maybe she'll have a fight with her boss at SKANX and bring the whole company crashing down," I said optimistically.

Dad rolled his eyes in a display of exasperation. "That would be great."

"Are you two okay?" I asked, hesitantly.

Dad smiled. "Yes, Crystal, we'll be okay. She's just rebelling, or something."

He did get it after all.

Chapter Thirteen

It was a little colder at around 7:30 p.m., and so I changed out of my shorts and into my light denim ripped jeans. I rummaged around in a mound of clothes for a jumper before locating my red cardigan with the hood.

I looked quickly in the mirror before I left and was struck by how long my hair had grown since coming to Starfish. It used to rest around my shoulders, but now it tumbled over my arms in these wild blonde waves.

I thought about Llyr and the inevitable tow of gorgeous mermaids that must swarm around him. Maybe he would like this look if Rosie's description of the mermaid on the rock was anything to go by. I hurriedly pressed pause on that thought.

I couldn't possibly go out with a merman, surely?

I ran my fingers through my mane. George would be able to tell me more, I prayed.

I came downstairs and saw Dad was watching the TV on

his own with a beer. I remembered Mum would be out all evening at the port.

"Dad, that beer will go straight to your stomach," I warned as I tugged on my boots in the hallway.

"I beg your pardon?" he said dryly sitting up and turning around.

I giggled mischievously.

"Your stomach!" I exclaimed.

"Where do you think you're going?" he said as I reached for the front door handle.

"I'm going to see Rosie," I said. "Is that alright?"

"Yes, yes," said Dad. "You are seventeen I suppose ... not that funny little girl anymore."

"Funny?" I said outraged. "What do you mean 'funny'?"

"Oh, you were such a funny little thing." Dad laughed. *Was he tipsy?*

He settled back down on the sofa and didn't appear to want to expand any further, so I said goodbye and walked out of the front door.

It was still light, but darkness was near. The residents of Lighthouse Lane all appeared to be indoors, probably having their dinner. It was so quiet that I could hear the waves lapping against the rocks, even from over the other side of the houses.

As I neared Seaman's Lodge, I heard a voice calling me from below. I walked around the building and towards the rickety wooden stairs which led down to the sea.

From above I could see George standing with one leg in

a boat and one leg on the jetty. I hoped he was getting out rather than in.

"Come on, kid," he beckoned. *He was getting in!*

I descended the stairwell. There was a giant creak with every step, and I froze.

"You're fine, come on! We fishermen have been making our way up 'n down that thing for about five centuries," he said impatiently.

I walked down the jetty.

"Where are we going?" I asked as I neared.

"We need to go and meet some people. And quick," he said, unwinding the rope.

The blue rowing boat bobbed away from the jetty, and I had no choice but to leap from the jetty into the departing vessel.

George grabbed the oars and began to row with big plunging strokes. I was amazed by how strong he was. He must be pushing seventy years old, yet he had taken us way out to sea within minutes.

Starfish looked far away now, and I began to wonder what on earth we were doing heading out to sea at dusk.

"I wouldn't worry, Crystal; I know these seas like the back of my hand. I could row us out 'n back with my eyes closed."

This all seemed highly unlikely as we had no compass in the event of the tide sweeping us off course, nor would we have any light to spot landmarks. However, yet again, my fate was in another's hands, and there was nothing I could do about it.

"We're heading to Gairdín bán-dearg," George announced after about five minutes.

"Oh, the garden something or another," I said remembering the map from earlier.

"Pink Garden."

That was what bán-dearg meant then. I realized we must be heading to the exact place Llyr took me. I gazed around us. The sea was calm tonight. Placid.

"Do you know Llyr?" I asked, unable to contain my curiosity any longer.

George continued to row, and I could hear every stroke as the silver water lapped beneath the oars.

"We'll be there soon," he replied to my question.

God, I wished people would be a bit more open around here. My life was turning out to be one big guessing game.

Suddenly in the water ahead, I saw three heads silhouetted by the sun which was in its final stages of descent behind them. I squinted. *Were they seals?*

George turned his head and nodded towards them, and then I saw an arm lift out of the water like it was signalling.

They were men.

George stopped rowing now, and we floated towards them. Detail began to fill in the shadowy faces, and I realized Llyr was among the three.

If he was shocked to see me, he didn't show it. Our eyes

met briefly, and then he turned his attention to George. They began to exchange words in a different language.

I had no idea what they were saying, or in what tongue. It sounded old fashioned, not like anything I'd learned at school.

George was now talking, and all three men in the water seemed to be listening intently.

As George spoke, I examined the other two.

One bore a strong resemblance to Llyr with long dark hair and a similar bone structure. I looked down and saw his big, strong arms were folded across his chest as he listened. I saw that he too had tattoos—only bigger, bolder Celtic patterns—and golden bands around his wrists. There was something very tribal about him.

I looked back up at his face. He had much thicker eyebrows than Llyr and was not quite as handsome, but there was an unmistakable similarity. They must be brothers.

The third man also had a broad, tattooed, and strong-looking upper body. He had long blond hair and was slightly unshaven. I had to admit, he was very good looking, and I hoped Llyr could not see my admiring glances. My attention shifted to a long, thin object poking out of the water beside him and realized he was carrying what looked like a spear.

I squinted and leant forward. I could see that there was a ring of white triangles decorating the upper part of the weapon.

I suddenly became aware that the men had fallen silent, and they were all looking at me.

"They are shark's teeth," said the blond man almost menacingly. He looked at me with suspicion, as though I were some intruder.

"I brought Crystal," explained George.

The man who bore a resemblance to Llyr began to talk back at George in their other tongue. He sounded irritable, holding out his hands. I got the uncomfortable feeling he was not happy that I had been transported along to this meeting.

I looked away; this was awkward.

Llyr swam over to me and rested his arms on the edge of the boat. "Hi," he said, looking up.

"Hi," I said back gratefully.

"Crystal, this is Ri," said Llyr, gesturing to the dark-haired man. He then nodded towards the blond guy with the spear, "and this is Spirit."

Spirit? How boho.

Spirit continued to watch me with suspicion.

"Who are you then, Crystal?" he challenged

"She is Keith White's daughter," George answered on my behalf.

Huh, they knew Dad?

"I have told them about your father and all the wonderful work he does in trying to stop SKANX," George said to me.

"Oh, yeah," I said awkwardly. "It's his ... thing."

Spirit laughed with what I sensed was scorn.

"Maybe we'd better go and do our 'thing' now?" he said to Llyr and Ri. "Where is this piece of crap leaving from, George?"

"Port Agatha," said George.

Port Agatha? That was where Mum was!

"What are you going to do?" I asked, with a tone of alarm.

Spirit rolled his eyes and sank slowly until he disappeared under the water. I grimaced at the bubbles where he had departed. What a jerk.

Ri nodded at me and lifted up a hand in a stern gesture of farewell before he too descended. At least he was relatively courteous.

"Llyr?" I said, my voice full of questions.

Llyr looked at me. I could not tell what he was thinking or feeling. There was a warmth, but he was not thinking of me tonight, he was preoccupied.

"We're going to stop the ship," he said calmly. "Our kingdom is under threat."

I nodded slowly, not because I agreed or understood, but because I wasn't quite sure what to say.

He winked at me, and then he too disappeared under the sea, leaving me once again full of questions and empty of answers.

We rowed back slowly. We were rapidly becoming entrenched in darkness but after what I had just seen, it felt like anything in the world was possible. Finding our way back to Starfish in the dark no longer seemed like such a big deal.

"So ... do you want to talk about what just happened?" I said, breaking the silence.

"The chaps?" came a casual reply.

I could no longer make out George's face; he was now dimming into a silhouette.

"Yes, the chaps!" I exploded. "The ones who were just bobbing about miles out at sea."

"Well, you know about all that Crystal," said George tiresomely.

"I've heard a story about it," I said.

"Yes, from your friend Rosie."

"She told you!"

"She told me she was going to tell you."

"Oh, well she did," I sighed in exasperation and leaned back against the stern of the boat. "You people tell me all these deep, dark secrets, and then you give me rations!"

"Rations?" said George bemusedly.

"Rations!" I reiterated in a squeak. "Scraps! I need details!"

"Oh, details!" exclaimed George, as though it had never occurred to him. "Well, they belong to a colony, a kingdom. And they've lived out here for many, many, many, many, years."

George rowed as he talked, and I could hear that he was getting a little breathless now, but I needed more info.

"A kingdom?" I repeated. "Like with a castle and a king and stuff?"

"Kind of," wheezed George. "It's called the Jeweled Kingdom. It is a place built with gemstones." George stopped rowing for a moment so he could talk. "And there's a palace. A palace made from amethyst. When the sunlight shines down through the water onto it, well, it is just the most glorious thing in the world."

I fell silent, stunned by the idea of such a place.

"Have you seen it?" I breathed.

George was silent.

"How do you know them?" I pushed.

"Okay, kid, if I tell you a secret, you mustn't tell a soul."

I leaned in closer.

"I will not tell a soul," I vowed. "But remember, if you tell me a secret I want details."

George sighed.

"Okay, I'll do my best," he said.

"Deal," I agreed. "Okay, how do you know them?"

"I'm ..." George stopped.

"Yessss?" I pressed. He was not getting off the hook with this one.

"I'm one of them," said George.

Chapter Fourteen

Life was getting weirder by the second.

One of them? George the fisherman—a merman?

"Well, kind of," George pondered, pulling out a torch lamp.

What did "kind of" mean?

We sat drifting in the dark. The lights of Starfish twinkled in the distance to the left, and a strip of orange dots to the right highlighted the mainland. It was like being on a plane looking down at the glowing patches of habitation against the wilderness.

"I mean, I have mer in my blood," George continued, turning on the lamp and placing it on the bench so that I could now make out all that was within a metre of us.

"Like, a relative?" I quizzed.

George clicked his fingers and pointed at me. "Exactly!"

"So ... How? Who? Huh?" I spluttered, my mind was flooding with questions.

"My mother," said George.

"Your mother was a mermaid?"

"Still is," George said. "She's out there somewhere. Probably at the palace; she likes to sing to everybody in the evenings. She has the most divine voice known to mer. It is so pure, so untarnished, like the jewels that surround her." I had never heard George speak with such passion. I leaned in, eager for more. "Ah, if I took you back out further you would hear it, even from up here," he said gazing behind me, at the sea we were leaving behind.

"So take me," I said, overwhelmed with intrigue.

George picked up the oars.

"No, not tonight. I need to get back."

I slumped back against the stern. I was being left high and dry, as usual.

I dipped my hand into the inky black waters. I still could not believe people lived underneath here. *How did they see anything?*

"So, if you're half whatever they are, do you get to swim down there?"

"Sadly not," said George. "I'm just a love child. I did not inherit many of the advantageous qualities of the pedigree mer. I cannot exist underneath the surface—I cannot even hold my breath for more than twenty seconds. I can't live for hundreds of years either—as you can see."

"Hundreds of years?!" I yelped.

"Yes, they're a bit like those big turtles, you know? The

ones that live for nearly a thousand years ... that kind of life span."

A thought crossed my mind.

"How old is Llyr?" I asked.

"Oh, he must be four hundred, odd."

I let out a high pitched giggle. *Four hundred? That was ridiculous.* I felt a bit weird all of a sudden. I know I wanted an older guy and everything, but Llyr was like, nearly ten times older than my dad.

"Yes, he's an antique," said George.

Suddenly there was a splash next to the boat. I gasped and sprang up, but as I did a wet hand grabbed my arm which was still dangling in the waters. I let out a massive scream as I felt a huge rush of adrenaline. It was the kind of rush where you are on a giant roller coaster, and it suddenly takes a massive plunge, and your stomach is in so many knots it hurts.

I saw Llyr's face looking up at me.

I let out a big gasp, which was actually bordering on another scream.

"Sorry," said Llyr, taking my hand in his. I put my other hand on my heart, trying to recover from the shock.

George chuckled. "He must have heard his name."

"Yes, I heard you telling her my age," he said smiling, as droplets of water ran down his face. He appeared to be more upbeat than earlier, like the Llyr I knew. "I'm only three hundred and twenty actually, but young in mind, body, and soul."

"Yeah, don't rub it in," said George with mock resentment.

"You scared the crap out of me," I said, my heart still pounding in my chest.

"Sorry, I wanted to see you," he said, placing my hand against his cheek.

"Did you stop the boat?" I asked, thinking it had only been a short time since I last saw him.

"It will not be leaving the port," Llyr replied.

I thought about Mum. She would be screwing.

"Where are you taking Crystal?" Llyr said to George.

"To her home, by the lighthouse," said George, picking up the oars again.

"Okay, I'll see you there," he said to me, letting go of my hand and disappearing again before I could say a word.

I shook my head. "I don't think I will ever get used to that, George."

George chuckled as he heaved back the oars. "Well, you might have to, he seems to be rather taken by you."

I said goodbye to George and watched as he and the little rowing boat disappeared around the curve of rocks.

I looked up at my house.

A light was on upstairs, it was probably Dad getting ready for bed. I thought of Mum and, despite everything, couldn't help but feel a little pity for her. She would be mortified right now.

A crescent moon now shone up above, and I heard the sound of water rippling in the illuminated waters below.

Llyr rose up just in front of the jetty, and this time, I didn't jump as much as before.

I sat down cross-legged at the end, and he swam closer.

"You coming in this time?" he said.

Was he mad? It was freezing.

"It's not so cold," he said.

"Okay, can you read my mind or something?" I demanded. *This was happening way too often for my liking.* "And anyway," I continued, "you're like, a fish, so it's obviously not going to be 'too cold' for you."

Llyr laughed out loud. "A fish? Is that what you think I am?"

"Well, obviously you're a bit human too."

"So then, I know that you will not find it very, very cold. In fact, I think you will like it."

I reached down and put my hand in. He was semi-right; it wasn't … freezing.

I suddenly remembered something. "Did you steal that boat that you brought the other day?"

Llyr smiled amusedly. "Borrowed it, yes."

I looked at him inquisitively. "Why?"

"Because I wanted to see you. I couldn't expect you to swim all afternoon. I couldn't think of another way. I took it back, don't worry." He looked at my face and could see that I was still not convinced. "You see, I have to stay by the water, just like you need to be by the land."

"So, what happens if you stay out of the sea for too long?" I asked slowly.

"I don't know; I've not had to be away from it for too long. But I've heard of mer getting swept inland by tidal waves and not surviving a day without water. We can be strong on our legs, but not for very long."

"Well, I'm not the greatest swimmer," I said, thinking about logistics. *How on earth were we ever going to spend any time together?*

"I loved swimming with you the other night," said Llyr.

I smiled as I thought about the night of the party. I guess if I really wanted to see him, I would have to meet him halfway.

I took off my cardigan. I had a black vest top on underneath. Next, I took off my boots and socks, and then I stood up to take my jeans off.

"I hope my dad doesn't see this," I said to Llyr as he waited below.

"It's probably a little dark for him," said Llyr distractedly, and I realized I had transfixed him.

I sat on the jetty in nothing but my vest top and underwear, lowering my legs into the water. I put the palms of my hands on the wood behind me and prepared to drop.

I closed my eyes; I couldn't believe I was doing this. I

momentarily wondered if I had gone mad and was simply hallucinating Llyr and this entire experience.

I lowered myself slowly into the sea, so as not to make a loud splash, and felt the chill of the water sting me from bottom to top as I descended.

When I was finally fully enveloped by the ocean, I swam out a little bit to get used to the cold. I turned and saw he was behind me, and together we swam further away from the island.

I was not afraid this time of sharks or currents. Knowing I was with Llyr, and what he was, made me completely fearless of the water.

We must have swum for about five minutes when we stopped, and I trod water. Just like last time, we were provided with some lighting from the moon, and I was able to make him out next to me.

"How do you know that I know what you are?" I said, suddenly curious.

"George said that you had come by the knowledge," he said calmly. "I was going to tell you, though."

I nodded and looked out to sea. We were quiet for a while, but there were other things on my mind.

"Why do you like me?" I asked, treading water. "Is it because of the information you can get from my dad?"

Llyr looked shocked. "No!" he said. "I would never make use of you in such a knavish act."

I giggled, sometimes he spoke in such old-fashioned tone.

He looked confused as to why I was laughing.

"Sorry," I said. "It's just the language you use; it reminds me of some of the manuscripts I read in my history class or something."

He smiled, and I had the feeling that once again he was not one hundred percent sure what I was talking about. But none of that mattered somehow. He reached out, drawing me closer to him, and I let myself be pulled into his arms. I rested my hands on his shoulders and looked into his eyes. Then finally our mouths pressed together, and I tasted the sea on his lips.

It was as I thought it would be, slow and sensual at first and then it became deeper and more passionate. I wrapped my arms around his neck, and his hands moved from my back to my hair and then they touched my face. I forgot who or where I was and everything else in my life during that kiss. It was everything I wanted and more.

We slowed down eventually, but he did not want to stop for one second, and his mouth moved from my face and down to my neck as I paused to catch my breath. Then we kissed all over again.

"In answer to your question, I like you for many reasons," he said when we finally withdrew from one another. "Your smile, your laugh, the things you say. I'm attracted to your beauty, obviously, but also your spirit."

I looked down, embarrassed by his words. No guy had ever said anything like that to me before.

"That night at the party, something drew me to you in

the dark, even before you were in trouble. It's like you sparkled or something," he continued.

"Is that why you said my name suits me?" I asked.

"One of the reasons," he said, retrieving my hand from the water and kissing it. He looked at me. "You really are getting cold now," he said.

I hadn't noticed in all the excitement, but it dawned on me that he was right. I was shivering.

We reluctantly started swimming back to my house, but as we approached the jetty, I heard the sound of an engine.

Suddenly the light of a boat came into view, and I realized it was a sea taxi approaching. Llyr pulled me behind the jetty, as the boat purred along to the other side.

Suddenly I heard the tapping of heels on the wood above. It was Mum.

Bugger—my clothes were on the jetty!

It sounded as though the boat was departing, and Mum's voice gradually became more audible as the engine faded.

"I cannot begin to express how sorry I am, Mr. Geake," said my mother.

She was talking on her mobile.

"I shall be down at the port at the crack of dawn, and we shall get to the bottom of this mess with the boat."

Her voice was just above us. I prayed she did not peer over the other side.

"Yes, yes, of course. And please, let me assure you that this is in no way an indicator of my performance ..."

My mother's voice and high heels appeared to travel away from us and down the jetty towards the ocean stairway. I breathed a sigh of relief. She had been too distracted grovelling to Mr. Geake to notice me or my clothes.

As soon as she had gone, Llyr turned to me.

"Is your mother one of them?" he whispered. I knew he meant SKANX.

"She just got a job there ... so like, she is paid money to work for them," I explained. "It's a total nightmare with Dad being the number one anti-SKANX activist."

"That must be hard," he said.

"Yeah," I agreed. "They are constantly arguing."

"You know, we had to stop that boat," said Llyr, now appearing worried about any problems he may have caused me. "Our people are getting ill from that poison they're bringing out there."

"Oh, I know!" I agreed. "I hate them too."

Llyr kissed me. "You'd better get in."

I was terribly cold now. "Yeah," I agreed, trying not to shiver too much.

He helped me climb onto the top of the jetty, and I wrapped my cardigan around me, thankful for the warmth it brought.

I looked down. "When will I see you again?"

"Sundown. The day after tomorrow?" he asked.

I nodded and gathered my clothes together. I was trembling.

I turned before pausing and turning back round again.

"Perhaps you'd better bring that boat along next time," I said.

Chapter Fifteen

I was aware that my English teacher was talking, but I could not process what she was saying. I was on another planet, and that planet may as well be called "Planet Llyr."

I must have played back every detail of last night a million times this morning.

I swallowed and was aware that it was slightly painful to do so. I seemed to have caught a chill, despite jumping in a blazing hot shower when I got home last night.

Maurice had bounded into the kitchen to see me after I said goodbye to Llyr. I had had to hold his tail as it was banging against the kitchen cupboards as it wagged. I did not want Mum and Dad to hear and see me coming home soaking wet. I had raced upstairs and spent about twenty minutes de-thawing under the piping water.

I ducked beneath the desk and hunted about in my bag for some paracetamol, failing to retrieve any.

I missed Llyr already and wished that he was coming

back tonight and not tomorrow. I had never felt so giddy for someone before in my whole life. It was like I was high on some kind of drug.

The bell rang, and I leaped up and tugged on my little sports jacket over my summer dress.

"Going somewhere, Crystal?" shouted the English teacher.

Everybody looked at me and laughed.

"Oh sorry," I said awkwardly. "I thought it was the end of class."

"I haven't set you your homework yet."

Homework? Over the summer holidays?

I smiled politely and sat back down again.

I walked down the corridor after class and saw Rosie standing with a group of people. I waved and headed over.

"School is officially over!" shrieked Rosie, bouncing up and down on the spot. "We are now officially upper sixers!"

"Yay," I said smiling, "and this time next year we will never have to do school again!"

"Oh my God! Stop it!" she screamed, her face lighting up like a Christmas tree. "You're so right."

"I have to tell you something," I said lowering my voice.

"Oooh okay," said Rosie, "we'll talk, we'll talk. These

guys all want to go for a drink, though, celebrate the end of the year."

"Oh, sure," I said, smiling at the small crowd. I was exploding to tell Rosie about last night but really couldn't be rude. "Let's go!"

Rosie linked one of the girl's arms, and they skipped off ahead while I walked along next to Lloyd and his friend Curtis.

They were both nice and fun, and we found ourselves joking about the Mrs. Vendercum and her strict ways.

"She was asking me about Pythagoras or something," said Lloyd, "and I didn't know what she was talking about, so she walked over to me, in front of the whole class and shouted *'Lloyd, you're an absolute banana!'*"

I giggled. I could just imagine her saying that. Mrs. Vendercum regularly seemed to throw strange insults at people, and in the process, her eyelashes would flutter really quickly, almost like a spasm.

"She called me a 'numpty' once," I recalled.

Lloyd laughed.

"Well apparently she called Rory an 'egg' once!" said Curtis.

We all cracked up.

"An egg!" I cried.

"Yes, an egg! I think it was over Pythagoras again; it really seems to get her going," laughed Curtis.

"Oh gosh, I'm dreading that class," I said, wiping away

a tear of laughter before a new thought entered my head. "Who's Rory by the way?"

I had never heard of or seen anybody by that name.

"Oh, he was a couple of years above us," said Curtis. "He finished school last year."

"How is he, anyway?" asked Lloyd, his brow furrowing.

"Getting there, I think," said Curtis. "His family are moving away, though. I think it's to get away from it all."

"Get away from what?" I asked. Curtis and Lloyd were silent, and I sensed I may have stuck my nose in somewhere it wasn't wanted. "Sorry," I said. "You don't have to tell me.

"No, it's okay," said Curtis. "Rory's dad died in a fire recently."

"Not that fire in the office?" I asked the article I had read the other week flashing through my mind.

"The VELO fire, yeah," said Lloyd. "That was the name of the company."

"How terrible," I said, remembering how I had read about a father with children. *Poor, poor Rory.*

"Awful," agreed Curtis. "Nobody even knows how that fire started."

We walked in silence for a while, haunted by our conversation, but as soon as we stepped out of the corridor and into the sunshine, our moods lifted again.

I suddenly felt ecstatic. *School was over, and the summer sparkled ahead. Oh, how I hoped that Llyr would be around to take me on more adventures!*

We walked out of the Coney School grounds and down the tree-lined streets towards the town center, laughing and joking the whole way. When we bundled into the pub The Dolphin, we grabbed a drink and settled on a table outside in the sun. Rosie nestled next to me, and I was able to tell her about my date, pausing here and there when the others fell silent between conversations.

"I can't believe you're going out with one of them!" breathed Rosie. "I don't know anyone who's done that before."

I frowned, as George's parents came to mind, but I knew that I could never say anything about that to Rosie.

I decided to change the subject.

"How's Will?"

Rosie smiled, "He's good. He's coming down a little later actually."

"Ah, summer love!" I sighed happily.

I chattered to some other school friends, now that I had lost Rosie to Will again. Rosie's bae had arrived about an hour ago, and we had all shuffled up so he could squeeze onto the bench next to her. He had been charming as ever, buying us all drinks and congratulating us on finishing school.

Will's hair was a much lighter blonde than I had remembered, perhaps it had been bleached during glorious sunny days at the beach surfing. I also couldn't help but notice that he had a super-hot body under his t-shirt.

I looked around the table and noticed, to my amusement, our female school friends giggled feverishly every time Will spoke. I inwardly laughed. They were all crushing on him, and Rosie was quite simply beaming with pride.

After a while, Will looked up and greeted someone. I leaned forward and realized that it was Allan.

"Hey!" I cried, jumping up. I was genuinely pleased to see him. We had really clicked that night at the beach party. "Good to see you!"

Allan looked at me and frowned. "Sorry, who are you again?" he replied breezily.

I recoiled, completely stung. *How could he not remember me?* The other girls around the table looked at me and smirked, and I stood there feeling humiliated.

After a few moments, I sat back down again, not even bothering to answer him.

"Harsh!" whispered Rosie, as Allan shook hands with all our school friends.

"Oh, whatever," I sulked, stirring my lemonade with my straw. I knew deep down he was punishing me for the beach party, but it seemed unfair. *It was hardly a criminal offense not to fancy somebody back.*

I looked up and caught sight of Jemima approaching the pub. *Oh great, more people to blank me.*

Suddenly I had a light bulb moment. Maybe there could be a solution to all my problems. *Could Hate + Hate = Love?*

"Introduce Allan to Jemima," I whispered to Rosie.

"Huh?" she squeaked, looking bewildered.

"I think they might like each other," I hissed.

When Jemima was close enough, Rosie stood up and hesitantly made the introductions. To my satisfaction, Allan immediately offered to buy her a drink, and I caught him shooting sideways glances towards me as she eagerly accepted.

I hope this works, I thought, chewing my straw nervously. If they could just both feel just a fraction of that dizzy sensation, that same one that I had had since last night, all animosity inside of them would dissolve.

Chapter Sixteen

The following morning, I lay in bed, congratulating myself. My plan with Jemima and Allan had worked a treat.

Just ten minutes had passed after they went into the pub, and I had turned and peeped through the window. Jemima and Allan had been perched on bar stools gazing into each other's eyes.

Jemima had actually looked really pretty with a smile on her face. Radiant, even.

An hour or so had gone by, and neither had left the bar. I had been bursting for the Lady's and had had to pass them on the way. They had looked up and to my delight; they'd smiled with an air of excitement about them.

"Hey, Crystal," Allan had said, appearing to have recovered from his amnesia.

Jemima had giggled. "Hello," she cooed.

They had appeared really quite taken by each other, and

I had no more enemies. *Two birdies, one stone,* I smiled to myself, as I stretched out my arms in bed. *How simple human beings could be, sometimes.*

My stomach rumbled and I decided to get up and go downstairs. I threw back the covers and opened my curtains; the sea dazzled under the midday sun. I thought about Llyr out there somewhere and felt butterflies in my stomach, as I remembered our date later this evening.

"Hi, darling!" said Dad, as I made my way downstairs.

"Hi, Dad," I smiled. As I descended, I saw he was putting on his shoes by the back door.

"Have you heard?" he asked. I sensed the excitement in his voice.

"Err, heard what, Dad?"

"SKANX still can't get their boat to work," he chortled merrily. "It was their very own brand new waste disposal tanker, and it's stranded in the port—a right eyesore, I might add—not popular with the locals. Anyway, they've got top engineers scratching their heads not knowing what to make of it!"

What on earth had Llyr, Ri, and Spirit done to that boat? I felt torn; I was so happy for Dad and the people of the Jeweled Kingdom, but I couldn't help but think of Mum. My father gloating like this would no doubt impact horribly on her mood.

"Now, now, Dad. Think about Mum." I warned.

"Oh, she'll get over it," said Dad, waving a hand and opening the door.

I sighed. A huge part of me wanted to get on board with Dad and the mers, but that could create even more problems here at home. I should stay neutral, at least until Mum was done with this stupid job.

She would give it up soon. It was the only way.

I decided to get dressed and look for a job. Maybe the more time I spent away from the whole situation, the better.

―――――

I caught the 1:00 p.m. boat to the mainland and walked for ten minutes along the beach towards Pearl Boulevard. As I neared, I checked my reflection in a boutique window. I wore a knee-length black skirt and a pressed white shirt. That afternoon, I had broken my four-year hiatus on ironing, and now I definitely looked the part of a classic waitress.

I took a deep breath and walked into Castello's, the same restaurant where Dad had taken us to celebrate Mum's arrival.

A waiter in a bow tie and tailed waistcoat glided towards me as I entered, his face was the absolute picture of hospitality.

"Good afternoon, miss, are you here for lunch?" he said charmingly with an Italian accent, a thick black eyebrow raised.

I smiled and looked down. "Actually no," I said in a lowered voice. "I was looking for a job."

The waiter broke into a smile. "Ah, I see. Have you experience in silver service?"

I frowned. "Er, what?"

He laughed. "Don't worry," he said kindly. "Let me fetch the manager, miss. You may well be in luck, some of our waitresses are leaving."

I smiled and relaxed a little. It all sounded very positive so far. I looked around the restaurant. Every table was full, and the waiters zoomed gracefully from table to table.

If they were stressed, they did not show it. I hoped I would be able to look that cool under pressure.

Suddenly a familiar leopard skin top caught my eye, and I recoiled as I realized it was my mother.

She was leaning forward and listening intently. I knew my mother well and could see that she was genuinely absorbed in whatever conversation she was having.

My eyes darted to the object of her captivation. He was a corporate type, dressed in a crisp shirt and tie. He was vaguely handsome, but he did not appear to have any warmth to his face whatsoever.

It suddenly dawned on me who this person was. I had seen him in many newspaper articles thrust angrily under my face by Dad. It was Mr. Geake, the Chief Executive of SKANX.

Ugh, so that was what mother was doing here, looking at him so intensely! I zoned in for a moment, and my eyes focused on her facial expression. Her brow was furrowed, and she was biting a lip. It was as though she were in a deep conflict.

The light caught Mr. Geake's golden watch as he lifted his hand to signal the waiter and I watched on with disgust as he clicked his fingers.

How bloody rude! I wouldn't even do that to Maurice.

I watched on as he lowered his arm and placed his hand on my Mum's wrist. I suddenly found it difficult to swallow. *Was that really the way you touched your colleague?*

I turned and raced back to the door. I could not stay here and watch them a minute longer. I broke into a run when I got outside, abandoning the boulevard, my job search forgotten. I hoped and prayed that I had been very much mistaken by what I had just seen.

———

That evening, I got ready for my date with Llyr, but instead of the excitement I had felt earlier, I was plagued with worry about my family.

Why had he touched her arm like that? And why was she looking so stressed by the end? Was it guilt? Had Mr. Geake been giving her some ultimatum? Leave your husband and run off with me?

I shuddered and pushed the whole thing out of my head. I couldn't just assume the worst. Maybe they were simply having a business discussion.

I had to just forget about it; I was finally going on a

planned date with Llyr, and I could not let Mum and that stupid company ruin this for me.

After a little wardrobe debate, I decided on a long navy blue tie-dyed dress. It was a halter-neck design, and it clung to my body. I let down my hair and brushed it so that it hung in two yellow curtains around my face. Like Will, my hair was getting brighter and brighter every day.

The house was quiet, and both my parents appeared to be out so, I let myself out of the door and made my way over to the jetty.

The sun was just about to connect with the sea, and I sat on the jetty and watched its descent. It was a burning copper-gold this evening and was truly sensational. I wished that he would hurry up and get here so we could watch it together.

After about twenty minutes, I began to feel a little nervous. *This was sunset, right? The day after yesterday, yeah? So where was he?*

As interesting as my unconventional love life was, I felt myself wishing again that Llyr had a mobile or at least a clock.

As the sun sank further, so did my heart and soon, I sat alone in the dark. Maybe he wasn't coming for me after all.

Chapter Seventeen

"Crystal!" a familiar voice called.

I turned around, now halfway back up the stairway to the garden.

I squinted, and in the dark, I could see a white triangular object gliding towards the jetty. *Where was he?*

As the triangle got nearer, I realized that it was a sail, and soon after I was able to make out a little wooden boat to which it was attached. Llyr was perched on the edge steering unsurely.

"Sorry," he said distractedly fumbling with a couple of ropes. "This is not the easiest thing to work."

"Where did you get it?" I asked.

"Oh, I just pulled it out of the harbor. I thought it looked like a very basic boat, but it's ... you know, fiddly?" He looked at me, as though to check he'd said the right word.

I giggled. "Yes, fiddly!"

He took my hand, and I lowered myself into the sailboat.

"I'll take it back later, don't worry," he said, tugging at a rope and pushing us away from the jetty.

After a bit of experimentation with the sail ropes, we set off, travelling slowly and slightly more surely over the still dark waters.

"Where do you want to go?" he asked.

"Somewhere where I can see you would be good," I said, looking around at the ebony night enveloping us.

"Of course, I'm sorry I forget you can't see in the dark."

"Why, can you?"

"Yes, I can see you perfectly."

"Okay, what color dress am I wearing then?" I challenged, just to be sure.

"Blue, with white bits," he said. "And I can see the shells around your foot as well."

I felt my anklet in the dark. *He really could see.* That was comforting, as traveling on the sea in the pitch black was highly disconcerting. I felt like I was blindfolded and had no idea where I was going.

"Don't worry, you know I'll look after you," he said, sensing my fear.

I smiled, which I trusted he would see.

"So I guess that's how you guys find your way about in the deep dark waters then?"

"Yes, it helps," said Llyr.

As ever, I wanted to know more about his world.

"Where do you live?" I pressed.

"In the Jeweled Kingdom," he replied. "In a palace. It's purple, and made from a big jewel."

"Oh, the Amethyst Palace?"

"Yes. The Amethyst Palace. Although those poisons have ruined it," Llyr said. He was probably angry, but he never showed it. "It's eroding in places. Maybe we will have Spirit restore it when we can be sure that those ships won't be coming back."

"I'm sorry on behalf of my species," I said guiltily. "You said they've been making your people ill?"

"Yes," he said solemnly, "some of the younger mer have not been able to survive."

I bit my lip. *That wretched company!*

"We tried to treat them with all the remedies we could source, but three passed last season," he said, his voice heavy with sorrow. He paused for a long time, and I began to wonder if he was okay. Although I could not see him, I sensed he were reliving the memories.

"You were there when they ...?" I trailed off.

"At the third death," he replied. "They brought her to the palace."

He fell silent again.

"How terrible," I said, softly.

"Well, it's not the first time we've had to contend with men and their poisons," said Llyr, his voice returning to its normal pitch now. "We used to get a lot of oil ships, maybe ten years ago. They always leaked all over the place. We could not see the jewels at one point because they were covered in a black slime. We messed with their boats, sent them off course. They kept getting so lost that they must have changed their route in the end. But still, there will be other mer out there now suffering because of these oil ships."

I remembered the SKANX tanker. "By the way, what the hell did you guys do to the ship the other night?"

"Well, Ri ripped out the engine, I took it apart, and then Spirit put it back together again," I heard Llyr laugh in the dark. "They will never be able to fix it."

"I'd like to see you in action," I said. "You seem so soft and gentle, but I bet you're actually really scary when you get going."

He laughed hard. "Ah, you're funny."

"Are you scary?" I asked.

"Why, are you scared of me?"

"No."

Suddenly something caught my eye ahead, and I gasped. A patch of water ahead was surging with white light from beneath.

"What the hell?"

"Well you wanted light," he said stopping the boat.

"Is this the Jeweled Kingdom?" I asked.

"No, these are just sea faeries," he replied.

"Sea faeries!" I shrieked. I could see his face now, and he was looking at me with great amusement.

"They're okay, don't worry," he said reaching out and

pulling me to him. "You probably won't even see them; they stay below."

I couldn't quite relax, and my eyes darted from side to side unsurely. *So now there were faeries too? Were these faeries nice faeries?*

"Okay, look," Llyr said, sensing my unease. He leaned over the boat and put his hand in the glowing water below.

"Look what?" I squealed, cowering in the boat.

He scooped about and eventually retrieved his fist.

"Are you ready to see a sea faerie?" he asked. We now sat on the floor of the boat, and his hand shook a little, with the movement of whatever was inside. I peered at it half intrigued, half terrified. He opened it slowly, but I got nervous and backed away. I don't know why, but these faeries were freaking me out. "Come on Crystal, it's fine, just trust me for once."

"Okay, okay!" I promised, sitting still again and forced myself to watch him open his hand.

Three little sparks shot out of his palm and straight back into the water.

"They were sea faeries?" I asked incredulously. "They were teeny."

"Yeah, it bit me, as well," said Llyr looking at his palm. I reached out and took it and saw a little blood spot.

"Sorry," I said.

"Oh well, I think I'll live," he said, putting his arms around me.

I looked up at him and was pleased that I could now see him.

"I missed you," I said.

"I miss you all the time when I'm not with you," he said, bringing me down so that we lay in the boat. "I always think of you and wonder how you are. Although I can often sense when you are upset or in trouble."

"Really?" I asked as we held each other. Although it didn't really surprise me, I had always felt as though he could read me like a book.

"Yeah, did something happen today?" he asked.

I thought of my mum and Mr. Geake.

"Family stuff," I sighed, "but I will just get upset if I talk about it."

"You can be upset if you like," he said.

"I know, but I barely get to be with you, I don't want to ruin it with all that," I said as we looked into each other's eyes. "Anyway, who else can you sense is in danger or upset?"

"Just people who I have a connection with," he said.

"That's sweet." I suddenly thought of something else. "Hey, do you have a tail?"

He sat up a little and smiled. "Yeah, why do you want to see it?"

I wasn't sure if I was ready for that just yet.

"Maybe some other day."

He laughed and lay back down. He ran his hand up and down my arm, which was wrapped around him. "Okay, another time then. Is there anything else you want to know?"

I racked my brains but couldn't think of anything else for now.

"No further questions," I said.

He leaned over me and placed his hand on the side of my face. "Sure?"

I nodded from below.

"Okay good," he said. "Because, I want to kiss you so very badly."

—————

We must have kissed for about an hour in that boat, but we couldn't get enough of each other, and every time we stopped we would have to start again.

He ran his hands up and down my body, and I knew we both wanted to take it further, but something was stopping me. I guess it was that old-fashioned worry of giving in too easily.

I did find myself wondering at one point if this dating etiquette meant anything in mer-land? They seemed to be a little more unrestrained than us; Llyr had always been all over me from the start. Maybe he thought me very bizarre and conservative.

As usual, Llyr read my mind.

"I know, you want to wait," he said between kisses. "I think we should, you know, make love when the time is right."

I giggled a little at his old-fashioned terminology. I had never heard anyone actually say "make love" before.

"Thanks," I said. I hoped he meant what he said, and wasn't just trying to make me feel better.

He kissed me again before leaning back a little.

"You taste so salty," I said, as he withdrew from me and I was left with a soft sting on my lips.

"I can't even find a word to describe how you taste," said Llyr. "Delicious, maybe."

As we lay there floating in the faerie glow, I suddenly thought of another question I wanted to ask him.

"Have you ever been with a girl like me before?" I said.

"A human?" he asked.

"Well ... yeah."

"No," he said. His mood appeared to change, and he sat up, suddenly with a sense of seriousness about him.

"What's wrong?" I asked worriedly, sitting up too.

"I have, to be honest with you, Crystal. They're not happy about it."

"Who?" I asked.

"Well, mainly Ri."

"Your brother?" I asked.

"Well, he's my father actually ..." Llyr explained.

Your father!" I exclaimed. Then I nodded slowly as I remembered that their life span was about eight centuries, and it was therefore perfectly possible for a father to look not a day older than his son. "So, why wouldn't he be happy?" I asked dejectedly.

"It's not that he doesn't like you," said Llyr. "In fact, he said he thought you were truly beautiful. It's just that he thinks mers making themselves known to humans is foolish, let alone, getting involved with them."

"It happened with George's parents," I argued.

"Yes, and look how that turned out." said Llyr. "The poor man has battled with identity crisis his whole life. He never knew where he belonged—with mer or man. He wanted to come and be with us, but didn't have the physical ability to survive beneath the surface."

I felt an unbearable sadness, and I put my hand on my chest. "Please, you're breaking my heart," I begged.

Llyr looked out to sea. "It's sad," he agreed.

Suddenly, my attention turned back to us. "Well, if you know of all these complications, then why did you come to me?"

For the first time, Llyr looked taken aback. He frowned uncomfortably.

"Well, everyone's different," he said. "That's what I keep telling Ri. Just because I am with you, doesn't mean the same thing is going to happen as with Nephys."

I nodded as though I understood, but really his words were still niggling at me. I guess a part of me worried that Ri was right, but I was not prepared to think about reality just yet. And it didn't seem like Llyr was either.

Chapter Eighteen

"Well I think he has a point!" said Rosie brightly, as she powdered her cheeks with the world's most humongous blusher brush.

"Who?" I asked. I was propped up on a purple gingham pillow on her bed, seeking counsel.

"Llyr, obviously," came Rosie's reply.

"Really?" I asked with surprise. I had been expecting Rosie to be in firm agreement with the seemingly more rational Ri.

"Yes, because, he's right. You and Llyr aren't exactly like George's parents, I mean you're not going to just immediately procreate!" she finished, blowing on her blusher brush. "You're only, like, seventeen."

A pink cloud had billowed out in front of her.

I became hysterical with giggles. *Procreate?* It wasn't just Llyr who had a funny way with words around here.

"No," I laughed. "I suppose we're not going to instantly just breed."

Rosie cackled. "Copulate!" she cried.

We were in stitches, and I wiped away a tear. Rosie was always so very funny.

"I mean, they probably didn't even have contraception back then," said Rosie reasonably.

I shrugged my shoulders. "Who knows? By the way, Rose, I actually feel really awful telling you that thing about George and his parents. Please never say anything to anyone," I said, in a more serious tone.

I had had to spill the beans to Rosie; there was no other way I could explain the whole crazy situation to her.

"I won't, I promise," said Rosie, putting on some mascara. "You had to tell me anyway; it's for your own mental state. You'd go mad if you had to keep all this stuff to yourself, right?"

"Right," I said, grateful for Rosie's justifications. I feared that George and the merfolk might disagree, but like Rosie said, I just couldn't process it all on my own.

"So, do you think this is the right outfit?" Rosie asked standing up. She wore a pink t-shirt with jewel-encrusted shoulders and tight black jeans.

"Of course, you look gorgeous," I said, with zero hesitation.

Rosie was off on a double date with Will, Allan, and Jemima. They were going for a drink and then to a party. I remembered when it had been just me and Rosie drinking wine and getting ready to go out, and I had to admit, I felt a little jealous.

"Thank you," said Rosie. "Gosh, I wish you and Llyr could come with us."

I laughed, this was a very weird thought. *Llyr in a pub or at a party?*

"Yeah ..." I agreed hesitantly.

"I know, I know, it's obviously out of the question," she said, picking up her phone and lipstick and popping them into a little pink handbag, "but you have no idea how much I would love to meet him."

I nodded and bit my lip. He was every bit as intriguing as one would imagine.

"Well, I bet Jemima's pretty happy that you guys are hanging out again," I said ultra-casually, so as not to show a hint of envy.

Rosie half smiled, and half rolled her eyes. "Yes, she's over the moon. You were such a genius setting those two grumps up!"

"Well, I just thought they had so much in common with their burning hatred of me ..." I said with a trace of sarcasm.

"And now they love you!" Rosie snickered, sitting down on the bed. "Jemima's like, 'Crystal's so nice, Crystal's so cool,' and I'm like about to strangle her, going 'Yeah nuh, I told you!'"

I laughed. "People are weird."

"So, Crystal," asked Rosie. "Have you and Llyr ... you know?

"Oh!" I said, looking down. "No. I thought we should wait a bit, right?"

"Yeah, okay that's a good idea. But how do they ...?" Rosie asked, her eyes gleaming with curiosity.

"I'm really hoping it's the same way as us," I said with unease. I had not assumed otherwise.

Rosie burst into giggles. "I'm so sorry. I'm sure it is the same from what you've told me. I just wondered that's all."

"Oh, gosh, please. I really couldn't cope with any more surprises," I said, trying to barricade the whole thought from my mind before it became an issue.

"No, no, it will be. Sorry!" Rosie said, putting a hand on my knee. "Let's just erase this whole conversation from our memories!"

"Okay. Erasing ... Erasing ..." I said searching my brain frantically for a new conversation topic. "Have you and Will?" I asked, suddenly realizing we had not touched base on this matter for a while.

Rosie looked at me and nodded.

"And?" I said, excitedly.

"Oh well, it was lovely!" she said.

I detected some hesitance in her voice.

"But ...?"

"It's just he's so much better at it than me," she sighed. "There, I said it!"

"No!" I wailed defensively. "Maybe he's just more experienced, but you'll catch up!"

"I hope so ..." she sighed.

"You will!" I insisted.

Yeah?" asked Rosie hopefully.

"I promise. And you'll probably learn all kinds of things ..." I added encouragingly. "I'm sure he thinks you're fantastic anyway."

Rosie looked at me and smiled. "Thanks. So when are you next seeing you're sea-bloke?"

I broke into a smile of excitement, as I remembered our next date.

"Tomorrow," I said brightly. "He wants to take me somewhere special."

Later on that evening, I looked painfully at the home-made fish pie that sat on the kitchen table. Two things were making me uncomfortable. Firstly, the fish thing, and secondly, the fact that my mother was nowhere to be found.

After a lot of fumbling on his mobile, Dad put it down on the kitchen counter.

"Well, she's obviously not coming," he said.

I felt my eyes fill up with tears, but I didn't want Dad to see, so I willed them to go away. He had spent all day preparing this meal and had been up at the crack of dawn buying the seafood.

"Nevermind," said Dad, picking up the spatula. "Shouldn't let it go to waste, eh?"

"Well, she'll come home later, she can try it then, I guess," I said encouragingly.

"Hmm," he said, "perhaps."

I wondered if I should tell him what I had seen at the restaurant. *Should I keep this from him?* I quickly decided that I needed to speak to Mum first, if anyone. *I mean, I could have the whole thing completely wrong, right?*

"So, are you coming on the demonstration on Friday?" Dad asked, slapping a huge piece of fish pie on my plate.

My eyes widened. "Huh?"

"There's going to be a huge anti-SKANX protest," said Dad, confirming my fears. "We're going to assemble here on the island and then take a ship to the mainland. We will then meet up with hundreds of other protesters and march through town, passed the council, where there will be speeches and a vigil. Then we will make our way through the countryside and, finish the whole thing at the beast itself."

Oh no.

"You're going to go and protest at the factory?" I said with alarm.

"Yes, I'm going to lead," said Dad proudly. "I've got a flag ready. And a megaphone."

"But ... what about Mum?" I said, worriedly. If anything

was going on with Mr. Geake, then this would only make things A LOT worse. Like, A LOT.

"This is the planet we're talking about Crystal. The planet."

Oh, my Gosh! While I totally got Dad's plight, I just felt like neither of them cared about keeping our family together anymore. *I mean, did he have to lead this demo? Couldn't he just march along discretely?* It was like SKANX had become the most important thing in the world. For both of them.

Chapter Nineteen

It was another beautiful day, and Llyr and I rowed over the waves. Today we were in George's blue boat, which was slightly more relaxing than "borrowing" from strangers, albeit much slower.

I could not believe how wonderful the weather was in this part of the world and was beginning to think Coney and Starfish had its very own microclimate. Since that wild storm last month, there had been nothing but ferocious sunshine.

Today I wore huge sunglasses and a headscarf, which was tied over my hair. I did not want anybody to see me out with Llyr, as this would quite possibly result in a lot of explaining on my behalf.

On second thought, given Llyr's tendencies to not even be visible, I may instead just appear as though I were sitting on my own in a boat, in the middle of the ocean.

I watched him row through my sunglasses, and secretly

admired the way his strong arms sliced the oars through the water as though each one was a knife through melted butter.

"You're watching me?" he asked.

"Yep," I admitted and giggled, "You're a good rower."

"Thank you," he said. "What are those things on your face, by the way?"

"Sunglasses?" I laughed. "How can you not know what sunglasses are?"

He stopped rowing. "I've watched people wearing them before, but I often wondered what they were. Can I see?"

I handed them to him, and he put them unsurely over his eyes. "They make things darker," he proclaimed, pulling the glasses off again and examining them.

"Yes that's the whole point," I said.

"So at night time you can't see, but then when it is the day you want to make everything dark again like it is the night?" he said looking very confused.

"Well, not exactly. It's just we don't like things too dark, or too bright." I said defensively. "I mean, we can't all just gaze into the sun, like you."

It was true; sometimes this man just stared up at the sky without so much a blink or a squint. It was as though nature and all its extremities were of no complication or hindrance to Llyr whatsoever.

"Ah, well it wasn't always this way for us," said Llyr, handing me back the sunglasses and picking up the oars.

"No?" I asked, putting them back on over my eyes.

Llyr looked ahead and sighed. "We're not too far now."

I looked around us and saw that, as usual, we were in the middle of a vast expanse of water.

"Really?" I asked. I hoped that we were going to be near some land, and not some underwater spectacle that I could neither view not visit. "Is it a place I will be able to see?" I asked.

"Yes," he promised. "You will love it."

The waves brought us closer into the cove, and we relaxed and let them carry us.

As we drifted inland, I gazed at my surroundings with awe. Mauve-coloured cliffs jutted out into the waters around us. I took my sunglasses off and leaned closer. They appeared to be made up of thousands of jagged chunks of marble.

I turned my head to the left so that I could see where we were heading. To my surprise, I saw white, sprawling sands. *Why was this incredible beach so deserted? And why on earth had I never seen postcards of it before?*

When we were near enough Llyr jumped into the sea, and began to pull the boat into the shore.

"Do you want some help?" I shouted over the roar of the breaking waves.

"No," replied Llyr, "just hold on."

"Are you s—"

I cut off mid-sentence as I felt the boat lift high out of the emerald water and into the air.

"Llyr?" I asked peeking up over the edge, wondering what in God's name was happening now. The boat appeared to land on the beach, and then there was Llyr again, standing on the same side as before.

"Did you ... just ... pick up ... the boat?" I asked slowly.

Llyr did not answer but held out his hand to me, and I took it in a daze. Seriously, I think he had just placed the boat on the beach in a similar fashion to which one might place a salad bowl on a dining room table or something. Jeez.

I used his hand to pull myself up and stepped onto the beach. The sand was warm on my toes, and I felt joy and happiness wash over me. It was beautiful.

He wrapped his arms around me. "It's called Crystal Bay."

We spent the whole day exploring "Crystal Bay." Llyr showed me little creeks in the cliff where there were all kinds of hidden secrets.

In one cove we found a waterfall which cascaded over the mauve rocks and into a deep emerald green pool. Llyr wanted to jump straight in, and I had to admit I was strongly tempted, that was until Llyr told me that sea fairies lived below the waters.

"They're like weird little mosquitoes!" I protested.

"They're harmless!" he pleaded, already with one leg in. "They're probably asleep at this time anyway."

I sighed and reluctantly took off my dress. I was wearing a bikini today as I knew Llyr would want to get me into the water. It was an inevitability.

After quite a lot of encouragement, I fully submerged myself in the pool, and once I was in, I had to admit, it was pretty lush. The water was cool, and it was refreshing after a day in the sun.

Llyr pulled me into the center of the pool, and we bobbed about for a while, enjoying the water. A beam of sunshine broke through the rocks like a little spotlight, and I swam into it.

I laughed, I don't know why I think it was just happiness. I looked up at my surroundings. The beam had cast a little mini rainbow in the waterfall, adding to the magic of the cove.

"I can't believe this place is called Crystal Bay!" I exclaimed excitedly.

"Well, it is now," he laughed.

"Huh?" I said confused.

"I named it after you," he said.

I was a little baffled. "You own this island or something?" I asked jokingly, squinting in the sunbeam.

"Yes, we consider it mer-territory," he replied with absolute seriousness. "Well, this part of the island anyway."

"No way!" I shrieked. "How on earth do you stop humans coming here?"

"Well the rest of the island is not so beautiful, and it is very rocky, which I believe makes it uninhabitable for your kind," he replied.

"Yes but this part is stunning," I argued, "even if only to visit."

"Well, the cliffs here are very treacherous," he said, looking up and around at the jutting purple rock.

"But can't they just sail in on a boat like we did?" I asked.

"I have had to work quite hard to keep it our secret place," he admitted, "but I have my ways."

"Well, I love it!" I declared. I couldn't believe he named the beach after me; this was surely the sweetest thing anyone had ever, or could ever, do. It also got me thinking about what kind of position Llyr had amongst the mers if he was in possession of land.

After our swim, we walked back to the beach through the little winding creek.

"There is one other reason I think this beach should be called Crystal Bay," he said, taking my hand and helping me climb down a rock.

"Yeah?" I said, wincing at the rocks on my bare feet.

He picked up a loose chunk of marble that had fallen from the cliff, and snapped it in half, as though it were a candy bar. A purple sparkly substance gleamed from within the marble.

"Oh my gosh!" I cried. "Is that Amethyst?"

"Yes," he replied handing me the one of the broken slabs and discarding the other. I was still struggling with the rocks beneath me, and so he scooped me up in his arms to carry me back to the beach.

"It is a crystal that does not usually form in this part of the world. However there is an abundance on this isle, both in its cliffs and surrounding waters," he said.

"Wow," I said, holding it up closer to my gaze.

"It is a wonderful gem," he said. "It keeps you clear-headed. In fact, George told me that humans used to drink from amethyst in ancient times, as they believed that it stopped you from becoming intoxicated."

"Well," I said, "it sounds kind of counter-productive if you are drinking wine from it."

"Yes, I don't think I would like an amethyst cup myself ..." said Llyr.

"You drink?" I asked bemusedly, trying to imagine him sitting in his underwater palace with a pint.

"Kind of," he said. "I know you do."

I frowned for a moment, not knowing what he was referring to. Then I remembered the night when we had first met, and how I had nearly drowned in my drunken hysteria.

"I don't drink that much," I said. "Only social, sometimes."

"I think your friend could have done with an amethyst cup," he said, with a smile.

I laughed, remembering the state of Rosie that night.

We had arrived back on the beach, and he placed me back on the sand. I turned and looked at him.

"Why were you at the beach that night?" I asked, suddenly curious. I had not given it much thought before.

"I saw the fire," he said. "I was returning from a journey way out in the Atlantic, and it caught my eye. Then suddenly all these people came running into the sea, and I was curious, I guess. I had never been to a human party before."

"Well, I'm glad you decided to swing by," I said, looking up at him.

He nodded. "I'm glad too."

Chapter Twenty

Sunset was approaching on Crystal Bay, and we sat on the beach together, looking out to sea. The cliff behind us was now flushed crimson by the sunset. The light must also have caught the crystal beneath the surface, as it twinkled somewhat.

I felt so blissful and chilled here with Llyr; it was almost like I was in a daze. When it got a little darker, we lay back on the sand and my eyes traveled over his gorgeous body.

I thought about how badly I wanted him, but Rosie's question kept playing on my mind. *Damn her.*

"Llyr ...?" I began. *Eugh, how was I ever going to ask him?*

"What's wrong?" he turned his head and looked at me with a bemused smile.

"Mmmm," I began. *Great start.* "Umm," I continued hopelessly.

He rolled on his back and closed his eyes. "Okay, wake me up when you're ready."

"I just wondered about merpeople and how they ... you know?" I said.

"I know?" he asked, his eyes still closed.

"Well, maybe you don't know ..." *Oh Gosh, this was awkward. Maybe I shouldn't ask; I should just wait to find out.*

He had now opened one eye and was looking at me, awaiting a full explanation.

I suddenly realized he knew exactly what I was talking about; he just wanted me to say it.

"Like, is it the same?"

"What's *it*, Crystal?"

"It!"

He began laughing hard.

"Yes," he answered finally.

I hit him on the arm with outrage. "See! You did know what 'you know' was. I hate you."

"Don't hate me," he murmured pulling me to his chest and kissing the top of my head. After a while, he turned and faced me. "You know, we were humans once, many centuries ago."

"Really?" I said, somewhat surprised.

"Yeah," said Llyr, running his fingers up and down my arm, before it rested somewhere in my hair. "And we're still very much human in the way we do things, only we dwell in the sea, and as you may have noticed, there are special things that we can do ... How we became mer is a long story, but I can tell it to you if you wish?"

"Yes, of course," I said, as I lay in his arms. I felt so privileged to be here with him, learning such secrets.

"Well, we originated from a Celtic tribe who lived inland on these very shores," Llyr began. "Our ancestors lived atop a mountain happily; I'm told, nearly two millennium ago. Your country was peaceful at that time; there were no wars. Everybody was happy, until one season there was no rain. The lands were scorched, rivers ran dry and most seriously, there were no crops."

"A drought that bad in England?" I asked doubtfully.

"Yes, as you may know, this was unheard of on such a rainy isle," he answered, "and our ancestors were deeply panicked. There was a shaman in the tribe who put himself into a deep trance so that he could contact the other world and ask them how this could be. He eventually began communicating with a spirit, who told him it was Carman, the witch who was responsible for the droughts."

"Huh, who's that?" I asked, feeling a bit spooked all of a sudden. He didn't say this was going to be a horror story.

"She was a malevolent warrior also thought to be a goddess of all black magic," he replied. "Carman and her sons, Dub, Dother, and Dain, roamed the lands bringing instant destruction to everything in their path. When they came to our ancestor's tribe, however, the spirit said she had decided to watch them suffer slowly with a hex."

I felt goose bumps prickle on my flesh, and he rubbed them away before he continued. "So, the spirit told the shaman that the only way she would cease the drought was if he were sacrificed to her. He bravely relayed this to the tribesmen but, of course, they refused to kill one of their beloved spiritual leaders. They decided to go and visit Carman herself and see if they could reason with her. They traveled down to one of her lairs on the ... brown expanses. Is it moors?" he asked, looking down at me.

I nodded and smiled. He continued.

"Here, they found her completely covered in a long black costume, with a—"

He put his hands over his head.

"A hood?" I guessed. It was all a little reminiscent of charades sometimes, and I could only imagine he was referring to a cloak.

"Perhaps," he said, shrugging a shoulder. "She was standing in one of her famous stone circles. She beckoned them in, but they refused to enter as they feared it to be thick with bad spirits. The tribe asked her to please relieve them, but she would not negotiate. It was the shaman or nothing."

"Why did she want the shaman so bad?" I asked.

"She did not like shamanism," he replied. "She did not like the way they could reach out to good spirits and learn about her magic. She perceived them as a threat. Anyway, the tribe's people left with no bargain, and they gradually became sicker and sicker until the only thing they could do to escape the great drought, was to leave their lands and travel towards the sea. This was four or five days walk away, but they hoped that they might pass water along the way. Unfortunately, Carman had summoned evil spirits and made sure all rivers ran dry, and they had no choice but to stagger towards the coast. As a last resort they had decided they would use fire to separate the sea water from the salt so that they could drink it, but some were now so weak they perished along the way. When the survivors did arrive they ran to the waters, desperate to gather it. Only to their horror, when they reached the sea, their lower bodies turned to fish, and they fell into the waves."

I turned and looked at him, my mouth now open. I had never in a million years imagined that the mer-people could be the result of magic.

Llyr continued, "According to legend, the skies opened right then and there, and the drought was over. The only person not to turn was the shaman and devastated and alone he quickly sought help to destroy Carman. He located a tribe who were said to be the people of Danu, the goddess of light. This colony had been able to fend off the witch with their superior powers and together they finally drove Carman and her sons out of these lands and across the seas."

"So where is she now?" I asked.

Llyr sighed. "Some people think she is in other lands, bringing misery to its inhabitants. We cannot be sure from the sea, but there have been tales of sightings over the centuries. I have heard stories of her standing on the rocks of faraway shores in her dark hoods, as you say."

But, I don't understand," I said. "Why would such a

horrible, evil witch give the mers all these incredible powers?"

"Well, for many, many years after the curse, the mer did not have any powers whatsoever. They could not even see under the water, and it was painful for them to be beneath the surface as the salt stung their eyes. They could not hunt and to make matters worse, they found themselves invisible to other humans and could not summon for help."

"So if you are not visible to us, why can Starfish islanders see you?" I asked, suddenly. I was actually surprised I had not asked this before.

"I know not," he murmured. "Anyway, things got better for the mers overtime," he said, pressing on with his tale.

I frowned, leaning my head back onto his chest. I was expecting a little bit more of an explanation on this matter, especially as it was so central to our romance.

"What happened next was part evolution, part magic," Llyr was saying. "Their eyes adapted over time until we ended up with the night vision that we now have. We learned to sense any danger too, like sharks. As a species, we grew a little stronger, but it was still tough. The shaman would visit them on a raft. He wanted to consult the spirits one more time, to see if they could become men again but many of the tribe's members begged him not to. They had become fearful of the other world and the aggressive spirits he may alert, just as Carman had hoped. There were many fights over the matter but eventually they agreed to hold a vote, and it was decided they should give it one last chance. This time, a water spirit was contacted."

"Well, I hope he was nicer than that other thing," I said.

"He was much a gentler phantom. He said that he could not reverse the hex but could gift them some powers which would allow mer not just to survive the waters, but to rule them. We would have assets that no other animals nor humans had. We could even shift and visit the lands, albeit not for long. But we had to do one thing for him."

"Which was?" I asked.

"Disband," he replied. "He wanted us to split up into sub-tribes and spread out across the oceans. He said the mers' presence in the region was too much. They were not a natural part of the ecosystem, and we were upsetting the waters. So that's what happened, and in return, he gave each sub-tribe a special unique set of powers."

"So ... your tribe is ...?"

"The Seuds. It means Jewel," he said, pointing to his pendant.

I played with the little backward "S" for a while, remembering that day on the boat when I had first noticed it.

"Makes sense ..." I said finally. "So, these powers then ... you, the Seuds can sense emotions, you're crazy strong ..." I listed. "Anything else?"

"There's one other thing," said Llyr. "We can start storms."

I couldn't help but smile. This was a little closer to the

mer-lore we heard about as humans. "Well, I wouldn't want to be in your bad books," I said, looking up at him.

"Impossible," he replied, squeezing me tight.

It was a little scary talking about all this stuff, but the moon was big and bright tonight, and we were bathed in its glow. The waves lapped gently at the shore and the warmth of the day still clung to us as we lay there. It was the perfect night for ... you know.

Chapter Twenty-One

"Are you sure?" said Llyr as we kissed under the stars.

I nodded, "Definitely."

I now truly felt like I could trust him, and after a day like ours, I didn't want to wait a minute longer.

He kissed my neck and tugged at one of the strings on my bikini. I lay back and sighed blissfully.

Suddenly a man's voice filled the air. At first, I was confused and wondered if I was hearing things, I sat up slowly and then I screamed. There were about a dozen big men standing in the waves.

Llyr put his arms around me.

"It's okay," he said. "It's Ri."

He shouted to the men in a foreign language and Ri, who stood at the forefront, answered him in what I could only assume was the same tongue. Now that Ri had transformed to man and stood out of the water, I could see that his dark, wet hair was as long as his waist, and he wore big metal bands around his wrists and neck. He was terrifyingly tall, and most certainly not somebody you would want to rub up the wrong way.

While they spoke, I looked at the rest of the congregation that stood before us. To Ri's right was Spirit. His blonde hair was tied up in a ponytail tonight, and he was watching me intently, arms crossed in front of his chest.

The rest of the men were, just like Ri, Spirit, and Llyr, muscular and inked up. I squinted in the moonlight and could see that some of them had little white dots painted on their skin. They wore cloths round their waists, which looked as though they were made of regular material humans used, but I could not be sure in the dark.

Llyr and Ri continued to exchange words, but I did not have a clue what they were saying. The language sounded old-fashioned, but perhaps there was a hint of British Celtic if I remembered correctly from my history class. I wondered why they were here.

Llyr turned to me.

"Crystal, there is another boat leaving the harbor full of poison."

"Oh," I said. *Great, that was going to make life at home all the better.*

"Yes, but they need me to go with them and stop it," he said softly. "I'm so sorry."

I looked at him and nodded. "It's okay, but how will I get home?"

"Bright will take you," said Llyr, nodding towards one of the smaller men, who stood on the edges of the gathering. "I will introduce you. He will get you home safely, I promise."

"Okay," I said, reaching for my dress. I looked at the mermen and then back at Llyr. "They're staring," I whispered.

Llyr turned. "Can you give us a moment?" he said, with a hint of annoyance.

Ri nodded silently, and they turned their backs on us so that they faced the sea.

Llyr helped me to my feet, and I buttoned up my dress, he picked up my sunglasses and scarf and handed them to me.

"I wish so much that I didn't have to go," he said kissing me on the cheek.

I hugged him. "Me too, but it's okay. I understand."

"I will come to you tomorrow, sundown," he said looking down at me. "But I won't be able to stay very long; I have to go on a journey."

I looked down disappointed but forced myself to nod and smile. He took my hand, and we walked down to the sea. The mermen turned back to face us again, and I felt around twelve sets of eyes fix themselves curiously to my face.

"Hi," I said awkwardly. *I had to say something, right?*

"May the spirit of the night reach out and bless you under its moon and stars, Miss White," said Ri with a friendly but boundaried smile. He was being polite but didn't want to give the impression he approved of me, I realized.

"This is Bright," said Llyr. Bright was of a more slender build than the other men. He smiled with a genuine warmth, and I relaxed a little.

Llyr squeezed my hand before joining the other men behind Ri.

"We need to take Llyr," said Ri. "I'm sorry for that."

"Oh ... no worries," I said, meekly.

Spirit threw back his head and laughed. "Oh, no worries," he mimicked in a high-pitched voice.

I suddenly had a little spell of dizziness, the type when overcome with rage. *This Spirit jerk was such a child,* I seethed. *How dare he mock me in front of everybody?*

"So Spirit," I suddenly heard myself say, "Where's your spear this evening?"

Spirit looked at me, with a look of sheer contempt. "Why? You need a toy to play with on your journey home?"

"No," I replied coolly. "I was just worried it had gotten stuck up your arse."

Oh my God, what was I doing?

There were a couple of seconds of shocked silence. *They were probably going to murder me.*

Suddenly the steely expressions the men wore on their faces cracked. They howled with laughter, and some even doubled over and fell into the waves.

One of the men next to Spirit slapped him on the back. "That told you, didn't it?" he said.

I raised an eyebrow at Spirit, who looked momentarily uneasy. He forced a sarcastic smile. "Not really," he muttered, turning away from the men and storming into the sea.

The other men laughed harder, before walking out behind him, disappearing one by one.

I caught a glimpse of Ri as he turned and was relieved to see that he too appeared to be shaking with laughter. Maybe he would like me a little more now, I hoped.

I looked at Llyr, and he grinned before striding into the waves after Ri and disappearing. The sea was still again, and Bright, and I were now left alone on a silent, deserted beach.

"Right," he said walking up to the rowing boat. "We'd better get moving."

His arms trembled a little as he picked up the boat and he then staggered bow-legged to the sea with it. Now, I could see why they weren't too reluctant to leave him behind. Although his strength was impressive, he didn't carry it with as much ease as Llyr.

I felt sad to have Llyr taken from me like that, especially given the timing. And I was also worried about what the mers would accomplish tonight, and how much this would rock Mum and Dad's marriage.

I waded through the sea, and Bright took my hands and

quite literally swung me into the boat, and onto the wooden bench.

"You look worried, Miss White," said Bright as we departed into the ocean.

"I am," I said, looking out to sea distractedly, my mind racing.

"He will come to you the first second he gets," said Bright, "let me not lie to you about that."

I smiled. "Thank you," I said gratefully, as we glided over the smooth waters.

I couldn't help but notice that the pressure had changed. Instead of that crisp, fresh air, it felt now as though a tension hung in the atmosphere. We rowed for another half hour or so when I saw a flicker across the ocean to the far West.

I jumped. *Please no, it couldn't be.*

The confirmatory rumble of thunder sounded in the distance some twenty seconds later.

"Oh my God!" I cried. I was out in the middle of the ocean, in a rowing boat! Bright seemed lovely and everything, but he did not have the reassuring, powerful presence of Llyr.

Nether-the-less, Bright rowed on, as cool as a cucumber.

"Don't worry yourself, Miss White. That storm will stay in the West, I guarantee it," he said with utmost confidence.

How could he be so sure? Maybe he was just trying to make me feel better.

I watched on rigidly for the next ten minutes, and true to Bright's word, the storm did appear to remain rather stationary. It was bizarre; I had always known a storm to travel.

"Look behind you!" said Bright.

I turned and saw the twinkling lights of Starfish, and breathed a huge sigh of relief, the tension slowly released itself from my body.

"Thank goodness!" I cried. I laughed, giddy from relief.

Bright laughed too. "What did I tell you? You didn't trust me did you?"

"I'm sorry!" I exclaimed. "It's just I'm terrified of storms, it's like my worst fear, asides from sharks."

"Poor sharks, no one cares for them much," sighed Bright.

"Well, they're not very ... approachable," I said, trying to find a neutral term to describe the animal. I didn't want to totally slag them off; maybe Bright liked them.

Bright laughed. "Of course. They're probably the greatest threat to the mer."

"Really? But you can sense them a mile off?" I said hopefully.

"Yes, we can. And also, even if one comes near us, we can usually put up a pretty good fight. There have been a few accidents here and there, but generally, they know not to bother us. There's a mutual respect."

"Oh, well that is good news," I smiled.

"Not always, though. You should have seen Llyr once,"

continued Bright. "He punched one in the face. It came charging into our kingdom one day—it was a Great White, as well. I think it was a bit of a lunatic, that shark."

My stomach did a somersault as I imagined such a scenario.

"It kind of recoiled but then it decided to advance again, and so he kind of hugged its mouth shut and then Spirit came at it with his spear," said Bright, before cracking up. "He must have pulled it out of his behind, you know."

I laughed too, as I remembered my earlier comment. "Oh God."

"Yeah, don't mind Spirit too much," said Bright. "He can be stupid sometimes. He'll start picking fights for no reason. But really, he's a nice man."

"Nice?" I squeaked.

"Yeah, honestly. He's got a soft side, most of our mers will tell you that. It's just that you just have to dig deep."

"Hmm, you must need a serious drill for that," I muttered, quite sure Bright would not understand what I meant.

Bright grinned. "I don't blame you for thinking that way. You did the right thing tonight. He was so rude, honestly ... to speak to a young lady like that ..." Bright sighed and shook his head in disapproval, "I'd have told him if you hadn't." He laughed again. "Even Ri was laughing, that's rare, you know?"

I grinned, pleased with this news. "I thought you were all going to kill me at one point," I admitted.

"No, we will always protect you," said Bright. "We all know how much you mean to him."

I smiled and nodded with gratitude, although somehow I knew Llyr's affections for me would not be enough to change Ri's mind.

Chapter Twenty-Two

Bright dropped me off on my jetty, and I waved him goodbye and thanked him. He had been such a sweetie.

I walked briskly up the stairway and across the garden; I had been outside in the night for a long time now, and I was cold.

I frantically unlocked the door, and Maurice bounded over and jumped on me. I bent over and kissed his fluffy head. "Hello, Moz!" I cooed to my excitable pooch.

I walked into the living room and saw that my Dad was watching the news and swigging from a bottle of wine.

"Hi, Dad," I shouted, as he had not appeared to notice my presence. I rubbed my arms to get warm. "Brrr."

"She's out there in that!" he shouted, raising a hand to the TV. Wine sloshed onto the floor, but he didn't seem to notice. His forehead was creased into about twenty lines, and he was almost an ashen colour.

I froze as I saw the headlines:

THREE HOSPITALIZED IN FREAK STORM

I suddenly remembered the flickers of light across the ocean and Bright's words: "Don't worry yourself, Miss White. The storm will stay in the West I guarantee it."

The mermen had created the storm to stop the boat!

"What do you mean 'she's out in that'?" I asked worriedly.

"Your insane mother got on the boat!" Dad shouted.

"Why?" I shrieked. "She didn't have to do that?"

"She called me up and said was obliged to personally see that the boat reached its destination," he said, rolling his eyes. "It's so she can impress that cretinous weasel!" The whites of his eyes could now be seen—so intense was his scorn.

My heart sank. *Could this be more of a disaster?*

A picture of a boat came into view on the TV, and Dad took a gulp from the bottle and turned up the volume with the remote. I watched on with alarm.

It must have been a huge, solid tanker, but it looked like a flimsy piece of driftwood in the humongous waves that crashed over it.

"Bloody hell," I said. I watched the tanker virtually disappear as a wave battered it. White froth erupted around it like a perilous cauldron. This was serious.

Dad stood there rigidly, his ear cocked towards the TV.

"The storm appears to be concentrated on this particular stretch of water," said the news reporter, "although reports are rolling in that it is also battering the

Port—Oh, incoming news, rescue helicopters are moving in. A rescue operation is underway for the passengers of the SKANX waste disposal ship. It is now thought to be sinking due to penetration in the vessel."

"Oh God!" I screamed. Please tell me Mum had managed to get a life jacket. Thoughts began to flood through my mind of Mum trapped in a room full of water, and I put a hand to my chest. *What if she died?*

Dad smashed the bottle onto the table and marched into the corridor. I watched with horror as he wrenched on his Wellington boots and scooped up his boat keys.

"I'm going to Port Agatha, Crystal."

"Huh, Dad, what?" I shouted. *Was he mad?* Dad did not answer me; he bolted straight towards the back door.

I chased Dad into the garden, just about managing to tug on my rain coat as we went. I was not going to lose two parents tonight.

"Dad!" I screamed as he shot down the ocean stairway. "You can't do anything, Dad!"

He was not stopping; he had ripped off the plastic that covered his boat and pounced onto the wheel.

"Okay, wait—Dad, wait!" I shouted, leaping in behind him. We sped off in the direction of the mainland, and I took a little comfort that we were not speeding directly towards the eye of the storm. He hadn't totally lost the plot yet.

I closed my eyes and prayed that Llyr would sense the devastation he was causing me and would somehow stop the bloody storm. I trusted he was not aware that my mother was on board, but another thought was beginning to manifest itself. *Had Llyr and his men ripped a hole in that boat deliberately? Were they trying to kill people now?*

———————

Once we reached the mainland, I was struck by how calm and settled the weather was, considering the raging storm just miles out of town.

Dad raced over to the taxi rank and knocked on the window of the first car. There was a whir as the window was wound down, and a sour-faced lady's face was unveiled. She wore a black flat cap and chewed gum.

"I need to go to Port Agatha!" he wheezed.

The window abruptly whirred shut again.

"I think that's a 'no' Dad," I said.

Undeterred, he banged on the next driver's window and received a similar reception.

Dad continued down the queue of cabs, until eventually, after a string of refusals, he reached the last car. He banged frantically at the door. When the window opened, I saw a familiar face. It was Roger, the silent skipper. He must have another job.

He recognized Dad immediately.

"Keith!" he exclaimed.

"Roger!" he shouted, now sweating profusely. "I have to get to Port Agatha."

"Watched the news lately?" he asked, a thick furry eyebrow shooting up.

"Yes, that's the whole point!" Dad squawked. "My wife is on the boat."

There was a click and we realized that he unlocked the door. We scrambled into the back seat gratefully.

"Thank you," said Dad as the engine started up, and we pulled out onto the main road that skirted the coast.

"What's your wife doing on the boat then?" said Roger suddenly, about ten minutes into the journey. "Was she doing a protest?"

Dad sighed. "No, she works for SKANX."

Roger looked in the mirror at me. "I hope you wear earplugs when you eat your cornflakes in the morning," he joked.

I smiled wanly in response and looked out of the window. We were now just around the corner from Port Agatha, and the sea was looking surprisingly flat and calm.

Roger appeared to notice the same thing.

"Must have passed," he said.

As we neared the port, I could see a line of flashing blue lights, and my heart rate accelerated. The cab had not stopped, but I opened the door and ran towards the ambulances, Dad in close pursuit.

There were people, presumably members of the crew, wrapped in foil blankets, sitting on the curb. They looked pale and traumatized.

"Bloody hell!" breathed Dad.

I looked around desperately for Mum but could not see anyone who bore her resemblance. It mainly appeared to be men. I looked inside an ambulance and could see that a burly man, dressed in a boiler suit was having his blood pressure measured. He must be a ship mechanic or something.

"Have you seen Sheila White?" I asked, tears running down my face.

He looked up and nodded. "She's fine; she's here somewhere," he said. "The ship went down, but they've just done a full headcount."

I collapsed into Dad with relief, and he hugged me. I felt his body slowly relax, and he kissed my hair, suddenly a parent again and not a maniac.

"Come on, darling, let's go and find her," he said, putting his arm around my shoulder and guiding me away from the ambulance. We made our way through the crowds, until eventually under the shadow of an ambulance, I saw a flash of blonde hair.

My heart stopped as we saw her small frame in a foil blanket and wrapped firmly in an intimate embrace with a tall, be-suited man. As they turned to face us, I recognized him immediately.

Mr. Geake.

The SKANX ship was not the only battered wreck that evening. It looked like my parents' twenty-year marriage was about to go down with it.

Chapter Twenty-Three

Starfish Island baked in the midday sun. Nobody here would know of the ferocious storm in St. Agatha the night before, were it not on the front page of every local paper. I had walked away from the corner shop hastily, as soon as I saw the headlines, cutting down a narrow little alley.

Now I pressed my nose against the shop window and let my eyes travel over the ornaments in the display.

I had never seen this little place before and had never imagined such a shop could exist on Starfish. Surely there couldn't be a demand for antiques on the island to keep it going all year round, I mused. My eyes stopped on the figurine of a mermaid. She was perched on a rock and smiling while running a comb through her hair. I sighed and looked away.

I had ventured across the island with Maurice as I couldn't bear to be in the house a moment longer. I could not even find the words to describe the tension. It was just so horrible, and I couldn't believe this was all happening to my perfect loving parents.

Just after we discovered Mum and Mr. Geake, she had been taken to the hospital in one of the ambulances for a check-up. Dad accompanied her ever-faithfully, but they were both completely silent for most of the journey and for the four hours that we waited in A & E. I think they were both in shock.

This morning they were both still pretty mute, and I had had to make awkward conversation at the breakfast table, something that I had never had to do in my entire seventeen years.

Mum had then rested in the conservatory with a newspaper as she had been given two weeks off to recover.

Maybe this week they would finally get to spend some time together and realize how much they love each other, I thought hopefully as Maurice and I wondered aimlessly down another back street.

I looked at my watch and realized that I had somehow managed to kill about three hours dawdling around the island.

I was near Rosie's house, so I stopped by. I had initially wanted someone to talk to, but Jemima was there, and the two of them were in high spirits, lounging about in the garden laughing and drinking tea.

I joined them for a cup but opted out of going into my problems, as I didn't want to ruin their fun. Instead, I listened to them compare Will and Allan and tried to laugh at the right places. Will snored, Allan didn't I learned as I sat in the deck chair feigning interest.

"Are you seeing anyone, Crystal?" asked Jemima, her grey eyes looking over at me inquisitively.

"Yeah, I guess," I said, hoping she did not pursue further detail.

Her eyes remained on me, prompting me to provide more information.

"Um, well, he's a really interesting guy. He's from, you know, another island," I stuttered, desperately thinking of how I could change the subject. I decided to pretend to be distracted by Maurice. "Hey Moz, don't dig over there!"

Maurice, who was sitting docilely under a tree behind the girls, looked up confused.

"Huh?" said Jemima, her eyes darted to Rosie confusedly. "Another island?"

"Yes," said Rosie brightly. "There are other islands about, you know."

"Where? I've never heard of any," replied Jemima, "certainly not one that anybody lives on, and my dad's a Search and Rescue pilot ..."

This triggered another topic of conversation that I did not wish to discuss. I closed my eyes.

"He was out in that storm last night, rescuing that boat!" Jemima exclaimed. "He said he's never seen such a vicious, concentrated storm in his entire career. The ship literally fell apart, can you imagine being on that thing."

I stood up.

"Girls, it was so good to see you, but I have to go," I said quickly.

"You only just got here!" said Rosie, with surprise.

"Yes, but I was just stopping by. I have to, erm ... go to a dinner," I explained awkwardly.

"Okay," said Rosie standing up and giving me a hug. She looked at me worriedly. "Have a nice dinner, and call me!"

I smiled at Jemima and waved goodbye, before opening the garden gate and ushering a tired Maurice through it.

I had to admit, I kind of missed having Rosie all to myself, but I had to learn to share her now that Jemima appeared to be a permanent fixture. I was still pleased I had set her up with Allan, but I didn't realize I would be losing my only real friend out here.

I wandered past the gawking locals and decided to quicken my pace until I reached the less populated part of the isle. Most of them would have no doubt heard about Mum and her near-death experience by now.

How could Llyr inflict that much trauma on a bunch of innocent people? I began to seethe as I walked. *It wasn't like Mr. Geake himself had been on that boat; it was just ordinary workers trying to get their day's pay.*

And I knew it was totally wrong, but in my traumatized mind, I was starting to point a finger at the mers for Mum and Mr. Geake's embrace last night. *If they hadn't started that storm then none of this would ever have happened, right?*

Wrong, a little voice protested somewhere, but it was

quickly silenced by more dominant thoughts looking for someone to blame.

I turned onto Lighthouse Lane and froze. I could hear shouting, and as I inched closer to my house, I realized that it was coming from within.

"I know what I saw," Dad was shouting.

"You didn't see anything!" screamed Mum.

Maurice and I rushed into the house where Mum and Dad were standing in the kitchen shouting at each other from either end of the table.

"I am sick of you interfering with my life!" Mum yelled.

"Funny, it seems that I've not been interfering enough," said Dad.

"Okay, guys—" I started.

"Oh, you've done plenty of interfering," spat Mum. "My secretary has you on speed dial, the amount of messages you leave for her, asking her to tell you my whereabouts."

"Well, I wonder why that is?" roared Dad. "Maybe because I never know where you are!"

They were both bright red and looked at each other venomously.

"Maybe you both need a holiday ..." I tried tentatively. "Make the most of Mum being off work."

"A holiday? I can't go on holiday. I've got the demonstration on Wednesday," said Dad, looking at me as though I had completely lost the plot.

"Oh fantastic!" cried Mum. "How much more do you want to embarrass me?"

"How much more do you want to embarrass me?" Dad shouted back and then they stood panting at each other.

Looking at them both, they must have been shouting at each other for hours, but it appeared they were now in deadlock.

I let out a long shaky breath. This was just awful.

"You know what, Keith. I think Crystal's right. We need a holiday," said Mum.

I felt a little spark of hope ignite inside me. *Was she coming around?*

Dad's expression softened momentarily.

Mum's voice broke, and her eyes became glassy.

"From each other," she said before turning and running upstairs.

I felt as though somebody had punched me a million times in the stomach, face, and chest. I could not explain the amount of pain that I felt throughout the rest of the afternoon.

The house had fallen into a deathly silence, and it reminded me of the placid sea last night as we had driven into Port Agatha. The silence after the storm.

I had sat in the conservatory, in a state of shock for the past couple of hours. I had no idea where Dad was, but Mum had not emerged from her bedroom since the argument.

At about seven p.m. I heard a door open and the sound of footsteps coming down the stairs.

I looked up and saw my mother fully dressed in black jeans and a white chiffon shirt. I looked down slowly and saw she was carrying a big bag.

"Mum, no!" I cried, tears pouring down my face.

She came over to me and sat on the arm of the sofa and cradled me in her arms as I cried.

"Darling, look after your father," she said finally, getting up and walking to the kitchen.

I sat in shock for about five seconds. *How could she be so cold?*

I stood up slowly, thinking I might faint if I wasn't careful. Tears surged down my face, now in a thick wall of water.

"Mum!" I whispered hoarsely, following her to the kitchen. "Don't do this."

Mum paused at the door, her hand rested on the handle, and for a moment I thought she may change her mind. She opened it and stepped into the garden.

I followed her down, pleading with her to stay, but she pressed on silently and descended the stairway. When I reached the top of the staircase, I saw that there was a sea taxi at the jetty waiting for her.

"Oh my gosh, Mum," I shouted storming down the stairs. "Why do you have to be such a bitch?"

There, I said it.

Mum dropped her bags and turned to me.

"How dare you speak to me like that," she snapped, her face now burning. I watched her expression; it was a combination of hurt, anger, and downright shock. I couldn't quite believe I had so much as uttered those words myself, but I bloody well meant them.

"Ever since you came to Starfish, you've been nothing but vile to Dad. I've had to sit there and watch you trample all over him and crush him for weeks now."

"Crystal, you have no idea what is going on," said my mother firmly, in a tone designed to make me feel like a hysterical brat.

"Yes I do," I cried. "I saw you with him, last night and in the restaurant."

My mother was silent for a couple of seconds. "Because you are my daughter, and I love you, I will forgive you for what you called me a couple of seconds ago, but that is the only reason. I will speak with you tomorrow when I have found somewhere to stay."

I wept as she boarded the boat, and the driver unwound the rope that attached the vessel to the jetty. He smiled at me sympathetically, before lowering himself in.

"Why would you choose him and that disgusting company over us?" I shouted at her hoarsely, as the boat pulled away. She was now too far out at sea to respond, but I had enough anger to rage at her for a week. "How could you?" I cried out, not even sure if she could hear me anymore.

I collapsed onto the jetty, my body wracked with sobs. I

watched the boat roar off into the sunset through my tears, as I sat there in a crumpled heap.

This couldn't be happening. Not to me. Not to us.

"Crystal?" came a worried voice.

Llyr was standing above me; he was dripping with water. For the first time since we met, I realized that I had forgotten he was coming to see me.

"I just overheard you with your mother. I'm so sorry," he said. His voice sounded full of concern, but I couldn't even look at him. All I could suddenly think about were the traumatized passengers of the boat last night.

I stood up slowly. I must have looked monstrous. I had been crying nonstop for hours, and my eyes were puffed out like two blowfish.

As I stood before him, I just couldn't take comfort in his presence, as I usually did. Instead, I just felt rage.

"Why did you do that?" I said angrily.

"Do what?" he said worriedly.

"The boat. That's what," I cried, fresh tears spilling down my cheeks. I wiped them away with the sleeves of my cardigan, which were already soaked, and Llyr tried to pull me to him, but I put out a hand.

"Crystal, are you angry with me?" he asked.

"They were just normal people, and you tried to kill them," I said accusingly.

"No," he said softly. "Crystal, no!"

I looked down; the tears just would not stop flowing,

and I could not think straight. I just felt anger and sorrow, and nothing else.

He put his hands on my shoulders, and I could tell he was trying desperately to get through to me, but I was in no mood for rationale.

"We never meant for that to happen," he insisted. "We were shocked when it starting collapsing. I have never seen a boat do that before. I promise, I—we would never do that. It was just meant to be a deterrent."

"Well, it worked well," I said, still refusing to look at him. "To think you all go on about your people, and how wronged they are by us, and then you nearly drown a bunch of innocent workers. They were just crew members and mechanics, that kind of thing. And, did you know my mother was on the boat?"

Not that she was so innocent, I inwardly fumed.

"No, I didn't," he said. "And I would never do anything to harm you. Or anyone, certainly not someone you care about."

I brushed his arms away from my shoulders.

"Whatever," I said abruptly, staring at the ground as we stood in silence. When I did look up at him, I was quite sure I could see hurt in his lovely green eyes. "Now they've broken up," I heard myself continue.

"And I'm so very sorry for you, but are you trying to hold me accountable for that?"

I turned and walked away from him. I just needed to be by myself.

"Crystal," he pleaded. In my head I knew what I was doing was wrong but I was just not myself at that very moment in time.

I walked up the stairs and back to my house, and as I opened the back door, I already began to feel a stab of regret.

Chapter Twenty-Four

I woke up to the sound of raindrops, pitter-pattering on my window. I looked outside and saw through bleary eyes that a grey smog had replaced the vibrant eggshell blue I had grown accustomed to.

Ugh. I grimaced sitting up groggily.

Suddenly the horrific events of yesterday began to creep back into my consciousness, and I remembered that my mother had left us.

I immediately sunk into a deep state of misery and lay back down on my side, letting a tear trickle over my nose and drop onto the pillow.

I picked up my iPhone and saw that it was two p.m. meaning that I had slept for about fifteen hours. *Jeez, I must have been emotionally shattered.*

Suddenly another memory came pounding back.

Llyr.

I sat bolt upright. *Was it all over?*

I had no idea what had happened between us last night, and who was in the wrong and who was in the right, but the thought that we may not be together anymore was unbearable.

I swung my legs out of bed, as though I were about to take some kind of action. This was my prime instinct, but as I stood up energetically, I was suddenly overcome by the feeling that there was absolutely nothing I could do. I couldn't rush to his house. I couldn't call him or text him.

I pressed my forehead against the window, and just prayed that he would feel my remorse.

The rest of the morning was not much easier. Having searched the whole house for Dad, I peeped into the garage where I found him sitting on a large white sheet with a paintbrush in his hand. He wore one of his scruffy old shirts, and his white hair shone silver under the bright garage lights. I guessed he was painting a banner for the demonstration, as he had been speaking about doing this all of the previous week.

Dad had had his back to me, and he was unaware of my presence. I was just about to call him when I realised his back was shaking, and to my utmost devastation, he was crying.

I backed away and went back into the house. My heart

was pounding, I had not seen Dad cry since Grandpa died when I was ten.

I could not work out what to do. *Should I go and comfort him, or did he want to be left alone?*

I realised I had to phone a friend for answers. As I scrolled through my phone book in the living room, my finger hovered over Jess, my oldest chum from London. I had known her practically my whole life and she knew my parents well.

"Crystal!" she screamed, as she answered my call. "I thought I'd lost you forever."

I immediately felt bad. Here I was, only contacting her when the going got tough.

"Jess!" I cried back. "I'm so sorry. It's been absolutely mental since I got here."

"Yeah, well, don't worry. Like I always said, we're family, you and me, we don't need to be in touch every day to know each other cares. I could call you up out of the blue, and I know you'd be right there for me. And vice versa."

"Erm, yeah. About that vice versa ..." I began wearily.

"Oh mate, what's happened?" said Jess, immediately clocking why I was calling.

I tearfully told her everything about Mum and Dad, right up until last night's grand finale. She gasped, as I told her how Mum had left us.

"Okay, Crystal," she said immediately "I know your mum's a little bit of a drama queen, a little bit difficult, yeah, but she loves you and your dad. It's obvious. She wouldn't just do that for no reason."

I felt momentarily uplifted by this, but then I realised Jess had not witnessed Mum's behaviour since she had come to Starfish. She didn't know the new Mum.

"Yeah, but Jess, she's been so awful since she arrived. I've been shocked too, but it's like she just suddenly decided that she hates Dad and is just out for herself," I explained.

"Yes, but that's what I'm saying. People don't just fall out of love like that," Jess argued.

"Until they meet someone else," I cried.

"But this guy Mr. Gawk—"

"Geake," I corrected her.

"Okay, Geake, even worse. Mr. Geake sounds so boring. Your mother likes her men to have a bit of charm, you know, a man with a sparkle in his eye. Even the film stars she likes all have charisma. I just can't believe she would just throw away her whole life for someone like that."

I was still doubtful. "Well ... she has!"

"I don't know, are you sure something else hasn't happened?" asked Jess.

I scanned my brain but there was nothing that came to mind. *Like what, anyway? What could possibly justify her actions?*

"You have to talk to her," urged Jess.

"I can't speak to her. I'm so angry with her," I replied. I thought of Dad crying on his own in the garage, and I knew that I could not talk to Mum for a long time after the heartbreak she had caused him.

I remembered the reason I called.

"Do you think I should go and comfort Dad, or do you think he wants to be alone?" I asked.

"I think Dad wants to go for a walk with his girl!" came a voice behind me.

I turned and saw my dad. He had put a cardigan on over his scruffy shirt and was standing at the living room door. I looked at his face worriedly and was relieved to see that, although he looked a little sad, there were no tears.

"Dad!" I cried standing up and walking towards him.

He smiled down at me. "Come on, finish your conversation and then we'll go."

Dad and I took the boat over to the mainland and tied it up in a little harbour just outside of Coney Bay. Here, there was a little walkway by the sea which led up onto the cliffs.

It was not the best day for a cliff walk, as the dull, drab light halved the beauty of the scenery. However, I think it did us both the world of good just to get out of the house and stretch our legs.

We didn't discuss Mum too much. I suppose there was nothing much to say on the matter. Or maybe we knew it was too painful to go into. Instead, we managed to distract ourselves with some history talk. Dad told me about how the Vikings had once ransacked the local villages around here, slaughtering everyone in sight.

Humans were so cruel back in the Viking days, I thought as we turned back. *In fact, they actually made Mr. Geake and his company look like The Salvation Army. And that was saying something.* This kind of topic of conversation also made my life seem really not so bad.

I picked some wild, purple flowers as we talked. I knew I shouldn't, but they looked so pretty, even in the grey light.

When we got back to the boat, it was getting quite late, and so we stopped at a pub for some dinner. We both ordered our favourite dish, lobster and chips. However, when it finally arrived neither of us could touch it. We clearly had no appetite, even despite an afternoon rambling around the cliffs.

After our meal and a lot of persuasion from Dad, I approached the bar to ask if they had any vacancies. It was just a teeny pokey pub and I felt embarrassed asking in front of the line of locals that were propped at the bar.

A burly woman leant over the bar. She must have been around fifty and had absolutely enormous boobs that filled the entire space between her chest and the bar. I could see she had a little love heart tattooed on the left one. The name 'Barny' was emblazoned on it. *Was that the name of her husband or her dog?*

She cleared her throat.

"Alright, my lover?" she chirped in a Westcountry twang.

I forced my eyes away from her chest and to her face.

"Yes, not too bad, thank you," I said, trying to sound as professional as possible. "I was, erm, just wondering if you had any jobs? I'm on my school holidays."

The whole pub had gone quiet. I grimaced and glanced sideways to Dad, who stuck his thumb up.

"Go on, Tamzin, give her a job," shouted out a man with a ginger beard. "A bonny girl like that wouldn't do this place any harm."

I thought I was going to die. *How embarrassing.*

'Tamzin' winked at me. "When can you start?" she asked.

"Well, tomorrow," I said, blinking. *Was she really going to give me a job, just like that?*

"Very well," she said. "See you tomorrow then."

"Wow, thank you. I'm Crystal, by the way," I said, smiling gratefully.

"Welcome to The Rose, Crystal," said Tamzin. "I don't imagine you'll be having our lobster too often, though!" she nodded at our plates which were now being carried away from our table.

I flushed red. They were completely full.

"I'm so sorry, we had a late lunch," I lied apologetically.

Later on, Dad tied up the boat and I clambered onto our jetty back on Starfish. The sky was getting darker, and it must have been about sunset.

Dad put the lock on the wheel and fastened the plastic covering over the boat, and I helped him clip it in place. He began to walk slowly up the jetty but I hung about looking out to sea. *Was he near?*

"I might watch the sunset, Dad," I called as Dad plodded up the stairs.

"You can't even see the sun!" he replied. "How are you going to watch it set? Oh, whatever ..." he appeared to give up and retreated up the garden path.

I stood on the jetty for about half an hour and the sky turned from grey to charcoal and then to black. I had half believed that he would come for me, that he was in as much despair as I was. I felt the tears come again as I walked back to the house. Despite the amazing connection that we had, maybe my tantrum last night had been enough to convince him that Ri had been right all along. Mer and humans were a bad mix.

Chapter Twenty-Five

"Crystal White?" said the cashiers at the bank.

"Yes," I said, leaning against the counter impatiently. I had come to check whether my first wage had come through.

The cashier turned the computer, and I looked at my balance.

NIL

"Oh, well that's just great," I moaned. I had now worked at The Rose for a week, and a half and payday was yesterday.

"Can I get an overdraft?" I asked, hopefully.

The cashier looked at me and then looked back at her screen.

"Not until you're eighteen, Miss White," she said firmly.

I turned dejectedly and walked out of the bank, rifling around in my purple leather bag as I walked. I had wanted to take out my money and head to the shops. I thought some retail therapy might go some way in cheering me up.

I retrieved my phone and called work.

"Hello, Rose Tavern. Tamzin speaking."

"Tamzin, it's Crystal."

"Oh, hello my lover!" she cooed.

"Hello. Look, I still haven't been paid."

"Teething problems, Crystal," she said dreamily. "Oh, can you work tonight? We've just got a booking for fourteen upstairs?"

"Umm," I said, searching my mind for an excuse. I was exhausted. I had worked every night this week.

"Come on!" she hollered coarsely.

"Okay, sure," I said reluctantly, unable to think of a reason why I could not come in. I hung up the phone and trudged to the harbor.

If I caught the two thirty p.m. sea-bus back, then I could probably catch a little nap before work. And besides, it wasn't like I had much else to do, asides from sit at home and cry.

In all honesty, my job had been a welcome distraction. It had now been two weeks since I last saw Llyr and I had not heard a thing. I was feeling pretty certain that it was over, and the thought that I may never see him again had been slowly killing me.

Had I not been at work, indulging chit chat at the bar or racing about with plates of food, I would have been at home torturing myself. Yet, even when I was at work, there had been times when he had surged into my thoughts. I had had to rush to the toilet, lock myself in the cubicle and dab away each individual tear away as they came, willing them to stop so I could get back to my job.

During the nights, I would be so tired that I would sleep, but in the daytime before work, I would lie in bed in a trance, and hours would pass without me realizing.

And of course, it wasn't just me who was nursing a broken heart in the house.

Just like I busied myself with work, Dad had thrown himself into his SKANX activism. The grand demonstration had been put back to this Friday, as organizers had felt they may be branded "tasteless" to demonstrate so close to the shipping accident.

Dad had not been too happy about this at all. I could sense that he was looking at this demonstration as an opportunity to get a lot to get off his chest. His quest against the company had now become deeply personal, and I had to admit, I was awaiting the date with apprehension. I hoped that he was not going to do anything stupid.

———————

"Table seventeen, Crystal!" squawked Tamzin. *Her voice was like nails on a blackboard; it was just so ... grating.*

"Like a fish wife, isn't she?" said Billy the regular, catching a glimpse of my pained expression.

"That's because I am a bloody fish wife!" she shrieked, and then cackled.

Billy chortled into his double scotch on the rocks, his blackened gappy teeth on full unashamed display.

I managed a smile. They were a pretty rowdy bunch, and Tamzin had a point—she was indeed married to one of the Coney Bay fishermen.

It was busy at the pub, and I had been up and down the stairs like a yo-yo. The customers upstairs were all plastered, and leery men had been slipping me tips all night, some of them quite possibly forgetting that they had already given me a good a note or two. I knew it was a little unethical, but I pocketed them all. *I mean, somebody had to pay me around here ...*

As the end of the shift finally neared, Tamzin uncorked a bottle of Sauvignon Blanc from behind the bar and poured two glasses.

"Get that down you, my lover," she said, pushing me one and knocking back the other in a gulp.

I took the glass gratefully and had a few large sips. I felt the wine instantly coarse through my overworked body. I had not had any alcohol for a while now—not since my one-time drinking partner Rosie had become so busied by Will.

Customers were filing out, and I began gathering glasses to stack into the big chrome washer. The machine itself smelt utterly rancid, and I held my nose as I opened the door and a great stinking billow of steam came out.

"So, Crystal White," said Billy, as I waited for my wash to finish. "How are you enjoying Coney?"

This was not the easiest of questions for me to answer at this present moment in time, and I took my time to dwell on it.

"Well," I began, "I think it's a very interesting place."

Billy raised his eyebrows. "Ah, well that's a first for a younguns. Kids your age are usually leaving Coney, not the other way round."

I raised my eyebrows and pretended to examine my nails. "Yeah, well ... I guess I'm a special case."

"So what's so interesting about Coney then?" he asked, his brow furrowed with curiosity.

I paused. "I guess it has its charm, you know, its history."

Billy swatted his arm. "Ahh, we've got all the pirates and smugglers stuff, I suppose. Keeps the tourists happy."

"We got mermaids 'n' everything!" came a voice from the end of the bar.

I looked up shocked. It appeared it was Charles, the elderly white-haired man, who had spoken up. He was looking at me from the shadowy corner with an eyebrow cocked mysteriously.

I stood behind the bar speechless, not quite knowing what to say. Maybe it wasn't an island secret after all. I looked at the two men; their faces were deadly serious.

Charles suddenly let out a wheeze and collapsed into laughter. *Okay, it was a joke*, I realized with relief.

Billy hooted and banged his hands on the bar.

"You really believed him!" he cried. He pulled an expression of sheer gormlessness, which I gathered was a highly unflattering portrait of me a couple of moments ago.

I forced myself to laugh along.

"Yep, must be the wine," I joked through gritted teeth.

———

I let myself out the back door, dropping the rubbish off and taking several gulps from the bottle of Sauvignon I had sneaked out in my bag. Since the mermaid joke, my mind had switched to Llyr, and I had felt my heart break all over again.

I chucked the empty bottle in the bin and stepped out onto the road. The glistening moonlit ocean caught my eye and pulled me across to the other side.

I rested my hands on the cool slate wall and gazed ahead. *Oh, if only he would just come to me one last time.*

The tears came again, flooding down my cheeks like a waterfall, but this time, I did not dab them away. I gave in, sobbing against the wall. I had never felt so alone in my entire life.

My family had completely fallen apart and both my parents were too angry to talk to each other or even to check in on me. I was hundreds of miles away from my old school friends, and the one pal I had made out here was barely around anymore. Llyr was the only thing that had truly filled me with happiness since

I came here, but he too had abandoned me, and it was all my stupid, stupid fault.

I walked slowly down the steps that led to the beach. Swimming was forbidden here. It was right by the rugged base of the cliffs, and there was sure to be all kinds of dangerous currents, not to mention falling rocks. But I was feeling reckless, and the wine had stripped me of any rationale.

I just wanted to be done with these long drawn out days of sadness, and I found, an idea was beginning to take shape within my foggy mind. *If I swam out a little further, would he rescue me like he did that night? Could I somehow make him come to me? He could sense when I was in danger, right? So then ...*

I walked to the water's edge, not quite sure whether I had lost my mind or not. But what I did know was that I loved him. That another day without hearing from him was unbearable. I needed to tell him that I was sorry, that I couldn't be without him.

I took a several big strides out into the water, and then I dropped. There was some kind of ledge, and I buckled startled, water sloshing in my face. I regained my footing and took some deep breaths, now waist deep.

The initial sting of the water did not shock me, unlike the previous nights that I had ventured into the seas. I took some more steps forwards until I was up to my shoulders. Here I let the waves break against my face for a couple of minutes until I eventually felt something. These cold slaps from the ocean gently alleviated the pain inside. It soothed me, and I liked it.

Now, I looked out to sea, my eyes raw from salt. I had to find him. I didn't want to be like my mum. I didn't want to just give up on love.

I stretched out my arms and launched forwards.

Chapter Twenty-Six

I had swum for about ten minutes. This stretch of sea was different. It was uncannily still and just felt plain hostile. Nonetheless, I continued slowly, paddling gently through the stagnant inky water.

I was starting to feel quite sure he would have come by now if he was going to. I trod water and looked to the side nervously. *Yep, there was no sign of him. Obviously, I had to be on death's door for him to bother with me these days.*

The Starfish Island lighthouse flashed across the sea, and I thought of Dad for a moment all on his own at home. I was really putting my life at risk out here. If anything happened to me now, then I was all he had left. I let out a long sigh. I would have to turn back.

Suddenly a splashing broke the deathly silence. My spirits lifted for a second. Perhaps my crazed idea would come to fruit after all.

I squinted, a dark fin broke the surface, and a large shiny body swished aggressively passed my face.

Oh my fucking God.

I let out a noise that was half cry and half muffled scream. *What was that?*

The waters were still again. I remained in the water, now hyperventilating. Although I was petrified of sharks popping up in Coney, deep down I had always thought my fear irrational. This was a) Britain, and b) these were shallow waters.

I craned my neck backward. *How far out was I?*

To my horror, all I could see was a huge black wall of rock. My head began to spin faster and faster as I realized I had been pulled along away from the shore and in front of the cliffs. If I were to swim backward, I wouldn't even be able to get out of the water; that's if I wasn't crushed against the rock beforehand.

There was another splash. The fin was back, but now to my left-hand side. Oh God, it was probably checking me out. I trod water helplessly. All I could do was hope that I didn't look juicy enough.

"Oh Dad, I'm so sorry," I whimpered into the night. My poor sweet father was going to be left on his own.

And what of me? What was it going to be like to be eaten? Would I die quickly, or slowly? Would I be able to distract myself somehow from the agony? I began to think of coping mechanisms for the inevitable horror that lay ahead but my racing mind could not offer up a thing.

There was another splash, and I closed my eyes, trembling with fear.

The unmistakable grip of a fist fastened itself around my wrist, and I was suddenly tossed up out of the waters like a rag doll. I saw the moon and stars as I passed through the air in what felt like one huge prolonged swoop and then SLAP. I was back in the water and being dragged along the surface at about five hundred miles per hour. It looked like we were heading back to shore.

Was this Llyr when he was angry? God, I must have REALLY pissed him off.

The hand finally let go, and I skidded the final couple of meters onto the beach.

I crawled along the sand, spluttering and coughing, trying to clear the seawater from my system. My head stung, I was quite sure the water had gone up my nose and into my brain.

I sat on my knees, trying to get myself together, and once I had regained my breath, I realized my hair sopped over my face, and I could not see a bloody thing. I put my hands to my face and managed to part it.

I turned expecting to see him there, standing angrily in the waves. I blinked. Nothing.

"Llyr?" I called shakily.

"Cooeeee!" came a girlish call.

I jumped and looked to my left. A half-naked woman was lying next to me in the sand, fingers wiggling in a little wave. "Sorry about all the pulling. I was running a little late, and you were, well, looking like somebody's din-dins."

"What was that thing?" I asked, feeling very lost.

"I'm not entirely sure, you know," said the woman, lying on her back in the sand and stretching, as though she were sunbathing. "A really big fish."

I looked my rescuer up and down, not quite knowing what to think or say. She was petite, yet curvy. Her shapely little legs were crossed, and her upper body was partly covered by long wet hair, while her modesty was protected by a skimpy jeweled band across her waist.

"I'm Nephys," she said, her eyes were closed, and long thick black lashes rested on beautiful high cheekbones. "No need to tell me your name."

Nephys. Where had I heard that name before?

"Thank you," I breathed, still traumatized.

"Oh, you're welcome, but like I said, sorry for the delay. I was in the middle of a gig."

I frowned. "A gig?"

She opened her eyes. "Yes, but don't tell Llyr I took so long!"

I felt a little flutter of hope. *He still cared for me?*

"Well, if I see him again," I said, raising my eyebrows.

Nephys laughed. It was a melodic high-pitched giggle, almost like a little song. "Good luck keeping him away! If you manage, remember to tell Ri how you did it."

I was confused. I had not heard a damned thing from him in weeks.

"Well, then where is he?" I demanded.

Nephys sat up, looking surprised. "He's on his dream journey!" she said, as though I should know all about this. Then her eyes widened as though she had remembered something. "Oh, yes, that's right. You were angry with him."

I leaned my head in my hands and let out a long trembling sigh of relief. Of course, he said he was going on a journey! *How, after all that time agonizing, had I forgotten such an important detail?*

My mind was such a mess at the moment.

"What's a dream journey?" I asked, after some time.

"Oh, it's a wonderful very important thing," she sighed, looking up at the moon. "I'm sure he'll tell you all about it."

"Well, when's he coming back?"

"Not long now. Another half of what's already passed," she said.

I did a quick calculation in my head. "A week?"

Nephys giggled again. "You're so cute!" she cried.

I smiled. "Erm, thanks."

Nephys reached over and touched my damp hair. "It's like the sun," she said.

I winced. "Really? I thought maybe, more like a haystack."

She giggled, but I sensed she didn't know what I meant.

"Hey, how did you know I was in trouble?" I asked.

"Oh, Llyr felt it and sent me a signal," she said.

I felt my body tense. *I hoped he hadn't sensed I was having a severe meltdown down over his trip. Talk about psycho.* "Hmm, so you can do that," I mumbled, frowning.

"Do what?" she asked, her hand still in my hair, now stroking it. These mers were very tactile.

"Like, project," I said.

"Yes, project, exactly," she said. She appeared to have had enough of my hair and now she took my hand and pressed it against her chest. I'm sure this was all perfectly innocent and normal in mer-land, but she was making me feel slightly awkward. "Crystal White, I have been dying to meet you."

"Really?" I asked, trying to cover my awkwardness.

She turned on her side and leaned on one elbow, and my hand was allowed to escape back into its comfort zone.

"You should hear the arguments Llyr and Ri have about you," she continued, drawing a love heart in the sand with her finger. "Ri says, 'leave that girl alone, this is no good!' and Llyr shouts, 'What do you know about what's good?' Oh, it's so romantic."

I was beginning to tire of the topic of Ri and his feelings towards me, although it had obviously caused a great stir amongst the merfolk. I changed the subject.

"So, how are you connected to Llyr?" I asked, curious. She was obviously quite close to the family if she was overhearing such conversations.

Nephys looked up at me, her big eyes dancing in the night. "Well, I'm his wife."

Chapter Twenty-Seven

"You're his—what did you just say?"

"Wife," said Nephys innocently.

I stared at her dumbfounded, tears gathering in my eyes. *How could this be? Llyr was married? How could I not know this?*

"Oh, my goddess!" she cried, watching my reaction. "You didn't know!"

I sat there completely stunned, unable to respond.

Why was this Nephys okay with this? Maybe they were in some kind of sordid open relationship, and I had just become his bit on the side. Perhaps she wanted a piece of me too and that was why she was so over-friendly.

"Look, it's not how it sounds," I heard her say.

Not how it sounds? Maybe she had been groomed by the Tribesmer to think this indecency was okay.

"Oh Crystal, I can just see it! You're torturing yourself!" she was wailing.

I had to get away from her. I went to stand up, but she grabbed my arms with her little hands. I battled against her, but I could not move an inch.

God, this little mermaid had the strength of about five thousand oxen.

"Right, I see what Llyr means now, you do jump to conclusions," Nephys was saying.

How dare this person just arrive on the scene and start judging me. Llyr could go to Hell, going home and slagging me off to the wife. I struggled to stand again, but she was like a bloody vice.

"Look, woman, take your hands off me," I snapped.

She would not let go!

"I think you need a little song to take the edge off this," she said contemplatively.

A song? Was I two now? I struggled on, determined to get away from her.

Suddenly the most incredible sound filled the air. At first, it startled me, just the volume of it but after a few seconds, it was the sheer beauty that overwhelmed me.

I looked at Nephys stunned, and I realized that it was coming from her full red lips. It was like a thousand angels were singing in perfect harmony.

Was that really her? Could this tiny creature really be producing such a heart-breakingly beautiful noise? And was it really possible for a singing voice to split like that, into so many notes? I swear I felt my spirit soar into the stars above.

I felt my body go limp and flop back onto the sand. *Wow!*

When she finished, I lay there glassy eyed.

"Oh, gosh, still crying?" she asked. She sat on her knees and extended a hand to my cheek, as the tears overflowed.

"No, it's not sadness, it's just that I've never heard such a beautiful sound," I sobbed. "Oh, no wonder Llyr married you."

Nephys sighed. "Oh yes, so about that ..."

I sniffed, I was coming down from my high a little. "Yes?" I asked tearfully.

"Llyr and I are old, old, old friends. We used to scream together as babes. Swim to the beach and play 'humans' together as children," Nephys said.

I sniffed. *Childhood sweethearts, playing 'humans.' Did she want to rub that salt in a little harder?*

"Don't get all sad again, just listen!" she said. "Right, I come from a beautiful, prosperous kingdom just south of Llyr's kingdom. Has he told you about that, at least?"

"The Jeweled Kingdom," I tremored.

"Right, yes, exactly, sweetness," said Nephys. "The Jeweled Kingdom is extremely important. Not only is it home to thousands of precious gemstones, but it is also a sacred city. Many flock there to be within its walls, they believe that the crystals there possess tremendous powers. It's all part of our religion that we must meditate alongside the crystals for answers. Anyway, Ri is the leader of course, like a king, and Llyr is his only son. I'm sure you know all of this ... "

The truth was I didn't, but I was listening, still monged out by her song.

"I come from the Evergreen kingdom," Nephys continued.

I didn't really know where this was going, but she needed to hurry up while I was still high.

"My kingdom is the nutrition capital. It's full of vegetation due to the minerals in the sand that it is built on. Most mers in the region get their food from our lands. All the buildings are covered in this luminous green moss, hence the name. It's just stunning."

I felt the song start to wear off, and I began to feel agitated again. *This was absolute bullshit.*

Nephys opened her mouth and omitted another minute of orgasmic vocals. I was back on my back again staring up at the stars. This wasn't fair.

"Basically, Crystal, my point is that most mer-leaders do not want to get on the wrong side of the Evergreens and risk losing their food supply. Similarly, we do not want to lose the support of the Jeweled Kingdom."

"Hmm," I speculated, still gazing up above. It appeared we were talking politics and I could feel this was vaguely taking some direction.

"My father and Ri are best friends, and they are both powerful mermen, leaders of their kingdoms. They have always been close, fierce allies. Not only do they need each other but they love each other, like brothers."

I rolled on my side to face her. I felt woozy; my vision was a little blurred.

"But there was one time, a couple of centuries ago that Father had heard that Ri was going to conspire with another kingdom to overthrow him and his tribe and take Evergreen for themselves," Nephys said, lying down on her side too, and facing me.

"And was he?" I asked doubtfully. I wasn't a massive fan of Ri but he didn't strike me as the conniving type.

"Well, no," continued Nephys. "But Father had intelligence from a reliable source, and he didn't know who to believe. So, to prove his loyalty, Ri offered up Llyr to be my husband."

I sighed. This was going some way to explaining things, but it was still nowhere near far enough.

"We were absolutely horrified!" Nephys told me, reaching my hand again. I hoped she wasn't going to put it on her chest. She played idly with my fingers instead. "We were like brother and sister. It was the most repulsive thought for us to be wed."

"They forced you?" I asked.

Nephys appeared distracted by my hand. She was picking up each finger and placing them down again on the sand.

"Yes ... " she sighed dreamily. "Can you imagine? We were supposed to start living as husband and wife, and have babes! I mean don't get me wrong, Llyr is the most gorgeous merman I have ever seen, but we could never love each other like that."

I gazed ahead. I had been brought up to think of marriage as a really big deal, not a stupid token. *Was this how Llyr saw it, a political match and nothing else?*

"So, you just pretend?" I asked, eventually.

"Well, yes for the next hundred and fifty years, we pretended, as you say, while begging our fathers to terminate our marriage," said Nephys. "I kept saying 'Come on Father, you know you can trust Ri now ...' We were living like siblings, not lovers and they knew it. I think over time they realized how unfair they had been to us, but anyway, they did not want the humiliation of a divorce. It's just not common practice for us."

"So the whole kingdom thinks you're happy together?" I asked, doubtfully. *They must all hate me, if so.*

"They believed that was the case, up until the scandal," said Nephys, her chirpy tone now serious.

"The scandal?" I asked. She announced this like it was some major history event I should be aware of.

"Oh, come on. You know, the great scandal?" she said, dropping my hand and gesticulating up into the sky, as though to indicate the scale of it.

I shook my head to demonstrate my ignorance over the matter.

"Georgie Porgie?" she said, raising an eyebrow as though this may ring bells.

I frowned, still totally perplexed.

"George," she tried again.

I snapped upright.

"George?" I shouted. "Fisherman George?"

I suddenly remembered Llyr's words.

'That's what I keep telling Ri. Just because I am with you, doesn't mean the same thing is going to happen as with Nephys.'

"You're ... George's ... mother," I said slowly.

"He's my baby!" Nephys confirmed.

I shook my head. "What the frig?" I said dazedly.

"We tried to pretend it was Llyr's," said Nephys wistfully. "Llyr even lied to Ri for me. It was celebrations all round at The Jewel. There were parties, processions ... Oh, I was receiving about a hundred gifts a day, right up until labor ..."

I cringed for her. "And then what?"

"Well," sighed Nephys, looking down, "obviously, he was born a human."

I could not get my head around this. Tiny fresh-faced Nephys was George, the ancient fisherman's mother. What a weird, weird world.

"How did your fathers take it?" I asked softly. I was really beginning to feel for her, even if she were Llyr's wife.

"They both wanted to banish me," said Nephys. "They wanted to throw me out of the kingdom and pretend I'd died during childbirth. Ri promised me enough jewels to last me a lifetime on my own. He said he would give me so many that I could build my own little kingdom, far away in the Pacific. Father said he would visit."

"But ...?" I pressed. I sensed that somehow Ri's plans had not come to fruit.

"Well, of course, Llyr would not hear of it. He said if I left then he would leave too, and that really got to Ri. He did not want to lose his only child."

I suppressed a snort. It sounded like all Ri really cared about was his kingdom so it would make sense he would want his heir to stick around.

"But I still don't get why Llyr didn't tell me about you?" I asked. This was all a sad and honorable tale, but I still needed to know how this was all kept from me.

"Honestly, Crystal, knowing Llyr, I think he forgets we're even married," said Nephys, running her hand through my hair. "I mean, it's been like two hundred years, and it's not exactly like we're in love, or ever have been."

I looked away. I still wasn't a hundred percent, even though Nephys did seem sincere.

"Why would he send me to rescue you if he felt he had anything to hide?" reasoned Nephys.

I nodded slowly. "I know, Nephys. It's just such a shock."

"Look, if it makes you feel any better, we were supposed to finally get divorced after the whole thing blew up with the baby sixty-five years ago," said Nephys. "As you can imagine, Ri was suddenly very keen for us to end our marriage."

This time I could not hold in a disdainful grunt. Ri, it seemed, was all about public relations.

"Oh, I know. He can be a big old pain sometimes," sighed Nephys.

Sometimes? Nephys was easy going. I would never speak to the man again if I were her. "So why didn't you get divorced anyway?" I asked.

"Well, we learned that you can only be separated by the same Shaman who wed you, but he had died a hundred years ago ... so we've been searching the world all this time for a sibling or blood relation—the next best thing. We were slowly making progress, last year we even had a lead that our deceased shaman had a brother who was living in a tribe in the Black Seas ... but then all this stuff started happening with the boats and the poison. We've all been rushed off our tails with that."

I looked up at Nephys. My instinct told me that she was completely genuine.

"Okay ... well, I'm sorry about George," I said, "and ... for you know, the rage."

Nephys smiled and shuffled forward to give me a hug, and I reluctantly let her press her bare body up against me.

"I'm sorry to give you such a surprise before," said Nephys withdrawing. "But you really have nothing to worry about, when it comes to me. You should also know, I think he's absolutely besotted by you. As you can imagine, all the mermaids have been throwing themselves at Llyr for centuries. We've got some rather scrumptious maids down there as well! Of course, he's had his fun but I've never seen him fall for anybody the way he has for you."

I could feel a smile spread across my face, and I looked down. I couldn't think of any words in the world that could sound better than this.

Nephys sighed and went back to drawing love hearts in the sand.

"It's so sweet, but yet so sad," she said.

"Sad?" I repeated back.

"Yes," said Nephys. "Because, as Ri keeps pointing out—winter will be here soon."

Chapter Twenty-Eight

This thought had swirled about here and there in the back of my mind, but I had never paid it much attention.

Winter.

The seas would indeed be much colder and rougher. Freezing, even. The beaches unpleasant, often unbearable to sit upon. *And what when it snowed?* I had just assumed Llyr had magical solutions to everything ...

"I mean, you can take it from me, it's impossible!" Nephys continued, crushing my hopes. "We spent an evening in his hut one September ..." she trailed off.

"And?" I fished.

"Dreadful!" she exclaimed, screwing up her little nose. "I hated being indoors. I felt like I was in a box and it made me paranoid. I kept thinking I was going to turn—you know, from legs to tail—and be stranded."

"Hmm," I mused reluctantly, suddenly having an image of Llyr turning in my parents' house. ... It did not sound good. I did some quick calculations; it was coming up to the end of July and we really only had a month left of summer.

"Who knows, though ... maybe Llyr has some ideas ... I haven't asked him," said Nephys.

I decided not to dwell on the thought of winter and buried it in the back of my mind again. *Maybe Llyr did have some ideas. He had to, why else would he pursue me?*

I shivered, I had been sitting here, soaking wet for about half an hour.

"Let's take you home," said Nephys.

"Do you have a boat?" I asked.

"Oh, I don't do boats, Crystal," said Nephys. "You will have to ride on my tail."

I hesitated. Firstly, I had never seen a tail before, and I had been putting it off for quite a while now. Second, of all, that THING was still out there.

"That shark ...?" I began.

"Oh, the fish has gone. I can't feel him," said Nephys dreamily, standing up and walking to the water's edge. She looked over her shoulder to check I was following.

I got up and trundled to where she stood. I bit my lip. *How was this tail thing going to work out?* I was nervous.

She put her hands to her mouth, as she realized the reason behind my reluctance.

"He hasn't shown you!" she gasped.

I cringed and looked down. "No. I'm a ... tail virgin!" I admitted.

She giggled that melodic little jingle. "Oh! Tails are wonderful. They are magical, beautiful things. As Nodun said 'to own a tail is to own the ocean.' That's a rough translation anyway," she said, swiping the air dismissively with her hand.

"Well then, I guess the world is your oyster," I joked gawkily, trying to cover up my uneasiness.

Nephys looked at me with her big sparkly eyes and took my hands, dragging me out into the waves. "I can see you're terrified. I'm just going to do it really quickly, okay."

"Okay," I said, my heart fluttering. *Don't freak*, I willed myself.

Nephys suddenly disappeared downwards; it was as though she had melted before my eyes. I blinked wondering if she were okay when I suddenly felt a tugging.

I looked down, and the first thing I saw was a shimmering flash. I squinted, and when I got my first clear glimpse, I just could not believe it.

It was a wonderful pearly white, and it was luminous under the moon, as though it were in its element in the night. It was a slender, curvaceous tail, just like her human form, and the bottom flared out into two large ruffled fins.

My eyes traveled upwards. The tail began just beneath her hips, and a few scales could be seen dotted around her flesh around the area, as the two forms merged.

She floated before me on the waves. "What I'm doing right now is rather miraculous," she explained. "Very few of us can stay mer on the surface. Most of us automatically shift—it's a protective instinct from humans."

I nodded, still amazed by what I saw. *Gosh, it really was true.*

"Isn't it brilliant?" she said proudly.

I nodded. It was not as scary as I thought.

"Yes, it's lovely," I said truthfully.

"Okay, right, we'd better dash," said Nephys, paddling forwards and lifting her fins up before me.

I trailed behind her for a while confusedly. *Did she want me to jump on her back or something?* I would await instruction, I decided.

She waved the fins just beneath my nose, and I squealed; they were tickling me.

"Hold on!" she cried, excitedly.

Hold on? It looked so fragile, almost like paper. I thought about the prawns they served up in restaurants; I could rip the tails of them with my bare hands. I didn't want to hold it, what if it broke off?

"Just grab it!" she called. "It is strong, don't worry."

It really was quite handy the way these mers read your feelings; you didn't have to bother communicating your worries. I realized that if Nephys could read mine, it must mean she felt a connection to me. I felt that we had indeed bonded during our short but dramatic time together.

I put my hands firmly over the two points. *She was right; they felt tough, more reminiscent of rubber than anything.*

Before I had time to speculate any further we were off,

plowing over the waves, which broke gently around us and then out into the open water. My body glided behind Nephys's, as though I were in a sleigh upon ice.

"We're going to go under!" she called.

Under?

Suddenly we dipped below the surface, and I held my breath and closed my eyes, as I felt our bodies' power through the icy water. And then we were heading up again and bursting upwards through the night sky, just as we had earlier away from the shark.

"We're going under again!" called Nephys, placing her hands above her head as though she were about to dive. I held my breath as we collided with the water and rocketed down below, only to scoop upwards again and shoot through the sky once more. This pattern continued for about ten minutes, like an invisible roller coaster. It was almost symbolic of my evening. I had emotionally gone from rock bottom to an absolute high.

I think my brain must have released a million endorphins and as soon as we dove through the sky, I would burst into gleeful shrieks, which I would have to stop when we lurched down again. We hit the water every time with such precision that there was never even a splash. We just cut straight through like knives.

Before I knew it, we were outside my house just beneath the jetty. I now giggled freely, and Nephys laughed with me. That had to have been the best experience ever.

"George used to love that when he was little," smiled

Nephys, placing a hand on her heart. "We used to call it the 'Big Wave.' He's a little old for all that now, of course ..."

I smiled sympathetically. It must be hard to watch your son age while remaining so youthful yourself.

"Thank you for everything," I said. "You have taught me so much, not to mention, saved my life ..."

"Yes, I can't imagine what you were doing out there, to be honest with you," said Nephys.

My stomach lurched as I thought about what an emo I'd been.

"I was looking for something," I said.

It was the truth in a funny kind of way.

"Hmm, you are quite a curious human, Crystal," she mused, hugging me. "Don't you worry about Llyr. I will send him straight to you when he returns."

I grinned and nodded, before hauling myself onto the jetty. I was quite a weight to bear with all my sopping wet clothes.

I made my way back up to the house, thinking of excuses as to why I was still fully dressed as a waitress but drenched from head to toe. I would have to tell Dad I fell off the sea taxi or something.

I opened the back door and was relieved that Dad appeared to have gone to bed. I tiptoed upstairs and jumped in a piping hot shower. *Oh my days, it was absolute bliss.*

When I got out I dried myself and put on my pajamas. I

realized it was the first time in weeks that I had felt a little bit like myself again. It had been such a relief to learn that Llyr hadn't written us off. Now that this weight was off my shoulders, I could focus on helping Dad through his crisis. Maybe I could even join the anti-SKANX cause.

It wasn't like I had to worry about rustling Mum's feathers anymore. I had barely heard a word from her since she left us, and I was beginning to believe that she had well and truly moved on with her new life.

Chapter Twenty-Nine

I had been curled up in bed with a cold for the past few days. I guess it was only a matter of time before one of my nighttime swims took its toll on me.

My dad had queried how I had ended up with a cold in the middle of summer, and I had simply shrugged mutely. I really couldn't think of a reasonable excuse so playing dumb seemed like the best option.

Fortunately, Dad had been completely obsessed by the anti-SKANX demonstration, now due to kick off tomorrow morning and hadn't really paid me or my cold too much attention. I had tried to help him paint some banners, but I had had a sneezing fit all over them, and Dad had ordered me upstairs to rest.

Over the past couple of days, Dad had been shooting around the island, mainly between Seaman's Lodge—to liaise with the other organizers—and home where he seemed to have had a string of phone conferences.

Yesterday, I had overheard a conversation with George, which I had to admit left me both baffled and concerned.

I had come out of my room to use the loo, and could hear Dad talking in a hushed voice in his bedroom. I had tiptoed along the corridor and put my ear up to the door.

"Now George, did you get the wire clippers—sorry—carrots and potatoes?" Dad was saying.

Wire clippers? Carrots and potatoes? Either Dad was going a bit batty, or carrots and potatoes were code words for wire clippers, which Dad was not very good at using. *What worried me was that if I was right about the latter then why, oh why, did Dad need wire clippers?*

———

The next morning, I still felt rough. It was Dad's big demonstration, but I wasn't well enough to go, and he had left the house before I had even woken.

I spent the day in bed with my iPad watching films. I was not up to much else, although I had forced myself to take Maurice around the block in the morning, and now he was curled up loyally on the rug by my bed.

Poor dog. He probably wondered what on earth was going on in this house and where Mum kept going. I wish I could tell him everything. Still, maybe ignorance was bliss in this case.

I was now on texting terms with my mother and had

learned that she had found herself a studio flat in Coney Bay, which, she reported, "enabled a nice quick taxi journey to work."

"Good for you," I had sneered, upon reading her text.

I wondered why she was still even here. Now she wasn't with Dad she could easily just go back to London. She had done nothing but moan about being here since she arrived. *Perhaps it was her boyfriend, Mr. Geake, now keeping her in Coney. She must like him so much ...*

I lay in bed thinking about it and began to seethe. *How could that awful man steal my mum away from my wonderful dad?* For the first time in my life, I began to have violent ideations. I pictured myself wielding a couple of samurai swords—Uma Thurman style—as he sat there quivering. It made me feel felt so much better.

Once I calmed down, I rewound my film. I had become so enraged that I had missed about ten minutes, but my iPad was playing up. It was being painfully slow and refusing to reload. I sat there impatiently as a little circle swirled on the screen. Not one for patience, I became too annoyed to persevere and flung it down on the bed. I was tired anyway and decided I would just go to sleep.

I must have drifted off quickly, and when I awoke, I looked outside and saw the sun was setting over the sea. Our jetty was lit up like a big orange block, jutting out into the water.

My thoughts travelled to Llyr and how he usually arrived down there with some borrowed boat. I giggled thinking about the "fiddly" one he couldn't operate. I wondered when he would next come to me. I missed him so much.

There was a ringing in the house. I sat up and listened. It was the sound of our landline. I decided to ignore it. *It wouldn't be for me anyway*, I thought, snuggling under my blankets. All my friends called my mobile.

I was just about to fall asleep again when I heard more ringing.

"Eugh, go away!" I cried from under my cover. *Who was this person bothering me? Surely everybody knew by now that Mum didn't live here anymore, and Dad was on his famous demonstration.*

It stopped, and I closed my eyes, relishing the silence.

There it was again. For goodness' sake, I suppose I was going to have to go and answer it.

I begrudgingly threw back the covers and stomped into the corridor and down the stairs. The phone was in its cradle in the hall, flashing as it rang. I picked it up and was just about to press the answer button when it stopped.

"Oh, typical!" I muttered slamming it back in its cradle. As I was now up, I wandered into the kitchen. *It must be Lemsip time by now*, I thought, flicking on the kettle.

I idly picked up the remote and turned on the TV. A cartoon of a sea monster was on channel three, and I hurriedly changed over, immediately thinking of my very own real life sea monster experience. I shivered, either from trauma or fever, or maybe a little of both.

The opening jingle of the local news came on, and I put the remote down on the counter. *May as well check out the headlines*, I thought, opening the cabinet and pulling out a box of Lemsip.

I was halfway through ripping open the sachet when I heard the commentator say the word "protestors." I turned, dropping the sachet on the floor when I saw the TV. Adrenaline pumped through my body, my heart racing a million beats a minute.

My father was pictured hundreds of feet off the ground, dangling in some kind of flimsy harness. He was splayed across the front of a very large building with an unfurled banner that read "SMASH SKANX."

"Ohh my God!" I shouted. "Oh my God!"

I rushed into the corridor and picked up the phone, dialing a code as fast as I could to find out who had been calling the house. I scribbled down the number and then rang it back as quickly as my trembling hands would allow me.

"Coney Police?" came a voice on the other end.

"Hi, my name is Crystal," I began. "Crystal White."

Chapter Thirty

I sat staring at the red plastic chair. Over the past three hours, I had pretty much thoroughly examined everything else in the police station, which included a couple of vending machines and a load of law-enforcing posters.

Being a Saturday night, a couple of aggressive drunks had been forced through the doors and out into the back, no doubt to the cells. I shuddered. I could not believe my father was back there somewhere with them.

Police had said that he would not be held for too long, overnight at the latest. They had urged me to go home but I couldn't be in my house alone while Dad was in jail.

Tired of looking at a chair, I pulled out my phone and saw that I had two missed calls: one from Rosie and one from my mother.

I would call Rosie tomorrow; she would understand. I was almost certain she had seen the news, no doubt along with everybody else at Coney Secondary School.

Now, as for my mother ... I debated returning her call. On one hand, I was still her daughter, and she may be genuinely worried about me, but on the other hand, she may just want to use the opportunity to slag off Dad and poison me against him. You just couldn't be sure with Mum these days.

I decided to send her a text instead, telling her I was fine. After the message had sent, I put the phone in my bag and went to the desk to ask the policemen for a cup of water.

The officer behind the desk was pretty decent about fetching the water and even brought it over to where I was sitting. They probably took pity on me, sitting there miserably waiting for my crazy dad to be released.

I was getting terribly sleepy and moved chairs so that I could sit next to one of the white concrete walls. Here, I rested my head against the wall and despite the bright glaring lights, I almost instantly fell into a deep sleep.

When I awoke, it was to the sound of two merry male voices. I sat up confused, trying to remember where I was and why. Slowly, reality came flooding back and I remembered how I came to be sleeping in this brightly lit room.

I squinted and looked up. Dad and George were standing in front of me grinning like a pair of Cheshire cats.

"You're free," I mumbled sleepily.

"Yes, darling," boomed Dad brightly. "They can't hold

me for more than twenty-four hours. They wouldn't have a leg to stand on!"

"Too right," chuckled George.

"What the hell were you thinking?" I hissed at Dad angrily.

"Well, I was thinking that we need to show SKANX that we're not a bunch of passive sheep here in Coney," said Dad as though this was the most reasonable statement in the world.

"You could have been killed!" I whimpered. "You scaled a two-hundred-foot power station!"

I had been petrified when I saw him up there.

George clapped his hands together and laughed. "What a legend!" he hooted slapping Dad on the back.

Were they having a joint mid-life crisis?

"And it was all over the news!" I added faintly.

Dad and George gasped with glee. They put their hands up to give each other a high five, only it appeared they were not too familiar with the whole procedure, and it took them about a minute to coordinate.

"Well done, that was the world's slowest high five!" I said, crossing my arms.

"I think we should all go and have a lovely fry up; that should cheer you up. We're just waiting for the officers to return our possessions," said Dad jollily.

"You were arrested too?" I said to George, with disbelief.

"I was up there with him, kid," said George. "I didn't

get as high, though, but I still graffitied 'R.I.P. CONEY MARINE LIFE!' Didn't they show me on the news?"

"No," I said flatly. "It would appear Dad was the poster boy this time."

I shook my head and looked away, but a giggle suddenly escaped my lips. I stole another look at them both sniggering away, eyes ablaze with excitement.

Oh, he had given me the fright of my life, but there was also something undeniably hilarious about it. I mean, this was the sort of thing students did, not old age pensioners. The press were certainly paying attention now. They didn't need me at the front of their campaign like George had once suggested.

I suddenly felt a little spark of hope for Llyr and his tribe. Maybe Dad could really stop SKANX after all.

———

I wiped the last table at the pub and returned the dishrag to the sink behind the bar. Everybody had left, and it was just myself and Tamzin in the dimly lit room. It was the night after the great arrest, and I was back at work.

I had been tempted to skive, but my cold had somehow cleared during my night in the police station, and Dad was having all the fishermen around for celebratory drinks. If I stayed at home, I might well join them for a tipple or two, and I wouldn't want that to get back to Tamzin.

I had learned over our fry-up this morning that Dad and George had teamed up with some green activists and buried six sets of wire-clippers by the fences a couple of days before. Unfortunately, it appeared that I had been right about the carrots and potatoes.

As the protest had moved towards the power station, this small group had broken away from the main march and nipped their way into the site. By the time the police had learned of the trespassers, Dad and George were halfway up the building.

Dad did not seem remotely worried about the consequences of his protest. In fact, he appeared to believe he had found a loop in the law which allowed him to do such things.

Now I rested my hands on the sink, lost in thought. *I was not quite sure how my life had ended up like this. We used to be such a normal family.*

"Crystal?" began Tamzin. She was propped up on a bar stool having her after-work Sauvignon.

"Yep?" I said, looking up and wringing out the cloth. I hoped she wasn't going to ask me to work tomorrow night.

"Was that your father on the news yesterday?"

I looked back down again. I didn't know what her reaction was going to be. News had it that some fisher folk thought Dad had gone a step too far.

"Erm, yeah ..." I winced, dreading her response.

Tamzin's face lit up. "I thought it were," she chirped.

"Well, you thought right." I smiled, drying my hands and smiling at her. She seemed pretty okay with it.

"Christ, if he were my father," said Tamzin. "I'd be bloomin' over the moon!"

"Yeah?" I asked. "He's pretty brave I guess. Slightly silly too."

"He'll go down in Coney history. That company is going to finish off this town if they carry on much longer. Trust me my Barney ain't had a good catch in months."

"I know, I don't like what the company is doing one bit. I just hope that Dad's efforts pay off," I said.

"Well, it might not stop 'em just yet, but it'll tell 'em," said Tamzin righteously. "He's my hero, anyway."

I smiled gratefully. It was nice to know Dad's efforts were winning him some fans.

I looked around the pub; it looked like my work was done, and so I said goodbye to Tamzin and headed down to the jetty where my sea taxi was waiting to collect me.

Tamzin was a good boss. She usually gave me half the fare for the taxis so it wouldn't cut into my wages too much.

I had seen that morning that my pay had finally come through and for once, I had some money. Perhaps I would be able to go shopping this week. Finally.

I felt a little buzz of excitement as I mulled over this prospect on the journey home. I had seen the most gorgeous jewellery down on the stalls by the harbour. There was the most wonderful silver ring with a big blue oval stone that could be mine.

It was a clear starry night, and by the time we pulled into my jetty, I was in much better spirits.

I searched my bag for my house keys, taking advantage of the cabin light in the boat. I retrieved them and stood up on the deck, ready to step onto the jetty. As I put one foot out, the boat suddenly rocked, and I shrieked as I lost my footing. My arms flew backwards and the keys out of my hand and into the sea below.

"Oh noooo!" I cried as the boat driver steadied me from behind. We looked below at the inky black waves.

"Anyone else home?" asked the driver. There was no way I was getting them back.

I looked up at my house. All the lights were out, and I was quite sure Dad must have gone to bed. I sighed; he would be out like a log, given that he had not slept in forty-eight hours.

I thanked the driver and walked slowly up the jetty. I was going to have to go around the front and ring the bell until he woke.

There was a gentle splashing sound behind me. I figured it must be a fish or something, so I continued my way.

"Were you looking for these?" came a familiar voice.

Chapter Thirty-One

"Llyr!" I cried excitedly rushing to the end of the jetty.

"Crystal," he said softly, lifting one hand out of the water and placing it around my leg. He tugged downwards, so that I sat on the edge, and I took my shoes off and dangled my feet in the water.

He handed me the keys.

"Thank you," I said, laughing. "I was just thinking I was going to have to sleep in the garden."

"Oh, well I couldn't have that." He smiled, running his hand up my leg. I instantly felt shivers up and down my spine.

"I missed you so much," I said, looking down at him. He had his hair tied up tonight, and he looked super, super gorgeous, as usual. Maybe even more so as I hadn't seen him in a while.

"Good," he smiled. "I had hoped your anger would subside."

I looked to the side a little sheepishly. Apparently, Jemima had told Rosie that her father had been investigating the incident, and there had indeed been something very wrong with the boat, just like Llyr said. I decided to change the subject.

"Where have you been?" I asked curiously. I still had no idea what this dream journey was all about.

"I took all the little mers on a trip," he said. "You know, we teach them to do stuff in the wild. Survival skills."

"How cute!" I exclaimed.

"Yes, there were less than usual, because of the poison crisis, but there were still maybe twenty. They were all lined up with their little spears," he laughed.

"Oh stop it," I cried. *This was too much.*

"Spirit made them their spears," he said.

I pulled a face of nausea. "Oh, yuck. Well, that's ruined everything."

"Yes, that's why I said it," he said, pulling himself halfway up onto the jetty, so one arm now wrapped around my waist and the other lay across my front. I felt water seep through all my clothes, but I couldn't be more unbothered.

He kissed me, and I kissed him right back. It had been a long time. Too long.

"Do you like children?" he said, between kisses.

I blinked, wondering if his trip had made him broody or something. I was only seventeen; I was in no place to think about children.

"Erm, yeah," I giggled nervously turning away. "Why, do you?"

"Yeah, of course," he said. He swung himself onto the jetty so that he sat next to me.

Perhaps he sensed how awkward his question made me feel, and he changed the subject. "Where have you been?" he asked, looking at my outfit skeptically. I wore a white shirt and a black knee length skirt. It was not my normal style.

I told him all about my new job, including full descriptions of Tamzin and all the larey locals.

"You know, instead of a job, I can just bring you some pearls," he said slowly when I was finished. "They are quite valuable to humans, are they not?"

I laughed. At first, I thought he was joking, but he wasn't quite smiling, and I sensed there was something about the job that he wasn't happy about.

"What's wrong?" I said suspiciously.

"I just think you should be enjoying yourself, that's all," he said.

Was he worried about all the time my job would take up? I was working four nights a week now, but it's not like he was around so much anyway. I had nothing else to do here apart from roam the island.

He seemed to recognize that he was stressing me out, and he put his hand on my face. "I'm sorry, I don't mind, Crystal. I only want your happiness. I promise," he said.

"Sure, I'm fine," I said distantly. *I never expected him to be remotely bothered about a job. He was supposed to be like, this free spirit. Or so I thought. Maybe it was the royalty thing. Kings probably provided for their women while royal mermaids sat at home and brushed their hair.*

Llyr started laughing. "I can see it in your face. You're imagining all kinds of things ..."

I couldn't help but smile. *How could he know me so well, in so little time?*

I leaned on his shoulder, the job disagreement forgotten. I still couldn't believe we were back here on my little jetty together. I had been so convinced at one point that we would never see each other again.

We watched a shooting star across the ocean. They were so quick that if you blinked you'd miss it.

I felt Llyr's hand on my leg again, light soft caresses making me feel amazing. His hand was around my knees, tugging my skirt up.

I really meant to tell him to stop. Part of me was worried about Dad waking up and looking out of his window and seeing us. The thing was, I just couldn't bring myself to end it, I felt ripples of pleasure with every touch. And he soon started on my shirt, unbuttoning it, his mouth all over my neck and chest.

"Lie down," he whispered.

I nodded, and there under the shooting stars, on my jetty, Llyr and I finally made love.

Afterwards, we lay there for a while. I was breathless and really quite overwhelmed by the whole experience.

I had never really taken so long to recover. In actual fact, within my limited sexual experience, it was pretty much always the other way around. Still, Llyr was a three-hundred-year-old superhuman, after all.

When I had resumed normality, we held each other. My shirt and skirt were somewhere on the jetty, and my underwear was in bits around us. He had literally ripped it off.

"That was amazing," he said, kissing my cheek.

I sighed blissfully. "Yes, it was definitely worth the wait. Although I was a little paranoid Dad would catch us."

Llyr sat up with alarm. "He's awake?"

"No, but I just thought maybe he would wake up or something ..." I said. "It's okay, anyway. I'm pretty sure we'd know about it if he had."

He lay back down. "How are your parents?"

"Oh, you know ... separated." I said.

"I'm sorry," he said.

"It's okay," I replied dismissively. I didn't really want to talk about it and ruin everything. "Hey, did you hear about my father and George?"

"No," he said, with interest. "What happened?"

I told him all about the saga over the last forty-eight hours, and he threw back his head in a bellowing laugh.

"Shhh!" I hissed, laughing myself and pointing to the house.

"That is beautiful!" he cried, thumping the wood beneath him with his hand.

"Really?" I said. "Beautiful?"

It wasn't quite the adjective I would use to describe it myself. Still this was the man who sank a SKANX tanker.

"You're beautiful," he said, moving so that he was on top of me. "Can I say that?"

"Yes, that's fine," I said, nodding with approval.

"And what about I love you?" he murmured, kissing me. "Can I say that?"

I smiled. They were the words that I had to stop tumbling out of my own mouth every second I was with him.

"Yes," I replied happily.

Chapter Thirty-Two

The next two weeks flew by in a whirlwind of fun and passion. I saw Llyr nearly every day. He would either pick me up at "sunhigh" meaning midday, or "sundown" sunset.

If it were sunhigh when we met then, we would head out to sea, spending hours cruising over the waves and swimming. We would then lie in the boat looking up at the sky, talking and laughing.

He would drop me home just in time to rush to work. After a summer like mine, life on the seascape was becoming second nature to me. I could chop and change between land and sea completely unfazed, as opposed to when I first arrived here at Starfish when everything would wobble for about half an hour after stepping off a boat.

Today he had collected me in George's blue rowing boat, and we headed out over the bumpy waves. I wore my new purple bikini, but there was a wind today, and I found myself shivering.

I had one of Dad's new SMASH SKANX t-shirts in my bag and I pulled it on over my body.

Llyr squinted at the thick black lettering, and I wasn't entirely sure if he could understand it. I translated the meaning to him.

"Very good," he smiled.

I gave him a dutiful nod and looked out to sea, rubbing my arms.

"I think we will be out of these winds soon," he said, looking over at me with his deep green eyes. He never appeared affected by the temperature, and in fact, I had never seen him wear anything on his top half. "Sorry," he finished.

"It's okay," I said, thinking how sweet it was that he always cared for me. "I don't mind so much."

After another half an hour of pushing on through the waves, true to Llyr's word, they appeared to ease a little, and I suddenly felt the sun on my face as the wind died down.

"That's better," I said lying backwards and resting my head on the stern. I ripped the t-shirt off again and let the sun warm my body.

Suddenly there was a big splash to my left, and something slippery touched my arm. I snapped upright and screamed.

"Oh, Crystal, I'm sorry I forgot how jumpy you are."

Nephys was draped over the side of the boat. She pursed her big red lips and leaned over to kiss my cheek.

"Nephys!" I cried. "Sorry, you startled me."

There was splash to my left, and I screamed again.

There was the sound of merry laughter.

"Sorry, I couldn't resist it!" came a friendly chuckle.

"Bright!" I shrieked, putting my hands to my heart as I felt it thud in my chest.

"Good day, Miss White," he said, propping himself up with one arm on the boat and shaking my hand with the other.

I shook it back a little wearily. *Why did everybody have to surprise me all the time?*

"She's very nervous, my Crystal," said Llyr.

"No, I'm not!" I protested. *Jeez, just because they were all mystical and magical or whatever ...* "I'm human," I finished.

"You're pretty scared of storms, even for a human," teased Bright.

"Yes, and you were petrified of that fish," added Nephys.

"Okay, that was not any old Joe Blogs fish. That was a shark!" I shrieked with outrage. *Who wouldn't be scared of that?*

"What shark?" said Llyr sitting up.

"Nothing ..." we chimed. I think we had both forgotten our promise not to mention my near death experience to Llyr.

I quickly changed the subject. "How are you both?" I asked.

"All the better for seeing you!" trilled Nephys. She was wearing a dark green band around her head. It looked like woven seaweed.

"We keep asking him to see you," she continued, "but he wants you all to himself. He's so greedy," she said splashing water at Llyr.

"How very possessive!" I said crossing my arms and looking at Llyr with mock disapproval.

"Don't listen to her," he replied. "I told her to come before, but she forgot and went off to some strange thing."

"Oh yes, yoga," said Nephys.

"Yoga?" I said curiously. *How on earth did she know about yoga?*

"Yes, my friend Silver started it. She calls it yog-mer, actually." Nephys let off one of her melodic giggles. "Silver always watches you people doing it on the beach—she's obsessed ..."

"Wow," I said. "Did you like it?"

"No. I was quite bored. I much prefer dancing," said Nephys. "Bright liked it, though."

I giggled and looked to my right at Bright, who scowled at Nephys. It appeared Nephys had let another cat out of the bag.

"I just went to watch the maids," Bright muttered hurriedly to Llyr.

"Llyr, you should go. It's all very meditative. You like that stuff," said Nephys.

"Maybe I can be Bright's apprentice," said Llyr, jokingly.

I put a hand on a forlorn Bright's arm. I felt sorry for him; he was already clearly considered the least macho mer.

"Well, I heard about George and your father," said Nephys, her sapphire blue eyes opening wide with the very thought. "I scolded him to the heavens. I can't quite imagine what he thought he was doing. He's not a young boy anymore. I was going mad down there sensing something was going on with him. But I have to say, I am quite glad I didn't know what exactly it was."

"I wish I hadn't known," I said, remembering the horror of turning on the news that night.

"Do humans go a bit funny at that age, Crystal?" said Nephys, frowning and looking at me. My heart went out to her; it must be so difficult to mother a child that you could not fully understand.

I smiled. "Sometimes. I think George is fine, though."

Nephys smiled gratefully. "Thank you."

"Well, anyway," said Bright. "We're not here to stay this time. We're here to drop something off."

"Drop what off?" I asked.

"Llyr, is she going to be able to handle this?" said Nephys, looking at him.

"Oh no, what now?" I said with alarm. Just when everything had calmed down, there going to be another bombshell.

Llyr looked at me. "She will like it."

"What? What will I like?" I demanded. *Did they have to talk about me in the third person?* "I am here you know?"

Llyr nodded at Nephys and Bright and they disappeared beneath the surface, leaving two little ripples on either side of the boat.

"Llyr?" I said.

"It's fine," he said, kneeling on the floor of the boat and putting his hand in the water. He began to make some clicking noises with his mouth to the water. It was like he was trying to communicate with something.

I sat up tensely. I had no idea what was going to come out of the water, but I knew by now that I had better brace myself for the unexpected.

Three sets of bubbles began to appear on the surface. This could only mean one thing: Nephys and Bright were not coming back alone.

Llyr looked at me. "Get ready to meet William."

I looked at him totally baffled. *What on earth was he going on about? Who was William?*

"Lean back a little," warned Llyr.

I sighed with exasperation and shuffled backwards into the boat.

Suddenly a sharp point punctured the surface. It was like a white ridged cone, and it kept getting taller and taller.

"What in God's name ...?" I shrieked.

There was a loud noise, and I closed my eyes. I knew that noise. It was a neighing sound. I slowly opened one eye.

There, swimming in the water next to the boat was a beautiful snow white horse. Even soaking from the water, this horse did not lose the sheerness of its colour.

There was something not quite right about this horse, though ... What was it? I opened my other eye to get a full look at the creature. Oh *my* ... crap.

"It's a unicorn!" I breathed.

"A sea unicorn," said Llyr proudly, reaching out stroking the wonderful William's nose.

Once my haze of disbelief had cleared, Llyr and I mounted William. At first, I was very worried. I didn't want to sink him with our weight.

I got on first, ever so gingerly, despite much reassurance from Bright and Nephys. Once I felt my legs on either side of him, I could feel that he was a big strong creature, and I probably wasn't too much of a burden to him.

I leaned forward and stroked the side of his face. It felt just like velvet. I felt another body behind me and turned and saw Llyr now sat astride the unicorn too. I leaned forward to check if William was coping with the weight and saw to my relief that he looked completely unfazed. In fact, to the contrary, he was looking rather alert, as though he were aching to get a move on.

Llyr rested a hand on my thigh. "Hold onto his hair," he said.

"Are we going to bareback ride him?" I asked, my eyes wide with worry.

"Bareback?" said Llyr, looking at Nephys and Bright for help.

"Without anything to sit on or leads to hold onto ... I think," said Nephys.

"Oh, yes, of course," said Llyr dismissively. "You don't need any of those things."

"Okay ..." I said, reluctantly holding onto William's silky, white mane. I was trying not to make a big scene, but I was a little apprehensive.

"Where are we going by the way?" I asked.

"To your beach," said Llyr. "It's not far. Bright can you anchor this boat for us please?"

Bright did a little bow for Llyr, his head dunking briefly under the water. I giggled, I think this was meant to be a *yes*.

There was a splash as Llyr kicked William in the side. He neighed and suddenly we began to move forward. I looked below us, and I watched in awe, as his little white hooves peddled through the water.

We waved goodbye to Nephys and Bright, and soon we were far away from them, my initial fears displaced with joy and excitement.

If someone had told me a couple of months ago that I would be riding a unicorn through the sea with a merman, I would have thought they were on drugs. It was trippy, let's be honest.

"Llyr?" I said.

"Mmm?" he murmured into my ear.

"How come he's called William?" I asked.

"Oh." Llyr laughed. "Yes, he has a human name. It's because George named him when he was little."

I blinked. William must be quite old in this case.

"I found him on a dream journey about sixty years ago," said Llyr, reading my thoughts. "At first, when I saw him, I couldn't believe it. I had heard of such things, but I thought it was a myth. He had a little foal by his side. I think something had happened to the mother."

"So you brought them back?" I asked.

"No, they just followed me ... I don't know why."

"Maybe they liked you," I said, leaning back into his chest as we moved along. "I would follow you too."

He kissed me on the cheek. "I wish you could," he said.

It wasn't long before the purple cliffs of Crystal Bay came into view.

As we got to the shore, William increased his pace; I think he was keen to get onto the land. As we got nearer, he put his feet down and cantered out onto the beach. I had been lounging back against Llyr and was caught off guard. I grabbed his hair and dug my knees in to keep myself balanced.

"Pull on his mane," shouted Llyr over the thundering of his hooves.

I gave it a little tug, and William slowed down, but we were now trotting up and down the beach. I let out an elated laugh. *This was so fun.*

Eventually, we dismounted William and left him to do his thing. He appeared to graze on some seaweed by the cliffs.

"Is that what he eats?" I asked laughing.

"That, and he loves sea cucumbers," said Llyr. "I have to go out far, even way past Evergreen to get him his treats."

I stood on my tiptoes and put my arms around Llyr's neck. I had never been so happy as at that very moment. He picked me up in his arms, and I wrapped my legs around him.

"You are the most romantic guy in the world," I said, beaming.

There were quite simply no other words.

Chapter Thirty-Three

The next day I woke up and was devastated to see big dark clouds in the sky. My window was splattered with rain drops like some giant had come and done a massive raspberry all over it.

It felt like that anyway.

I had worked until one a.m. last night at The Rose as it had been a Saturday night. It had been tiring, but the one thing that had kept me going was the excitement of today. I was supposed to meet Llyr at sunhigh and go to Crystal Bay with William.

How would we do this now?

My phone beeped. It was a text from my mum.

"Eugh," I grumbled, as I opened the message. I had not heard from her in a while now.

Hello, it's your mother. I just wondered when I was going to get to see my baby girl? I miss you. xxxx

I felt my heart soften a little. She was actually displaying a little sorrow.

What do I do? Run to her with open arms and condone her actions against Dad, or be cold and brutal, punish her? *This was family,* I thought. *Not politics.* There was a time to think with your head and a time to think with your heart. And I knew my heart wanted my mum.

I slowly texted her back.

I miss you too Mum. When are you around?

I turned off my phone. That was all I could handle for now.

I trudged to the bathroom. I thought I may as well get ready to meet Llyr; it was nearly eleven thirty.

I thought about my family as I stood under the jet. Since Dad had scaled SKANX, he appeared to have calmed down a lot. Maybe it had helped him get all the rage out of his system. But it didn't fix things. Now I was seeing a sadder, more subdued Dad. The reality was hitting him.

I felt guilt flush through me. I hadn't really been here for him the past few weeks. I had been out with Llyr and then ducking into the house to shower and race off to work. *Was this really wrong?*

I didn't know what my role in this house was supposed to be anymore. As much as Mum was the perpetrator, perhaps there was no better person to tell me what to do.

At around 12:30 p.m. I went down to the jetty. I could not see the sun under the clouds but knew by now that it peaked at around this time.

It was still raining, so I wore my sweatshirt for the first time in months and pulled the hood up. The other thing I noticed as I stepped out of my back door was the temperature. It was cold.

I walked down through the garden and could feel goose bumps prickling up on my tanned legs. I felt worried. *Was winter kicking in early?* It was mid-August now, after all.

When I got to the jetty, I could see him sitting on the end. He looked at me and pointed to the sky.

I responded with a big shrug. *What can you do?*

I sat next to him. He kissed me, but even his lips on mine did not feel pleasurable in this weather.

"I know," he said, zoning in on my disappointment. "We can still go if you like, though?"

I didn't know what to say. If we didn't go I would feel sad and depressed all day, but then if we went, I would be cold, wet and no doubt grumpy. It was a no-win situation.

"The first day it is clear again, I will be straight here at sunhigh," he offered, as though to help me make up my mind.

I looked at him. Water ran down his face, like a little web of rivers.

"You think there will be more rainy days?" I said, wiping his face with my sleeve.

"It may go on for a little while," he said. "I can feel that it will, yes."

I nodded sadly. "Okay."

"What will you do today?" he asked.

"I don't know," I replied truthfully. "Maybe go and see my friend Rosie, I guess." I looked up at him and smiled. "What will you do?" I asked. I wondered what mers did on a rainy day.

"I will go and see Ri, I think," said Llyr. "He has been asking to see me."

"Is everything okay?" I asked.

Llyr raised his eyebrows. "Oh, he hasn't been talking to me for a while but maybe he wants to start again."

"Because of me?" I asked. Llyr had not mentioned this before.

Llyr looked down. I could see he didn't want to hurt me.

"I don't care. I love you," he said, looking at me again.

I leaned my head on his shoulder. *We sure had had a lot of hurdles to jump over ...*

We sat like this on the jetty for a few more minutes but then the rain began to get heavier and so I sat up straight again.

"I should go in," I said standing up.

He stood up too and I wrapped my arms around his neck.

"I love you too, by the way," I said.

Chapter Thirty-Four

With Dad out at the dentist, I had decided that today was as good a day as any to reunite with my mum.

Now I let my iPhone guide me through the back streets of Coney to her new house. Like many classic English fishing towns, it comprised of two main roads and a labyrinth of narrow, winding, cobbled back streets.

I had texted Rosie earlier after Llyr had left. I'd asked if she wanted to have lunch, but she texted back with a sad face and said that she was in another town all day.

"Probably with Jemima," I had mumbled, grumpily.

I wondered how school was going to be now that Rosie and Jemima were besties with bestie boyfriends. *It was like bestie squared, you know like in Maths—bestie².*

"Stop it!" I had warned myself. There was no point in thinking about these things. Now I had become the petty one.

I had not ventured down these Coney back streets

before as I had never had any purpose to do so. The houses on opposite sides of the roads were so close together that you could easily skip from one into the other, and I had to squish right up against a wall to let an old man pass me.

Eventually, I turned down Josephine Avenue. Hanging baskets of red and pink flowers spilled onto the mossy walls of the stone houses.

It was cute but cramped, a little bit like somewhere I could imagine an imp or hobbit may reside. I double checked the address. Yep, this was definitely it.

I couldn't help but wonder how happy my mum was living here, on this pokey little road. It was so ... not her.

Mum was into her space. She liked big light rooms and a large garden to look out onto. Still, perhaps I had best not judge a book by its cover.

I took a deep breath and knocked on the door. It had been about a month since I'd last seen my mum.

The door opened with a creak, and there she was, smiling in the doorway.

The first thing I noticed about my mum was that she looked a little gaunt. She wore one of her favourite tailored dresses, and I could see that today her body did not quite fill it.

Well, I guessed people often lose weight when they fall in love, during that honeymoon period. I mean, I had certainly shed a pound or two these past couple of months, so maybe the excitement of her own fling was also suppressing her appetite. I felt a little bubble of rage, and I distracted myself. This was not the best trail of thought to start this visit.

"Darling!" Mother cried, throwing her arms around me. I smelt her perfume and felt the most overwhelming sense of comfort being back in her arms. My anger dissolved.

"Mum!" I cried, hugging her back and resting my head on her shoulder.

She eventually pulled away, and I could see her eyes well up, just as mine probably were. It was just like that day at the station when she had greeted Dad and me, before dropping the big bombshell.

I followed her up through a narrow beige painted stairwell and up a couple of flights of stairs. She definitely wasn't her usual chatty self. In fact, there was a sense of seriousness about her.

I entered her new studio flat. It was fairly nice, perfectly presentable. There was a double bed in the centre and a large fitted wardrobe to the left. A kitchen with all the mod cons graced the far right and there was a nice set of French windows which overlooked the sea.

I still couldn't quite understand why Mum would choose to live here in this weeny flat in Coney, rather than move back to the big smoke, or even back to Starfish with us.

She made us a cup of tea, and we sat at her little kitchen table catching up on basic stuff. I told her about my job and that in my free time, I had been exploring the area.

She asked me where exactly I had explored, and I

became a little flustered. I mumbled about beaches and cliffs and she looked at me suspiciously.

"Hmm, and what about that chap you liked?" she asked, knowing me all too well.

Oh bugs, I had forgotten about our conversation all those months back on the jetty. *Should I tell her there was still a guy, or not?*

"He's about," I said, turning a vase of lilies on the table. I didn't want to lie outright.

"And ... ?" pressed Mum. Of course, she wanted to know more.

"He's really sweet. He's kind of local," I struggled. "He's a ... sailor."

"A sailor?" said Mother dubiously.

"Yes," I said. *There was still such a thing as a sailor, right?* All I really knew about sailors is that they wore those old fashioned navy and white suits and that Popeye was one.

"In the Navy?" said Mum.

"Yes," I replied firmly. *Okay, so sailors worked in the navy.*

"Oh, maybe I know him; he could have rescued me that night the ship sank?" said Mum. "I've met most of the sailors since the accident. Some of them are gorgeous. What's his name?"

"I mean ... no," I said, panicking. "No. He is not in the Navy. He's just a sailor."

"You don't sound very sure about that, Crystal," said my mum sternly.

"I am!" I protested. "I am sure."

"Okay, if you say so," she replied. *What was with the third degree anyway? I hadn't seen her in months. I wasn't going to grill her about her stupid boyfriend.*

"I wanted to talk to you, anyway," said my mum. She sounded serious. My heart lurched into my stomach. *What was she going to do now?*

"Oh God!" I cried. *She was getting married or pregnant with Mr. Geake's child.* I swallowed trying to calm myself down and ended up making a big gulping sound.

Mum examined my face; she appeared to be evaluating the situation. "Do you know what darling, it's nothing."

"What?" I gasped.

"It's just that I miss you, that's all."

Deep down I knew she was lying, but I did not delve deeper. Maybe it was because I didn't think I could cope with any more drama. I had enough on my plate with the separation, a crazy Dad and my own really complicated relationship.

Whatever it was, maybe I just didn't want to know.

"Do you want to play a game?" she said suddenly.

"Huh?" *A game?*

"Yes, I thought we could play a game. I've got cards, backgammon ..."

This was all very peculiar. Even as a child, Mum and I had never really played games. This was more something that I had done with Dad. We would spend hours playing marble wars, the entire living room being our battleground.

"Are you okay?" I asked.

She raised her perfect eyebrows and tilted her head to the side. "Yes, I just wanted to do something fun with my girl," she said looking at me fondly.

I half smiled, half frowned. Maybe she wanted to avoid talking, as the topics of discussion that would arise were inevitably painful.

"Okay ..." I said, nodding. "Backgammon."

———

Mum and I spent the whole afternoon playing backgammon and drinking tea. Neither of us had ever played before, and we soon became preoccupied with working out the rules of the strange, medieval-looking game.

Once we had figured this out, we quickly became addicted and poured hours of our energy into moving the little counters across the zig-zaggy board, taking each other's pieces and learning new tricks every time.

I had to admit, it was a genius idea. We had spent all this wonderful quality time together and not argued about Dad or SKANX once.

At about seven p.m., Mum walked me down Josephine Avenue and through the snaky little streets of Coney back to catch the boat to Starfish.

It was still raining, and we huddled under her red umbrella. I linked her arm as we strolled happily along. Finally, I felt like mother and daughter again, and in the absence of frustration and anger, I realized how much I had missed her.

When we got to the boat stop, she put her arm around my shoulders and pulled me to her. I leant in and we embraced for a good couple of minutes. When I pulled apart, we found ourselves in a gap of silence which we both knew was the place that should be filled with questions and answers.

We stood there mutely. The questions were on the tip of my tongue. *Are you coming home? Do you still love Dad? What are you doing?*

Yet somehow, the moment just seemed to pass us by, and I found myself saying goodbye to her and getting on the boat.

The boat was like a mini ferry, dropping Islanders back and forth from Starfish three times a day. There were about five rows of plastic benches, and I took a seat towards the right, just by the window.

I rubbed away the condensation and waved to my mum through the window as the boat pulled out. She looked sad as she stood there alone under her umbrella. My mother usually had the poise of a lioness, standing tall, proud and resilient. But today she looked small and vulnerable.

I thought I had known exactly what was going on with

her, but today had left me somewhat doubting the angry conclusions I had jumped to. I was more confused than ever.

"Crystal!" squealed a voice, interrupting my thoughts.

My head snapped to the left where, to my delight, I found Rosie perched on the same bench as me.

"Oh my gosh!" I cried shuffling down closer to her.

Rosie was halfway unzipped out of her raincoat and struggling to get the arm off. When she finally freed herself, she hugged me.

We both sat there giggling for a while. We were amused for some reason to bump into each other like this on this dreary old day. I don't know why this tickled us exactly.

"So, how are you, Crystal White?" said Rosie finally, breaking up the silliness. She leaned in and whispered, "How's the mermance?"

I giggled all over again. *Mermance. How cute!*

"At present it's a total washout," I informed her. "How's your ..." I paused; what could I coin a regular relationship? "Hum-ance?" I finished lamely.

"It's good," said Rosie slowly. She didn't seem quite so sure.

"But?" I prompted.

"He wants to go to Australia for a few months ... check it out," she said dejectedly.

Hmm. I could actually see why this would trouble her.

"I don't know, he just came out with it the other day," she continued. "He wants to go surf out there. But Crystal, if he goes, I just don't see him coming back in a couple of months. I mean he keeps saying he really likes me and everything, but that he has to go over there, it's his life dream ..."

I thought this over for a bit. I didn't want to agree and crush her, but I kind of sensed she could be right. *What twenty-something-year-old surfer would come back after a few months? Will worked for his father, and this was the type of job he could easily pick up again, at any time.*

"Oh Rose, I'm sorry," I said, "but if he is planning on going for longer, he has to tell you that now. He can't just string you along."

Rosie nodded firmly. "I know," she said. "I'm meeting him tomorrow, and I'm giving him an ultimatum."

I nodded, supportive. "Good for you."

"Thanks," she said, pulling her glossy brown hair to one side, and exhaling wearily. "You must be feeling worried too ... with winter round the corner and all."

I felt a stab of anxiety. It was blatantly obvious to everybody, it seemed, that me and Llyr could not make it into the next season.

Was it just me that was in denial about this? Perhaps Rosie and Will weren't the only ones who needed to have a serious discussion about their future.

Chapter Thirty-Five

It had rained and rained and rained the past week. I couldn't believe it. Every day, when I had opened my eyes, the first thing I had done was rip open the curtains to check the weather, and every time my heart had sunk.

At the end of another grim day, I tucked myself up in bed early. I lay on my back staring at the ceiling thinking about Llyr. I wondered what he was doing right now. Maybe he was with some other mers, having a get-together. Maybe they had a bar, or something, where they all met up. I hoped that there were no—in the words of Nephys—"scrumptious maids" at this bar.

My phone bleeped. It was Jess, inviting me to a festival this weekend with some of my old London friends. They were leaving on Friday, which was ... gosh, tomorrow.

Hmmm. I felt like I should actually be excited about this, like any regular seventeen-year-old would be. *But what if it* was beautiful and sunny, and I wasn't here when he came for me?

My mind quickly became conflicted. *Was I too readily available for this man?* He could be having a lovely time down there, frolicking about with these maids, whilst I was sitting around waiting for him. *Maybe I should be off having my own fun.*

But the thought was unappealing. I wanted only to be with him.

I googled the weekend weather forecast. Three big yellow sunshine symbols immediately popped up. Friday, Saturday, and Sunday were going to be glorious.

I texted Jess back, saying I wouldn't be able to get out of work. This was true anyway, I reassured myself. I was working Sunday evening.

I snuggled under my covers and closed my eyes. I hoped the weather forecast was right because if it was, then tomorrow he would be here again.

Chapter Thirty-Six

I sat on the end of my jetty and stretched my legs out happily in front of me. All I could see in front of me was endless blue skies across the seas.

Hurray!

It was around midday, and he would be here soon. Although it was hot, that intensity of the heat from the earlier summer months had gone. I could definitely feel that this part of the world was cooling.

I touched the wood next to me and had a flashback of our midnight moment on the jetty a couple of weeks ago. I remembered his strong arms gently and effortlessly lifting me, and his lips travelling all over my body. Even in the heat, I felt goosebumps just thinking about it.

Suddenly I heard something calling my name. I leaned forwards and listened, now alert. It had come from across the waters, but it didn't sound like a human voice, it was more like a bell or something.

"Crystal."

There it was again. It was almost like a wind chime, but I could hear my name in there somewhere. *What on earth?*

Suddenly I saw a familiar face in the waters ahead. Nephys.

Of course, she was singing. Her voice was doing that weird thing where it split into a hundred notes.

She disappeared and then reappeared, now just a couple of feet away from me.

"See, I didn't want to scare you," she said. "Especially sitting there daydreaming like that, I'd have given you a heart attack."

"Thank you," I laughed, "Although I'm getting used to surprises now."

"Hmm, I don't think you're quite broken in just yet," she said, bobbing in the little waves that lapped at the jetty.

Suddenly something caught my eye and I squinted closer at her chest. There were two orange shiny things clamped to her breasts.

"Are those ... ?" I began.

"Starfish!" she finished excitedly, arching her back and lifting herself further out of the water so that I could get a better look.

I leaned in and could see that they were indeed Starfish that had their little plump triangular legs squeezed around each one in a firm grip.

"Ouch!" I winced. *And, Eugh!*

"Oh, they don't hurt, they're actually really supportive," she said.

Hmmm. I was not convinced.

She plucked one off and handed it to me.

"Try it!" she urged.

I backed away. "No, no. It's fine," I said, holding up my hand.

"Seriously, they're marvellous."

"I'm good, thanks," I said, laughing.

"Oh whatever," she said placing the animal back on her chest. I grimaced as it quickly regained its clasp.

"So ..." I said, changing the subject. "To what do I owe the pleasure?"

"Oh, to Llyr," said Nephys. "He can't come today."

I felt my heart sink to the bottom of my stomach. *Couldn't come?*

Nephys had become preoccupied with my wedge heels that were placed next to me on the jetty.

"Oooh, these are nice!" she said, picking them up and examining them.

"Nephys?" I prompted. I needed to know what was going on with Llyr.

"He's busy, angel. He will come later. He said sundown," she said, swimming backwards with a shoe.

I relaxed, satisfied with the memo and my attention turned to Nephys and my shoe. *What was she doing with it?*

"I always wanted a pair of shoes, Crystal!" she said,

flapping her foot out of the water, trying to put my shoe on it.

"Nephys, you're a mermaid, what are you going to do with a pair of ... oh, come here!" I said as she fumbled about with the wedge. I didn't want her to drop it in the sea.

She reclined backwards in the water with her leg on my lap, as I fastened the shoe onto her foot. They were pretty red wedges with bows on the front. In fact, they very much suited her personality.

When I had finished, she swam around on her back with her leg stretched up in the air, admiring herself in my shoe.

"Very lovely, Nephys!" I laughed watching her. *It was like Swan Lake.*

She giggled with delight, and her eyes sparkled. It was really quite adorable.

"You can have them," I said. I didn't suppose they would last long under water, but she could probably enjoy them for a day or two, show them off to her friends.

"Have them?" Nephys screamed.

"Yeah," I said. "Keep them, take them home."

Within a flash, she had thrown her arms around me, and I was absolutely drenched

"Thank you, thank you, thank you!" she was squealing into my ear.

"It's okay ..." I laughed. "I can see they make you very happy."

"Oh, yes they do! But you know that it's not just me

you make so very happy, Crystal!" she said, withdrawing from our embrace and looking at me with misty eyes. "I just wish you were one of us."

Chapter Thirty-Seven

I riffled through the dresses in my wardrobe. I didn't know which one to wear tonight; I thought Llyr had seen them all by now.

I could have popped to the mainland earlier and browsed the shops, but I had been scared of anyone from work catching me—I had had to pull a sickie earlier!

"Alright then, Crystal," Tamzin had said flatly, as I had reported my sudden stomach bug onset. I had cringed. I think this was the first time she had ever called me by my name, and not "my lover."

"Sorry," I had then croaked. I don't even know why I had bothered to croak. People with stomach bugs don't croak, they groan, or something. Anyway, I'm sure she knew I was bluffing, whatever the case. I would have to work extra hard on Sunday to get back into her good books.

I came across a long navy dress with little spaghetti strap

shoulders which I had bought in Notting Hill a couple of years ago. I had definitely not worn this out with Llyr before. I hadn't worn it in years, in fact. Maybe I should try this one ...

As I pulled the dress over my body, I wondered if he even liked my clothes, or clothes at all for that matter. He had seemed rather fond of my t-shirt the other day, but other than that he rarely commented. I had only ever seen him in the same pair of shorts, and I had the feeling that was just to make me feel at ease.

I looked at my reflection. It was tight fitting and had a split from the thigh down. It was a sexy dress that surely even a merman would appreciate. And even if he didn't, I wasn't going to swap in my clothes for a pair of starfish. ... There's only so far you can go for love. Surely.

───

Later that night, I let Llyr guide me down the little creek off Crystal Bay. I could not see a thing in the dark, and we were going to the cove with the waterfall where Llyr had taken me before.

When we reached our destination, I was relieved to see the fairy pool below the fall was filled with light enabling me to see most of the surrounding area in the cove. The light caught the waterfall, and it dazzled in the night.

Llyr found us a mossy patch nearby, and when I stepped

onto it, I was surprised by how springy it felt under my toes. It was like a mattress.

Llyr sat down on it and leaned back on his elbows to look up at me.

"Do you like it?" he said.

I giggled. "It's bouncy!" I said, still standing.

He smiled and took my hand. "A little," he said, pulling me downwards.

I knelt down next to him, and now, on the same level, we gazed at each other. It always felt so surreal to actually be with him, given the amount of time I spent agonizing about when we would see each other again.

I had wanted to talk to him about winter, but as he ran his fingers up and down my arm, my mind travelled to other places.

I moved one of my legs over so that I straddled him. We started to kiss slowly, one amazing kiss at a time and then they became deeper and more urgent. The straps of my dress fell off my shoulders, and I now felt his lips move downwards.

"Do you like my dress?" I asked, remembering my thoughts from earlier.

"Yes, but I like you better without," he replied, pulling it down further.

Sometime later, we lay on the moss, and I cuddled up to him. I was feeling really quite cold. He rubbed my arms, and I started to warm a little. I was happy and content despite the chill, and after a minute, I felt myself doze off in his arms.

When I woke, I felt an intense heat behind me, and I turned my head slowly. I jumped and sat up; there were giant flames.

"I built you a fire," came Llyr's voice.

I searched around confused until my eyes found him, just to the left, sitting by the pool edge with his legs in the water.

"Oh, thank you," I said gratefully. *Was there anything this man couldn't do?*

I lifted my hands up to the heat. The night air was crisp, and I was seriously glad he had thought to do this for me. Perhaps this was an appropriate moment to discuss the changing temperature and our situation.

"Llyr?" I said, kneeling by the fire and pulling off a hairband that was around my wrist.

"Yeah?" he said from behind me.

I twisted my hair up and tied it. I was quickly warming up by the flames.

"I was just wondering about, you know, the cold and stuff," I began, turning my head back to look at him.

He got up and came and sat back down on the moss just behind me. I continued to face the fire; I was enjoying its warmth on my bare skin.

"What stuff?" He said, kissing the back of my neck.

"Um, you know ...?" I said, now a little distracted. His

arms were now encircling me, and he didn't appear to want to talk.

"Oh, stuff ..." I finished, giving in to him. I would try again later.

———

We collapsed back on the moss again. "Do you want to go swimming?" he said, nodding to the pool.

"No!" I protested. "I want to talk."

He pulled me to him. "Okay," he said.

"I'm worried, Llyr. Winter will be here soon," I began. There. He couldn't distract me now I'd said it.

"Hmm," he replied.

"Hmm"—Was that it?

"I don't know how we will see each other," I said looking up at him.

He looked away. I didn't get it—it was like he didn't want to talk about this.

"I don't know, maybe we can run away somewhere hot," I tried. I was kind of joking but I just wanted a response.

"How would we do that?" he asked.

"I don't know, I could get a house by a beach ... You could bring me some pearls, you know, like you said? Then I could pay the rent with them," I said, tracing my finger over one of the tattoos on his chest.

"I can see you've been really thinking about this," he said.

"Well, I can see that you haven't been," I said, a little stung. *What was his problem?*

We were silent for a while, and I lay there tensely, waiting for him to say something. I'd never known him to be so un-reassuring.

"I'm sorry, Crystal ... I guess I just don't want to think about it," he said finally.

I felt my heart sink. *Did this mean that there wasn't a solution? No magic answers?* My hopes that this could go on were being slowly shattered.

"Well, maybe I can just wait for you until next summer?" I said, trying not to cry.

He sighed and sat up.

"I don't want you to do that," he said.

Chapter Thirty-Eight

I felt like someone had slapped me in the face. *He didn't want me to wait for him.* And if he didn't want me to wait for him, then what he was basically saying was that he wanted us to break up.

He turned around and glanced at me, and his expression immediately changed.

He put a hand on my cheek and looked worriedly at my face. The hurt must have been evident. "I don't want to waste your time, your life," he said. "That's all," he finished firmly.

"You won't be wasting my time," I said hoarsely, trying to fight back the tears.

He was shaking his head. "No. I couldn't do that. It would be wrong of me. It would be very selfish."

"No. It would be my choice," I insisted.

"Crystal, you have your whole life ahead of you. You are

so beautiful and so amazing, I can't keep you for myself," he replied, running his fingers through my hair.

"Why?" I asked. I didn't understand.

"Because I can't give you what you deserve," he said. "What can I offer you? Really, in the long term? I can't offer you anywhere for us to live, and even if I could, I wouldn't be able to be with you half the time ..."

"You can offer me you," I said. "That's all I want."

"That will change, the closer we get and the more you grow up," he said, shaking his head.

"Well ... why did you do this then?" I said, my hurt turning to blame and anger.

He sighed as though he knew that this was coming.

"You were in trouble, I helped you," he said, clearly referring to the night he rescued me at the beach party.

"So, it's all my fault?" I glared at him angrily. *He knew what he was doing. He would have known full well all along that this would not work out.*

"Look we found each other, that's all I'm saying," he said, his hand falling from my hair.

I was beyond reasoning. My mind was racing one hundred miles an hour right now.

"I bet you don't even like me," I said, a tear finally escaping and running down my face. "You just wanted what you couldn't have."

For the first time, he looked angry. His jaw clenched, and his eyebrows were raised. He looked away. "You sound exactly like Ri," he said. "That's just the kind of thing he would say."

We were both silent for a while, and I sat there wiping tears away, not really knowing what to say.

Maybe I was being a little harsh, but I was angry with him. He was the one who had been in a position to know where this was all heading. I had just had to bat about in the dark the whole time, guessing how things would work out. I had put my faith in him, and he had known all along that this couldn't last.

"Can't you see how much I care about you?" he said after a while.

I tried to think straight. I forced myself to rationalize through the pain. I thought about all the things he had done for me—the secret places he had shared with me, the beach he named after me and the way he had disobeyed his father, just to be with me.

Eventually, I nodded slowly in agreement. "Yes, but I just don't understand why you did this when you knew that it was just a summer thing."

"I just couldn't help it," he replied, looking down. "I was obviously intrigued by you to start with, being a human, but I just loved being with you so much; I wanted to see you more and more."

I sat cross-legged, listening—my elbows were rested on my knees and my head in my hands. I didn't know if there was anything he could say to make this easier.

He reached over and took one of my hands so that I looked up.

"I guess I never really thought I would fall in love with you," he said, putting my hand to his lips. He kissed it and pressed it against his face. "I never even knew I could love like this."

My eyes welled up all over again. "So why don't you want to be with me then?"

He lay down and pulled me to him. I lay down too and relaxed slightly. It felt good to have his arms around me, comforting me, even if he was the source of my pain.

"Because I want you to have a normal happy life. I have already been greedy, having you like this all summer. I have to be responsible now," he said.

I exhaled a long shaky breath and hugged him tight. The thought of this ending was just unbearable. *And for what? So I could go out with some regular boring person?*

"Pretty soon I'm going to cry you a whole new ocean to live in," I said. My tears had already made a massive puddle on his chest.

"Let's enjoy what time we have left and cry later," he said squeezing me tight.

It was dawn when we finally got back into the boat and headed home. We had laid by the fire all night until it finally burnt out and then we had reluctantly dressed and weaved our way through the cliff back to the beach.

Now I sat looking ahead as Llyr rowed with his back towards the direction we were travelling. I was transfixed by the thick pink line on the horizon where the sun was rising. I really loved being awake at dawn; it was something about a new fresh day that excited me.

"What are you thinking?" he said.

"Just that I love the dawn," I replied wistfully. "Although it's a little ironic given the circumstances."

He looked at me and laughed. "You mean us?" he said.

I frowned. "Yes," I replied. "I'm glad you think it's so funny."

"Of course I don't think it's funny. It's just you're so sweet sometimes, the way you sit there philosophizing."

"It's pretty," I protested, pointing to the candy smudge that parted the sky from the sea.

He stopped rowing, turning and looked at the horizon. After a few seconds he turned back again. "I still prefer to look at you," he said, moving the oars again.

He suddenly did a double take as he looked over at me, and I jumped. *What was wrong?*

He nodded at my knees, and as I looked down I screamed. They were bright green. *Were they mouldy? Gangrenous?*

"Hey, hey, calm down." He laughed. "It's the moss."

The moss. The moss. Of course. Phew. I breathed a huge sigh of relief.

"I can't think what you were doing to get knees that colour," he said, raising an eyebrow at me.

I giggled. I think we both knew what I had done to get my green knees.

"Hey, how's Ri?" I asked. We hadn't spoken about how their talk went the other day.

"Oh, he's okay," said Llyr. He paused and looked around us at the sea. "The ocean has ears, you know?" he said.

"Oh," I said. I got off my bench and crawled closer to him so that he could talk quietly.

"He is just angry that I went against his advice, that's all. He worries a lot about humans finding out about us," Llyr said in a hushed voice. "He thinks that they will try and put us in captivity or something."

"He's probably right about that," I said, looking up at him. *I'm sure there would be plenty of people who would give an arm and a leg to bung Llyr and Ri in a tank in Sea Land.* "Still, you guys would probably annihilate anyone who tried to catch you."

Llyr smiled down at me and nodded. "I think you're probably right."

"Is that why he has been so anti-me?" I asked.

"I think it's that and just that he is very cynical about love." Llyr was whispering now, and I had to concentrate very hard to listen. "He's very bitter, ever since my mother ... you know?"

I didn't know. I had never heard Llyr speak of his mother before. I shook my head.

"Oh, well she passed," he said. "She got caught in the Red Tide on a trip to visit the Mexican tribes. She died out there about two hundred and fifty years ago. It was terrible. The tide just came on out of nowhere. Virtually her whole party was poisoned. I have never travelled anywhere near there since."

I racked my brain. *Red Tide, Red Tide. Yes, I had heard of this in my biology classes, it was some kind of natural toxins that appeared every now and then, killing all the fish.*

"Oh," I breathed, I came up on my knees and kissed him on the cheek. "I'm so sorry."

"Mother was from a very ordinary family, but he doesn't see the purpose of being with someone because you love them anymore. He just thinks it should be about political convenience," he said. He had stopped rowing and withdrew the oars into the boat. "It's kind of sad, but I can't make him see any differently. I've tried, but I can't."

He put his arms around my waist and rested his head on my shoulder. We held each other for a long time, me kneeling up against him as the boat rocked in the waves around us. I thought about all the sadness he had been through in his life, from his mother dying to his long loveless marriage to Nephys, while all the time having this emotionally backwards father.

And now he was about to lose me, but he never complained. He had never ever complained once.

"Do you think that we will see each other again before summer's out?" I asked, looking hopefully into his eyes. I could see they were filled with sorrow this morning; they were not quite sparkling like they usually did.

"Yes," he said, looking back at me, deep into my eyes. "Let's meet in three days, sunhigh."

Chapter Thirty-Nine

"That's how we're going to end up," grumbled Rosie, pointing at an advert on TV. Two old ladies were sat alone together on a bench, looking out to sea.

I had to laugh. It could well be us in sixty year's time, especially with the setting.

"I hope I'm the one with the purple rinse," I said.

"No, that one is totally me!" cried Rosie. "Just look at my room."

Hmm. She was right; purple was definitely her thing if her bedroom was anything to go by.

Rosie and I were curled up under her purple duvet having a pity party. To the right of us was a bottle of wine and to the left was a huge box of chocolates.

Last night Will had broken the news to Rosie that he had booked his ticket to Australia. A one-way ticket.

"I hate him!" Rosie declared with a mouth full of chocolate.

"I hate him too!" I cried downing my glass. "Why did he lead you on like this?"

"Because he's a selfish little man, that's why," Rosie replied. "He probably wanted a little fling to keep him busy throughout the summer, and he probably thought he would get away with it easier with a young helpless school girl."

"Oh, come on, Rose," I protested. "He was definitely really into you."

"Oh, he talked the talk, but the truth of the matter is, if he really liked me, then he wouldn't be going to Australia," she said righteously. "I mean, he just wouldn't be, would he?"

"Well, I think that he is just young and putting adventure before getting serious," I offered.

"He could have had it both," argued Rosie, "he could have waited one tiny little year until I finished school and then we could have gone together. He didn't even ask."

She had me there.

"I don't get it," I said shaking my head, "I just don't understand how he could just leave you behind like this."

"I told you, Crystal, it's because he's a stupid, selfish man," she reaffirmed.

"Well ... so is Llyr," I said. I said this to reassure her but instantly felt guilty.

"Eugh, they are both so stupid," Rosie ranted. "They just think with their ..."

"Yep, absolutely," I cut in, pouring myself another glass and topping up Rosie's.

Hmm, had I let Llyr off the hook too easily? Maybe he just wanted a bit of fun this summer, too, and now he was spoon feeding me with all this sentimental stuff to soften the blow. Something in my heart told me this was not the case, but perhaps I could pretend for Rosie. Just for tonight.

"Men!" I despaired.

"Bloody men!" agreed Rosie. "Still at least with your one, it's relatively understandable. My one is buggering off voluntarily."

"Maybe we should watch a fun film," I suggested. "I think we may need cheering up."

"Okay, well as long as it's not *The Little Mermaid*, or er, *Australia*," said Rosie.

"Yeah, or *Splash*," I chipped in.

"Or *Crocodile What's-His-Face*."

"Got it." I giggled and got up to inspect Rosie's DVD collection.

"At least we have each other," said Rosie from the bed. She had been lying in the same position for hours. It was like she was ill or something. Literally love sick.

Despite all the upset in the room, I felt a flutter of happiness. The one good thing about all this was that I actually got my friend back.

———

I stayed at Rosie's the whole of the next day. In the end, we had borrowed *Sex and The City* boxsets from Rosie's older sister, and we had been unable to able to stop watching them.

Of course, we had likened every plot to our current situations with Will and Llyr, and we had also decided that Rosie was the character, Charlotte, and I was Carrie. Jemima could be Miranda, I had offered generously, but we were yet to find a hilarious Samantha.

I now walked home at around five, and I was feeling pretty square-eyed.

As I crossed the island, I looked out through the trees and saw the sun was low in the sky.

The days were getting shorter.

When I got home I found Dad in the living room watching the football with Maurice. Maurice had been allowed on the sofa next to Dad, a very rare treat.

"Oh, Maurice!" I squealed from the entrance. "What's all this?"

Maurice was looking at me, and his tail was moving, although with much more restrained wags than usual. I got the feeling he didn't want me to draw too much attention to the situation, in case Dad changed his mind.

I grabbed Dad a beer at his request and myself an orange juice, and I settled down next to them and stroked Maurice's back. He gave a big blissful sigh and me and Dad laughed.

"He's with his pack," laughed Dad fondly, petting his head.

"Not his whole pack," came a familiar voice from behind us.

Dad and I jumped, and Maurice let out a loud bark. *What the hell?*

We leaped up and spun around.

My mother was standing in the entrance of the living room. For a moment she looked like that small sad woman I saw on the mainland the other day, looking over at us meekly.

"Sheila!" exclaimed Dad.

"Mum!" I squawked, at exactly the same time as Dad.

There was a pause as we all looked at each other.

"I see," she said suddenly, raising her eyebrows as though she were unimpressed by our reaction. Dad and I watched on as she sauntered over to the armchair, next to the sofa, her steely exterior now returned. She sat down, crossing one leg over the other.

Only my mum could have the nerve to try to swagger back into a broken home like the Queen of Sheba.

Dad and I remained standing for a while, still in shock.

Everything was a bit of a daze, but I noticed she had a big white package in her hand.

"You're both making me feel very on edge standing there like that," she said all matter-of-fact, like a headmistress. "Can you please just calm down and sit down."

We looked at each other and then sank back onto the sofa at the same time.

"What is that dog doing there, anyway?" my mother said, as her eyes travelled downwards with our descent. Maurice closed his eyes. I could see the poor hound was trying to pretend to be asleep.

"What are you doing here?" Dad retorted, ignoring her question.

"I need to talk with you both," she said firmly, gripping the package in her hand. It was an A4 envelope, I realised.

"Okay ..." said Dad unsurely, "but I wish you would have given us a little notice; you scared us."

"Oh, don't be such a pansy, Keith," spat Mother, swiping the air with her hand.

"A pansy?" cried Dad. "I climbed up a two hundred foot building last month."

"Please don't remind me," said my mum putting her head in her hands.

"I am not sitting here if you're both going to argue," I said, placing my hands on the sofa to stand up.

"I don't want to argue," said Mum, putting up a hand.

"Could have fooled me," mumbled Dad, looking down at his knees.

"Okay, believe it or not, I'm here to make things right," said Mum.

"Oh, are you now?" said my dad. "How are you going to do that?"

I watched my mum's face carefully. It softened slightly

as Dad said these words, it looked longingly at him for a split second. *Did she still love him?*

"With this," she said firmly, placing the mystery envelope down in front of him.

Dad picked it up, and opened it up. He looked up at her suspiciously.

What the hell was in the envelope? Divorce papers, or something? Great.

"You wanted insider information," said Mum. "Well, I said I'd give you it didn't I? The documents that are in that envelope will bring down SKANX once and for all."

Chapter Forty

"They are false inspection documents," said Mum as Dad thumbed through the papers, "and one real inspection document too."

Dad was silent as he read through them.

Inspection Documents? Was this like, school inspectors? Did inspectors come and inspect SKANX too?

"Ha! World class equipment ... ethically sound disposing devices," Dad guffawed, as he read the papers out loud.

It seemed I was correct. SKANX had been inspected.

"Yes, darling. That's the fake document," said Mum dryly.

Darling? She just called him "darling!"

Dad looked up at her as though he suddenly understood the significance of what she had brought him.

He shuffled through the papers excitedly, until he

appeared to locate the covering letter of the genuine report.

"VELO Inspectors," I read peeping over his shoulder at the red and white logo.

VELO ... That was the company which had burned down in the fire. The same fire which had taken Rory's dad.

"*Dear Mr. Geake,*" Dad began reading. "*My colleague and I visited your factory this June 15th. You will find enclosed a detailed report of my visit.*

I would, however, like to put in writing how thoroughly disturbed we were to find the majority of your equipment was greatly flawed, to the brink of dysfunction. Not only is this extremely dangerous for your employees but also violates international industrial law.

In addition, we were particularly concerned to find false certificates, which indicated that you meet essential safety requirements when this is clearly not the case."

Dad stopped reading and looked at my mother, and with wide, starry eyes. "Unbelievable!" he whooped. "I knew it! They are dodgy as hell."

I sat there stunned. *Well, it had always been obvious their equipment was not exactly up to scratch. Just look at their leaking waste disposal boxes and their shambolic sinking ship. But now Dad had actual proof!*

Dad carried on reading.

"*I am ordering you to suspend all industrial duties within your* factory as a matter of urgency, until we have completed further investigation."

Dad and I looked at each other confused. *If SKANX had been ordered to close down their factory, then why was it still open?*

Mum sighed and picked up the documents again. I couldn't help but admire her, for putting together all of this and smuggling it over here. It took guts.

We watched her rifle through the papers. *What did she have for us now?*

She placed an article in front of us.

FIRE AT LOCAL OFFICES KILLS FOUR

It was the very same article I had read that day in class when Mrs. Vendercum had bollocked me.

"They burnt down their offices," said Mum. "The two inspectors and their bosses were killed."

Dad's face darkened. "What?" he barked, his white eyebrows knitted together.

"You knew about this?" I gaped at Mum.

"By no choice of my own," she replied. "I was making tea and I overheard Geake and his friend Mr. Sherman—a hideous creep, I may add—discussing the whole thing. I tried to keep quiet in the kitchen so that they wouldn't know I was there, but then I dropped the cup on the floor."

"Sheila!" Dad cried, putting his hand on her arm. His face suddenly blackened again. "Did they hurt you?"

Mum looked ahead. "No, but they threatened to kill me, you, and Crystal if I said a word."

I felt nauseous. I couldn't believe it. *Kill all of us!*

Dad nodded slowly as though everything was falling into place.

"Why didn't they just get decent factory equipment?" I asked faintly. I didn't get it. *Surely that was much easier than going around killing everybody.*

"They would be saving millions, Crystal, with that botched up equipment," explained Dad, "millions that would no doubt be going straight into their greedy little pockets."

The room was spinning. I was in complete shock. I couldn't believe our lives had been under this threat and that Mum had been dealing with it all by herself.

"So you weren't having an affair?" I asked.

Mum rolled her eyes to the high heavens.

"Er, no," she said. "That night of the shipwreck, Mr. Geake came down to the harbour to look all responsible in front of the media. I had moved away from the crowd, trying to calm down and get my head around what had just happened. But he snuck up behind me and put an arm around me. He whispered in my ear, 'I had hoped you would have gone down with the ship.'"

Dad stood up, overcome with rage.

"They put you on a faulty boat deliberately?" he barked.

"Well, the containers would finally have gone into the sea, and so would I," said Mum. "Kills two birds with one stone. Genius really."

Dad's face was like a beetroot, and his eyes were

popping out of his head. I grabbed his hand to pull him back down again.

"Dad, you need to chill," I said firmly. He looked as though he were heading for a heart attack.

Dad allowed me to pull him back down, but he was nowhere near calmer. "I will rip out his throat!" he roared.

"And this is exactly why I didn't tell you about this," said my mother.

"Huh?" yelped Dad.

"Because you have been acting like a madman over this company, and I was scared you would do something really stupid. It is only because I now have this evidence that I could finally come to you. But you had better not let me down, Keith. We need to go about this the right way. If we put a foot wrong then I think we all know the consequences."

I shuddered and hugged Maurice. "Does he know you're here with these papers?" I asked.

"No, it's Saturday, and he shouldn't realize until Monday at the earliest when he returns to his office," she said.

I still couldn't relax. I felt tense all over and some of my muscles were actually twitching.

Dad walked over to the drinks cabinet and retrieved a large bottle of scotch. He took three crystal tumblers and poured us all a drink. He walked back over to the sofa, and we took them gratefully. He had the right idea.

After knocking back the scotch, we sat there silently for

a while, letting the alcohol and the shocking news absorb into our systems.

"I love you both so much," said Mum eventually. "I admit, when I initially took my job, I enjoyed tormenting you, Keith. I was so annoyed I had to leave London and everything behind. I wasn't ready, and when I got here, you were acting like a child. I had intended to start looking for another job and put you out of your misery but then ..."

Dad nodded. He took Mum's hand and kissed it.

I felt tears welling up just watching them, and I reached for the scotch bottle. I could not cry anymore tears this week.

"Crystal, put that down," ordered my mother.

I sighed and lowered it back onto the table. Yes, my mum was a bossy, domineering woman, but she wasn't such an awful person. In fact she did everything with our best interests at heart.

She still loved Dad after all, and oh, we still loved her.

Chapter Forty-One

That night I lay in bed with my ear phones in. I wasn't too sure if Mum and Dad would be "making up" down the corridor, and I certainly did not want to find out.

I played some music and lay on my side facing my window. There was the occasional flash of the lighthouse, but otherwise it was mainly darkness outside.

I thought back over the past three months and how much time I'd spent out there at night in that black expanse of ocean.

It was really kind of crazy. When I first used to lie in my bed here in Starfish, it seemed like such a hostile, scary place. It was like being out there in the dark would be your worst nightmare.

But now it didn't seem so bad. In fact, on the contrary, it just made me think of my love, Llyr.

Tomorrow was the day we were due to meet at sunhigh. I sighed and turned off my light. I was half excited to see him, but at the same time I was nervous. *Were we meeting to say goodbye?* I couldn't even bare to think past goodbye, when there would no longer be Crystal and Llyr, no longer the long hot days of mystical adventures and salt kisses.

I would just be normal old Crystal White, the school girl again.

I rolled over onto my back and blinked as a flash from the lighthouse penetrated the darkness. I wondered if it was even worth bothering to get up tomorrow. I was only going to have my heart broken into a million pieces.

Would it be better to just never see him again? Was I just prolonging the inevitable that little bit longer? After a little consideration, both options of saying goodbye and not saying goodbye seemed equally as painful.

———

The next morning I woke up at around 10:30 a.m. I tried to wrench myself out of my sleep but ended up dozing off for another ten minutes.

It was getting increasingly difficult to get up early, and I needed to start trying if I was going to return to school again in the next week and a half.

I threw back my covers and immediately hunted for my dressing gown. *Brrr, it was cold.*

I threw it on and headed groggily down the stairs. Mum and Dad didn't appear to be about. Perhaps they had gone out, or maybe I thought, pausing with horror, they were still in bed.

I shuddered and put the kettle on to make myself a cup of coffee. As I opened the kitchen drawer to get the spoon, I saw the envelope hidden away beneath the cutlery. I felt another shiver travel through my body, but this time it was not from the cold.

I shut the drawer. We were really sailing close to the wind with all this. I just prayed we were able to pull it all off on Monday.

I made myself a drink and headed upstairs again. Once I got back under the covers, I put my music on and sipped from the mug. I loved that sensation of lying in bed, waking up with a cup of coffee, even if the day ahead was a little scary and overwhelming.

I gazed out to sea. It was a greyish day, but the clouds were just a thin veil behind which the sun glared through. The sea was silver and twinkly, and there were a couple of boats dotted on the horizon.

Suddenly there was a hand on my shoulder, and I screamed and jumped. My earphones fell out and my coffee flew up into the air and back into my mug again with a big brown splash.

"Oh Crystal, you really are a jittery little thing," came my mother's voice from above me.

Jeez, why was everyone always calling my nervous, jittery, or jumpy? It was so unfair, especially when I had been dealing with some seriously dicey situations of late.

I looked up at Mum. She looked much more relaxed and fresh-faced today than she had in previous weeks. Coming home and offloading her burdens must have helped her.

I realised I owed her an apology. "Mum, I'm really sorry I called you that thing," I said looking up at her.

She sat down next to me on the bed. "Apology accepted, so long as you never call me that again."

"I won't," I said looking down ashamed.

"Now, your father and I are going to the mainland. We thought we'd go shopping, grab some lunch ... what do you say?" she said brightly.

I smiled up at her. I wanted to go, but I had to meet Llyr.

"I er, need to stay home and finish my holiday homework ..." I lied.

My mother raised her eyebrows at me. "Does this holiday homework involve this sailor friend of yours?" she asked knowingly.

I bit my lip. I had forgotten my silly story about the sailor.

"Um, no," I said hesitantly "I don't think we're going to be seeing each other anymore. It looks like he may be ... sailing away."

"Well, Mrs. Hart from next door said she saw you down the jetty with a man one night looking very ... shall we say together."

I flushed scarlet and looked down. *I seriously hoped it wasn't THE night.*

"Oh darling, things aren't always what they seem," said

Mum. "Look at your father and me. You thought that was all over, and now we're all fine and dandy."

I frowned. It was a nice thought, but Llyr seemed pretty serious about breaking up with me. "I don't know," I mumbled.

"Well, what *I* know, Crystal, is that when two people really care about each other, they usually find a way to make it work no matter what," said Mum. "You will know when you find that person."

I did know. That person was Llyr, I thought sadly.

"Plenty of fish in the sea, anyway," she said, ruffling my hair and floating out of my bedroom.

I shook my head as she shut the door behind her. *More fish in the sea, huh? If only she knew …*

I lay in bed listening to Mum and Dad getting ready and then I eventually heard the door shut. About five minutes later, the engine of the red boat started up outside, and they were off.

I got dressed in jeans and a cardigan and headed downstairs. It was 11:30 a.m., and I decided to make myself another coffee and take it down to the jetty. I could watch the boats and wait for Llyr.

I put my sandals on for probably one of the last times this summer and fastened the straps. I had not been able to find my hairbrush, and my hair was a mess. I scooped it up into a messy bun and headed out of the back door.

Once I got down the ocean stairway, I felt something bumpy in my sandal and realized it must be a stone from the garden. I limped to the end of the jetty and then sat down at the end, taking off my shoe. I removed a small pebble and flicked it off into the sea, sighing irritably.

I took a sip of coffee and went to put my sandal back on, but something just wasn't right. I couldn't quite put my finger on it, at first. Everything looked fine, but there was just this feeling in the pit of my stomach that there was something amiss.

Someone was here, waiting for me. I felt it coming, but I didn't know where from.

The hairs on my neck stood up on edge, and I sat there for a second completely frozen. The ocean was still and flat before me. I swallowed nervously before turning my head to the side, but as I did, a hand planted itself over my lips.

I wanted to scream, but the hand was blocking any sound from coming out. I tried to struggle, but an arm was suddenly around my body, restricting any movement.

My mind was racing a thousand miles an hour. *What was happening to me? Who was doing this? Oh, couldn't anybody see?*

A piece of fabric was pressed up against my face, and I breathed in something horrible and toxic. It smelt like Tippex ... strong, vaporized Tippex. And then there was blackness.

Chapter Forty-Two

I was aware of a whirring noise, and that was it. It grew louder and then quieter as I drifted in and out of consciousness.

Everything was black, and I felt numb. My only sensory experience was the sound from the whirs.

This must have gone on for about an hour until I gradually became more aware of other things. A sharp stabbing pain in my back, for instance, and a dull thudding in my head.

Slowly I heard other things too. Voices. Male voices.

I groaned. I felt as though I had had some kind of terrible accident. I couldn't move a muscle.

"She's awake," said one of the voices. *Was I in the hospital, maybe?*

I wanted to shout out, but there was something in my mouth.

Never in my whole life had I felt so uncomfortable and

disempowered. Slowly I remembered the hand around my mouth on the jetty and the poisonous vapour in my nostrils. I groaned again.

The sound of footsteps approached, and I felt something touch the back of my head, fumbling at something. I whimpered, terrified of what it might be.

And then there was light.

I squinted as I struggled to adapt to the brightness. Slowly shapes began to form, and I was able to make sense of my surroundings.

There were two figures looming above me. I blinked a few more times, and my vision became clearer and clearer. A pair of smart shiny shoes stood on the floor in front of me. They were brown and had little leather laces, which were fastened neatly and tightly.

"Pretty, isn't she?" said one man. I'm quite sure it was the one in front of me. He squatted down to inspect me further.

My eyes widened as I recognized the face before me. I went to scream, but the noise would not come out. I was gagged.

Mr. Geake lifted a hand to my face and gently squeezed my cheek. It was a creepy feeling, and I tried to scream again, but I just couldn't force it out.

"Yes, even if she does look half dead," came the other voice. I strained my eyes to the left and could see a be-suited individual overhead.

"Only child, aren't you, Crystal?" said Mr. Geake, his

finger still fondling my face. *Ugh I just wished I wasn't gagged. I would bite it right off.*

He reeked of cologne, a horrible overpowering type that someone sloshes on when they want their presence to be felt. I quickly examined his face before I looked away again. I was so close to him that I could see every pore in his flesh. I noticed his eyes were green, a similar shade to Llyr's, only void of any character and sincerity.

"You must be very, very precious to Mum and Dad," he continued, his finger slipping down from my face and onto my neck. I twitched as I felt it around my collarbone.

He turned to his loathsome companion. "Take a photo of precious, will you?" he said, removing his finger and standing up.

The other man came before me. He was short and overweight with a head of gelled, black hair. I had never seen him before.

"Pleasure to meet you," he chirped. He was coarse and brash, your dodgy dealer stereotype. "Simon Sherman, by the way."

I recognized the name. It was the guy who Mum had overheard discussing the office fire with Mr. Geake. The office fire that they had started to kill the inspectors and their bosses.

I watched on terrified, as Simon Sherman pulled out a phone from his suit pocket, and aimed it at me. I heard the phone make a snappy sound as he took several photos.

He let out a sinister laugh and then he too squatted so

that he was on my level. "Which one should we send to your mother and father?"

He thrust the phone before me, and my breathing rapidly increased as I looked at the images.

I was pale and red-eyed with a white piece of cloth tied round my mouth. And worst of all I was bound to a huge metal object by my wrists and ankles. My breathing became tighter as I realised what the metal object was. I was strapped to an anchor. A really, really large anchor. *Oh shite almighty, what were they planning on doing with me?*

Simon Sherman sat next to me, and I felt the thump through the floor as he connected with it. He began typing on his phone, his chubby fingers sliding clumsily across the keyboard.

"Your girl is safe and sound," he recited, before continuing, "let's hope we don't have to … anchor … the … boat … anytime … soon."

I cried out as I realized why I had been attached to the anchor. They were threatening to throw me in the sea with it. *We must be on a boat, but the question was, where was this boat?*

"Maybe we won't have to if you … cooperate," Mr. Sherman finished. "How's that?" he said turning to Mr. Geake. I felt a humungous lump in my throat as I thought of my parents opening the text message.

"Yes, yes, fine send it," said Mr. Geake. "Oh precious, it's only a little caption—let me get you a tissue."

"No signal," said Mr. Sherman with annoyance. "I'll

have to take the shagging dingy and head towards land. It will probably take a good hour."

A good hour? We must be way out at sea. What about Llyr? Surely he must have picked up that something was wrong by now ...

"You can take that gag out of her mouth, now the photo shoot is over," said Mr. Geake. "It's not like anyone will hear her out here anyway."

Mr. Sherman nodded, and he reached behind my head and fumbled with the knot. I hated that this creature was so near me, but at the same time I was desperate to get this thing off. My mouth was agony; it had been stretched for hours now.

I gasped with relief as the gag was removed. It was an almost heavenly sensation to have my lips fall back into place again. I moved my jaw around; it was so stiff.

"You know I have a boyfriend," I shouted out. It hurt my face to talk, but I didn't care.

The two men now looked at each other and simultaneously erupted into laughter.

"I'm happy for you, sweetheart," said Mr. Geake, his voice dripping with sarcasm, "but he's not going to be much use out here, is he now?"

They hooted again, and I choked back a sob. *Maybe they were right. Where was he anyway? If he was going to rescue me then surely he would be here by now. Maybe he was getting some back-up or something.*

"I'm afraid some fellows only want one thing, you know
... " Mr. Sherman chided, standing up.

I glowered. *Llyr wasn't a pig, unlike them.*

"She's only young," said Mr. Geake. "She'll find out
soon enough, well providing Mum and Dad do the clever
thing, that is."

They began to cackle maniacally, so hard that the veins
in their necks became visible. They were like a pair of
suited and booted male hyenas, and I wondered if they
even found each other funny or if they were just trying to
intimidate me. I stared at the floor helplessly. I really didn't
know what to do ...

Chapter Forty-Three

Simon Sherman had delayed his trip inland on the dingy so that he could knock back a beer with Mr. Geake. They now sat at a little table openly discussing their sordid business affairs. Simon boasted about how much money they had saved this past year through "cutting corners."

"What, with your useless equipment?" I challenged them from the anchor.

"Yes, exactly," he replied, a smirk spreading across his bloated face.

"Do you not realize how much you have hurt the sea life?" I demanded.

"Oh sea life, shmee life," said Mr. Geake, sounding bored. Simon pointed at him and laughed at this pathetic crack while Mr. Geake held out his beer to me. "Would you like a sip, Crystal? You seem a little agitated."

I scowled at him in response. I wasn't used to this type

of human, one which had no morals whatsoever. I couldn't believe I was here at the mercy of such people.

"Well, I've got plenty more tricks up my sleeve for when we open up our new plant in St. Carolinas," said Simon to Mr. Geake.

New plant? What new plant? I don't even think my parents knew about these plans. It certainly hadn't been in the news. Otherwise, everybody would be talking about it. I closed my eyes thinking of the misery a whole new factory would bring to everybody in the region, and in particular Llyr's people.

They couldn't get away with this. Mum and Dad needed to take those documents to the police immediately, but I knew that they would prioritize my rescue above all else. *Llyr really needed to get here and save me. He could save all of the merfolk too if he would just hurry up.*

I heard the shameful duo crack open another beer, and I did my best to zone out. I had realized now that by engaging with them, I was just playing into their game.

Eventually, they got up and walked out of the cabin. I heard the door open and felt the cool breeze from outside. They were stepping out onto the deck. The door clicked shut, and I opened my eyes again, craning my head to look at the ropes that bound me to the anchor.

They looked like quite fat knots to me, but I tugged my arm to test how strong they were. They tightened further around my little wrists with every pull, leaving a searing pain on each one. Thankfully I was at least able to stretch my legs out, but I could see ropes lead from my ankles to the metal structure behind me. I kicked but found a similar tightening effect and stopped before it became unbearable. I slumped back defeated. I couldn't do anything; my only hope was some kind of intervention.

Come on Llyr. Please. I knew he wasn't exactly psychic, but if he could, at least, sense my desperation, then he may get a move on. *Oh, I just couldn't believe this. Why did I have to go and be kidnapped, just as everything finally seemed to be going well again at home again? And how had they even found out about the missing papers?* It was supposed to be the weekend; they weren't supposed to have discovered their disappearance today. Poor Mum and Dad would be kicking themselves for leaving me alone like that. *Still, if these crooks hadn't taken me, they would have done something else tonight*, I thought as I leaned my head on the metal spine of the anchor. *If it hadn't been me, then they may have tried to harm my mum or dad. It was better this way.*

It was dusk now, and I had been here for many hours. There was no heating, and my body temperature was starting to dip as the heat from the sun faded. I looked down at my trembling arm. I didn't know if it were the fear or the cold that was causing me to shake.

Simon Sherman had traveled off in his dingy to send the diabolical text to my parents, and he had now returned.

The pair seemed to be dividing their time between the cabin and the deck and were now outside watching the sunset.

I suppose now that Mum and Dad knew what was going on, they would offer up the documents, and Simon said he would travel inland again tomorrow morning to check their response. But even despite my suffering, I still found myself not wanting my parents to hand them over. I wanted SKANX to go down, and even more so now I had met the evil people behind it.

When Simon first came back, I had hoped Mum and Dad may, at least, make copies of the papers, but apparently, Simon was two steps ahead. I had overheard him boast to Mr. Geake that one of the conditions he had laid out for the exchange, would be a signed letter from my parents, stating any copies were fakes.

I sighed, it was nearly dark now, and I was starting to confront the unbearable idea that Llyr might not be coming for me. *Surely he would be here by now.* My thoughts were disrupted by the sound of them clambering about on deck, no doubt getting ready to come back in. I braced myself for a torrent of their passive-aggressive comments.

"Oh pretty precious," came the dreaded voice, as the door opened. He was clearly drunk now, and he was getting more and creepier with it, if at all possible.

"She is pretty isn't she?" said Simon. "I wonder if we should make more of having her out here to ourselves."

My head spun, and I began to shake uncontrollably. *No, no, no. He couldn't possibly mean what I think he did.*

Suddenly my terror was interrupted by a loud smashing. I jumped, and as I looked up, I saw that the ceiling of the boat now had a large hole in it. I screamed; it was being ripped off in huge chunks, and I could see the night sky.

Mr. Geake and Mr. Sherman fell silent as we stared upwards, awaiting whatever lay on the other side with baited breath. Mr. Sherman ran his fingers through his slicked-back hair, and it cascaded over his brow in big stuck-together clumps. "What the ..." he trembled, awash with perspiration. He turned to Mr. Geake, holding out his hands.

Suddenly there was a shout and a body flew through the top of the boat and landed in the middle of the cabin.

I cried out his name, overcome with relief. The rage on his face made him virtually unrecognizable, but he was here. It was Llyr.

I knew now that everything was going to be alright, but my heart hammered through my rib-cage all the same. It was partly his anger that made me so nervous. The veins in his neck were popping out through his flesh, and his eyes were so wide that you could see all the whites. Every muscle in his body was tensed, from his big strong arms to his rippling torso. Llyr now appeared more muscular than ever, so intense was his fury.

"Well, here's that schmee life," I said, through rapid shallow breaths.

But my captors were not paying any attention to me anymore. Mr. Sherman had quickly realized he was no match whatsoever for this terrifying intruder and he let out a yelping noise, like a frightened puppy. He was all bark no bite, I realized with disgust, as he backed away, tripping over Mr. Geake, who was in turn, frozen to the spot. They fell to the floor together and scrambled towards the door. They had messed with the wrong people, and Llyr was not going to let them go.

He began with Mr. Sherman grabbing him by the ankles and whipping him up into the air above his head. He then brought him down hard onto the floor as though he were wielding an axe. I screamed again, as blood splattered everywhere.

Llyr lifted him up once more and brought him crashing back onto the floor of the boat. The floor cracked with the weighty impact, but he hauled Mr. Sherman's limp, bulky body into the air again, regardless.

"Llyr!" I squealed.

He looked over at me. "What?" he shouted.

"Enough, please, I'm going to be sick," I begged.

Llyr sighed and flung Simon Sherman up in the air. He disappeared through the hole where the roof had been and into the sky above.

There was a suspended silence before we heard a splash somewhere in the distance.

Llyr rushed over dropping to his knees and putting his arms around me. "I'm so sorry," he said, his face softening slightly. "I couldn't find you. I've been searching all day long. I couldn't sense you ... or feel you. Were you not awake?"

"Not to begin with," I explained as quickly as my trembling lips would let me. "I think they drugged me or something."

"I'll kill them," growled Llyr, snapping the humungous rope in half which bound one of my arms to the anchor.

"Well, I think you're halfway there," I said, inhaling sharply as I stretched out my arm.

"Who are they?" Llyr asked, his brow furrowed into deep angry lines.

"The owner of SKANX and his henchman," I tremored, every muscle in my body still contracting.

"I'm definitely going to kill them," said Llyr reaching for one of the ropes that tied my legs. I breathed a sigh of relief as he snapped it and I was able to lift my left ankle. *I was nearly free now. Oh, I was lucky to have a superhuman in my life right now.*

Suddenly I heard the unmistakable clash of broken glass and Llyr collapsed on top of me. My heart ceased to beat for several moments. *Oh my goodness, what just happened?*

"I told you he wasn't much good out here, didn't I?" Mr. Geake was standing above us with a broken beer bottle in his hand. I let out a choked noise and felt my whole body turn cold. Llyr was limp in my lap, and there a dark, damp liquid seeping from his scalp. My instinct was to put my hand on his head to stop the blood, but somewhere in my dizzy, terrified mind, I had the sense to hold it behind my back as though it were still tied. "He put up a very good fight, though," said Mr. Geake. "Extraordinary. I'm not quite decided whether or not I'm going to kill you both after that. I'll have to go away and think about it."

"What about my mum and dad?" I despaired. "Don't you want the papers back?"

He knelt down and grabbed my ankle, fastening the rope around it again.

"Yes, good point. I may keep you alive a little bit longer then, just to seal the deal," he said, tying the other end of the rope back to the anchor, "it looks like it might be lights out for your boyfriend, though."

I could now feel Llyr's blood dripping onto my leg. It was a cool sensation, almost like rainwater. I took a long, shaky breath and brought myself to look down at him. His eyes were half open, but I could see he was out cold. His tanned skin was paler than I had ever seen it, and as I looked at the wound, I knew I had to stop the bleeding immediately or else he would die.

"Are you going to be alright with that dead weight on your legs?" said Mr. Geake with mock concern.

"Yes, leave him there," I shouted, aghast. "Don't you touch him."

Mr. Geake chuckled and walked out on the deck shutting the door behind him. The whirring noise began again as the engine started up.

Chapter Forty-Four

I had managed to stop the bleeding by pressing my hand to his scalp, but Llyr was still unconscious. I knew I had to stay strong for us both, but I felt so helpless. *Now that Llyr was injured, what hope did we have?*

I had initially wondered if the other mers would come, but if Llyr was unconscious, then I realized that they probably wouldn't be able to find us, just like he hadn't been able to find me.

"Come on!" I begged him, but there was no response. It was so hard seeing him like this, weak and lifeless.

Oh God, what if he never woke up? What if he died? I had to do something, but what?

I looked up at the sky through the battered roof. I could see little pockets of stars here and there, but they mostly obscured by cloud. It was now well into the night, and Llyr had been out cold since dusk.

I tried for the hundredth time to undo the ropes but it

truly was impossible and to make everything just that little bit worse, I could barely see a thing. It was dark now.

I slumped backward. *We were screwed.*

The boat had been still for a while, and now I heard the sound of snores coming from the front. It seemed as though the beast was sleeping. I could see the broken bottle glinting a few meters away. *Oh, if only I could grab it but there was no point in trying. I knew already that it was out of my reach.*

Suddenly the inside of the boat was bathed in a ghostly white light. I looked up and saw that the moon had come out from behind the clouds. I quickly seized the opportunity to check on Llyr's condition, but when I lowered my gaze, I noticed something. Strange marks were appearing on his skin, just by his waist. I strained forward to look closer. It was like blue circular shapes were appearing on his hip. *What on earth?*

I gasped as the circular shapes suddenly became more pronounced, and I realized what they were starting to remind me of.

Oh my God. It couldn't be? Please, no. Not here. Not now.

He was turning.

———

"Frigidity frig!" I squeaked for the third time.

Llyr's long smooth tail now glistened under the moonlight, and all I could do was gape at it. The shift had all happened within a matter of seconds, and I sat there stunned, trying to adapt to what was happening. It was the moment I had been putting off for a long time, but it had finally arrived, and it couldn't have been at a worse time.

I extended a shaky hand towards his lower half. The night only permitted me to see that it was a dark shade, and I was unable to distinguish the exact color. When I placed my hand on it, I realized that despite the subtle outlines of the scales, it was smooth, toned and really quite masculine.

I shook my head in wonder. All this time I had known in my head, he was a merman, but part of me couldn't truly believe it until now.

I remained transfixed by his lower form, and I ran my free hand over it as far as the ropes would allow. It was kind of beautiful and just completely extraordinary.

After a few moments, I began to regain my sense of urgency. *If he was turning like this, how long did that mean he had left?* I remembered his tales of the mer who had been swept inland by tidal waves, and had died, stranded without water.

I scoured the room with tired eyes. If I could just get him a splash of water, it may just keep him going that little bit longer. I looked around the cabin. There was a table, chairs, a fishing rod and a few dusty old books. None of this would help.

I leaned forward and turned my head backward. *What*

was there behind me? I couldn't see much, and so I resorted to groping about with my free arm.

I heard myself grunt. My arm was at a seriously awkward angle but suddenly my hand clasped at something plastic, and as I grabbed at it, I realized that it was a soft, hollow shape. My heart lifted. *Had I found something?*

I managed to retrieve it and felt a surge of victory as I realized it was a bottle of water, but only a quarter full. I forced the top off with my teeth, but it was tough, as though someone had screwed it on really tight. After some time, I managed to wrench the lid off the bottle and splashed it on Llyr's head. It washed over him and dripped onto my lap.

There was still no movement. *At least, he's getting something on him*, I told myself, trying not to let despair get the better of me.

I leaned back and closed my eyes. I didn't know how much longer I could take this.

I had drifted off when I was awakened by cold irritating splatters on my face. I grumbled, touching my face with my free hand, and opening my eyes slowly.

It was rain. I sat up, shielding my face and looking up at the sky—it was a cobalt blue. Dawn was here.

"Crystal," came a soft, hoarse voice.

My heart soared through the battered roof when I saw him. He still lay in my lap, weak but awake.

"Llyr," I cried, trying to suppress the volume of my voice. "Oh, thank God."

He remained on my lap for a while, and I realized he was confused. I stroked the side of his face. "You got hit on the head," I said softly.

He sat up gradually, and his eyes moved from side to side. I could see he was starting to piece together the events that led to his injury. He looked down at his tail and shook his head. I knew he must be shocked. This would be the first time he had ever been vulnerable enough for this to happen.

"Where is he?" he said groggily.

"Outside, driving the boat," I explained in a hushed voice.

He nodded and reached for rope on my wrist. He lacked the strength from yesterday, but as he pulled at it, I felt it loosen.

"What are we going to do?" I asked as he worked at the rope.

"I think we should wait for Ri," he replied, his eyes fixed on the ropes. His voice was heavy, and I knew that this was the last thing on earth he wanted to have to do. Finding Llyr in this dire situation would no doubt reinforce all Ri's feelings about us. "They will sense me now that I have woken," he finished.

I looked up at him, my eyes moist with tears. I opened

my mouth to say how sorry I was for him when I heard the sound of thumping on the deck. I felt that feeling of dread return as I stared towards the door, utterly horrified.

It opened slowly, and Mr. Geake staggered in. At first, he looked at us frowning sleepily before his eyes slowly widened as he registered what awaited him.

He lifted a finger slowly and pointed at Llyr. His mouth then opened as though to say something, but he was unable to choke out the words. Silence hung in the air for what felt like an eternity, and then he laughed. A loud hysterical cackle. I froze as I watched his face. His evil, little eyes had turned from a mirror of disbelief to one of pure greed.

The dollar signs flashed in his pupils as he eyed up Llyr.

Chapter Forty-Five

"Well, well, well. I'm not even a fisherman and look what I'm bringing home with me today," Mr. Geake sang, as he looked on at Llyr. He let out another high-pitched laugh, clearly very elated by his discovery.

I didn't know what to say or do. My legs were still bound to the anchor, and it was not like Llyr could get up and fight him. We were both immobilized.

Mr. Geake reached into his trouser pocket and pulled out his phone. "I must get a snap of this ..." he said, giggling.

I looked at Llyr and took comfort in the fact that somehow he looked as calm as ever, despite this horrific chain of events.

He was leaning on an elbow, staring at Mr. Geake with a look boredom. He didn't even dignify him with a response. Mr. Geake hitched up his trousers and squatted down leveling his phone at Llyr. I reached out and clawed at the camera, but he laughed and moved it away from my reach.

"Say 'cheese,' Neptune," said Mr. Geake.

There were a large splash and the boat rocked. Mr. Geake lost his balance a little in the sway and had to put his hand on the floor to steady himself. I seized the moment, reaching out and snatching his phone, but suddenly a large, dark shadow appeared. I looked up just as a huge mass of a being flew through the air.

At first, all I saw was a mane of long, black hair and a mound of muscles. The mass landed on top of Mr. Geake, and I heard the cracking of bones. I cried out and looked away, as long whiny moans penetrated the air.

When I looked again, I saw that Ri had mounted Mr. Geake with a fist to his face. I didn't know whether to be happy or worried. Ri looked livid, but I didn't think all his anger was channeled at Mr. Geake.

He looked at Llyr, with a face of thunder.

"Who is this little man?" he said coldly, nodding at Mr. Geake.

"He is the leader of the poison bringers," said Llyr. He looked pale and stressed, and I knew he was going to get bollocked for the next century.

More bodies flew through the air, landing on board, like flying fish. I recognized some faces. Nephys was here next to me, tending to Llyr and pulling his body away. I let him go, knowing he was in safe hands. The loathsome Spirit had also arrived and had taken over from Ri, pinning Mr. Geake's arms on the floor above his head.

Ri stomped towards me, and I looked down. *Should I say hello? Maybe just silence was the better option right now.*

His huge, bare feet came into view, as he stopped by my side. I felt relief ripple through my body as he snatched away the ropes in a matter of seconds and then without a word he reached behind me and retrieved the anchor, with one hand.

"Thanks," I said quietly, pulling the ropes away from my limbs, but he was gone.

I felt a wetness through my jeans and noticed that water was starting to appear in the cabin. I wondered if the mer had created a hole somewhere as they had pounded on board. Maybe it was just all the water they were bringing over the side with them. I didn't know what was going on anymore.

Ri began to tie Mr. Geake to the anchor with a long rope that Spirit had retrieved from the deck. They were wrapping him like a caterpillar into a cocoon. A feeling of dread washed over me as I realized that I might be about to watch an execution. *I mean, there were no police out here, no law or court to stop the mers from seriously harming him.*

I felt troubled for a moment as Mr. Geake's eyes caught mine.

"Crystal," he begged. "I was never going to hurt you, or him. I was just trying to get those little papers back."

Eugh, now what did I do? I knew he was lying. He would

have had no problem murdering us, but whoever he may be and whatever he had done, I just couldn't condone his demise.

I suddenly felt like an emperor in a coliseum—the crowd waiting for a thumbs up or a thumbs down, to decide whether or not a fallen gladiator should die.

I looked up at Ri, I didn't say a word, but I think my sorrowful expression communicated a plea for Mr. Geake's life.

Ri raised one of his eyebrows at me, as though I were the most pathetic thing that had ever lived. *Really?* His expression read. He picked up the anchor with Mr. Geake bound tightly to it, and carried it out onto the deck. It looked like Mr. Geake was going down, and it also seemed that Ri could not give a damn whether I approved or not.

"Please, sir," begged Mr. Geake. "Please."

"This is for all our children you have killed with your poison," Ri boomed, lifting the anchor overboard.

"I didn't mean to hurt anybody. I love children," Mr. Geake spluttered, as he was suspended over the water.

I looked away.

A high-pitched scream pierced the night, and then a splash.

I exhaled wearily. *Well, I guess he was gone.*

The mers now began to leap off the deck, and I suddenly became aware that I was sitting in about ten inches of cold water. The boat was flooding.

I looked around for Llyr, but he was nowhere in sight, and so I stood up, calling out his name.

"He's in the water."

I turned. Spirit looked down at me with his ocean colored eyes, and for a fleeting moment, I caught a bit of kindness in them.

"Thanks," I said, forcing a polite smile. *I suppose he had just saved our lives.*

"I'll take you to him," he said coolly, grabbing my hand and scooping me up into his arms before I could utter a word. I did not like to be so close to him, but right now, I had more pressing things to care about. I let him hold onto me, and he leaped up through the roof, and out of the boat.

I held my breath, squinting as we travelled through the bright morning air and into the ice-cold seas below.

When I first surfaced, I felt numb from the cold of the water, but after a while, it began to hit me like a thousand little razor sharp needles, pricking at my skin.

"Crystal," it was Llyr's voice.

I turned and saw him immediately. He didn't look good; he was being propped up by Ri who now hovered next to him. Nephys swam over in a flash and pulled me across the small stretch of water that separated us.

"Oh darling Crystal," she said, putting a hand on my arm as I shivered. "You've had a rotten night, haven't you?"

"Too bloody right," I tremored.

Llyr left Ri's side and put his arms around me. I wrapped my arms around his neck and held him tight. *Oh, thank God he was alive. I thought we were both going to die on that thing, but we were going to be okay. We were going to be okay.*

"I'm sorry," he said eventually in my ear.

"Sorry?" I spluttered with disbelief. "Why would you be sorry?"

"I was so angry I forgot to make myself invisible. If I had been able to think straight then they would never have been able to attack me," Llyr explained.

I shook my head, unable to find the words to protest.

His face was tired and full of worry, but there was a flicker of a smile, as our gazes met. *If we could survive such an ordeal, then we could surely conquer all.*

Suddenly Ri was by his side, speaking sternly in that funny ancient language. He pointed at me and shouted.

"You can speak in human to her," said Llyr angrily, tightening his arms around me.

I knew what Ri's rage was about; there was no need to explain.

"I'm sorry," I whispered hoarsely to them.

Llyr held me. "You have nothing to be sorry for," he insisted.

"There is a boat coming," said Ri suddenly. "It is humans. Rescuers."

I turned and saw a large white boat traveling over the distant waters. A blue light flashed from its bow. It looked like the Coast Guards.

Ri turned to Llyr. "You have to come now," he said. "Nephys can wait with her."

"No, I'll stay here," said Llyr.

"Son, you are weak. You may not be able to make yourself invisible. Do you seek to be discovered again?" said Ri firmly.

"I'll be fine," he said.

"Llyr, go," I said. *I didn't want to cause any more trouble.*

"No," he said, turning away from Ri and resting his head on mine. "Leave us."

Ri shook his head; his eyes were burning with anger. He looked at the other mers who now swam in a circle around us.

"We will be beneath," he said in a stone-cold tone. He nodded to the others and one by one they each disappeared under the waves.

When we were alone, I kissed Llyr. Even despite the freezing cold, I still felt a surge of love. *He truly does care for me,* I thought as he kissed me back.

"Thank you," I said after a while. "For coming for me."

"I would do anything for you," he replied, looking into my eyes.

"Well then, will you wait for me?" I asked, looking at him pleadingly as I shivered.

He looked down and ran his hands up my arms. "Except that," he said.

I felt my eyes fill with tears. *How could he still be intent on ending this after everything we had just been through?* I let go of him and trod water, in a state of disbelief. "When two people really care about each other, they find a way to make it work no matter what," I whispered, echoing my mother's words in desperation.

"When two people care like that, they do what is best for one another," he argued softly. "This is better for you Crystal. I promise."

He pulled me to him slowly again, and we held each other for a while, as I cried.

"Is this it then?" I asked, staring at his chest, dreading the answer.

I looked up and saw that for the first time, his eyes were also glassy. "I think so," he said slowly.

I shook my head, and my tears tumbled down my face into the seas below.

"I have waited my whole life to meet someone like you," he said quietly in my ear. "Even though we weren't able to be together long, I will learn to see you like my little diamond in the sands of time."

I tried to speak but I was too upset, the most horrendous emotional pain was crippling me. I leaned my forehead helplessly against his.

I could feel the waves now from the approaching vessel.

"You are young, you will find somebody else, who can give you everything that I can't," he continued.

"No," I managed to cry. "I will never find anybody like you. You are my diamond too," I could barely get my words out, I was so cold and tormented.

"Then we will be each other's diamonds. And we will never forget each other," he said, holding me by the shoulders and looking deep into my eyes. "And we will never regret each other."

"No, never," I sobbed, as tears ran down my face.

The boat was close now. I turned my head and could see the orange decking and a couple of men leaning over the railings waving at me.

Llyr kissed my cheek. "I am invisible," he said. "Look, they are throwing you a ring."

I turned and saw that one of the lifeguards was chucking a buoy over the ship railings.

"Go," he said. "You are freezing, you need to get out of the water."

I shook my head. I couldn't bear to leave him, even despite the cold.

"Please," he said.

"No," I protested.

"Do it for me, Crystal," he said. "Please, go."

I let go of him slowly. I knew that I would remember this moment forever, and wish that I could have stayed.

"I love you. Be happy," he said to me, as I turned.

I caught hold of the ring. I could not even feel it my fingers were so numb.

I turned to Llyr to tell him I loved him too, but he was gone.

Chapter Forty-Six

A couple of weeks had passed, and I was now back at school. It was difficult getting back into the routine, but it helped to keep my mind off my heart ache.

Following the rescue, I had spent five days in bed with yet another terrible cold, but the truth was, I had been sicker from sadness than anything else.

Mum and Dad had spoiled me rotten, of course, believing that my ordeal was all their doing. When I had arrived back with the lifeguards they had hugged me with the strength of a pair of anacondas. I can't imagine how difficult it must have been for them—their only child taken hostage out at sea like that.

On the bright side, their fight against SKANX had not only brought them back together but even closer than ever. Mum had given up her funny little studio flat on the mainland and moved back to the house. In typical Mum-style she had turned her nose up at all of Dad's decorating and had insisted on a "full revamp," which was already underway.

As for SKANX, well, the factory had been closed once Mum and Dad had submitted their evidence, and it was pending a full investigation. The prognosis, I'm told, was not looking very good at all.

Of course, nobody knew the truth about how I had come to be in the water that evening while the boat had sunk, and Mr. Geake had disappeared entirely.

I had told the lifeguards and police about the kidnapping, of course, but I had added my own little twist at the end. The boat had been dodgy, I had reported, like all of SKANX's equipment and Mr. Geake had drowned trying to patch up the sinking vessel.

"I guess he fell on his own sword," I had said while everybody had murmured in agreement.

It was all highly feasible, especially given Mum's stolen documents, lifting the lid on the shambolic truth behind the company.

Nobody knew what had really happened that day with the mer, except one person, that is.

"Heard you've had quite a colourful time of late, kid," said George, as I popped my head round the door of his fisher hut one day after school.

"I don't know, George," I said, walking inside the warmly lit room. He was sitting down with his trusty mug, and an aroma of liqueur hung around him. "I'd say more blacky-greyish."

He smiled at me sympathetically. The sorrow must have been written all over my face. "You're not holding up, are you?" he said.

I sat down opposite him and put my head in my hands. "I just don't know how I'm ever going to get over him, George," I said.

He reached over the table and rubbed my arm. "I heard you two fell for each other very deeply," he said, "but it's for the best, kid."

I looked up at him.

"Yeah?" I asked, searching his face for answers, for some reinforcement that this pain was somehow worth it.

"Yeah," said George. "You don't want to get too messed up in that. You'll end up like me. A sad, old, lost man."

"Well, I'd have to have a sex-change but yeah ..." I managed to smile, putting a hand on his. It was a wrinkled, leathery hand, and I still found it incredibly hard to believe that he was the offspring of the radiant Nephys.

"Well the good news is, they took his body away from the crime scene, you know?" said George in a hushed voice. "So that things don't get complicated for you."

I nodded. I had been a little worried about what would happen if they found Mr. Geake wrapped a million times to the anchor. It was good of them to do that for me.

"George?" I asked.

"Yep?" he said brightly.

"Did your dad ever get over Nephys?"

George rolled his eyes. "Well, I wouldn't know. He was

a bit of ladies man, my father. He always had some lass on the go. It was hard to tell who he was in love with but what I do know, is that whenever he talked about her, he would go all misty eyed and gooey."

"Do you think I will ever be able to find anyone who compares to him?" I asked. "Llyr, I mean."

George laughed. "Well, he's quite catch that's for sure," he answered cocking an eyebrow.

I giggled at the pun, the first time I had felt a pinch of amusement in days.

"But, I mean you're young, gorgeous. I'm sure you could have anyone you wanted," he continued. "You may well find a charming young land-dweller one day and forget all about our Llyr."

I shook my head firmly. There was no way I could ever forget him.

"George?"

"Hmm?"

"You said you went to the Amethyst Palace once ...?"

"No, my dear. I said that I had seen it," he explained mysteriously.

"Well, how could you have seen it without going there?" I cried.

"Well, how do you see the Taj Mahal without going there?" he asked.

I was baffled. "Um, TV ... or something ...?"

George got up and walked to a shelf of books in the

corner. He pulled down an ancient book about trouts, whilst I watched on confusedly.

He fanned through some old brown pages, and a cloud of dust puffed out all around him, causing a coughing fit. When the dust cleared, I saw a little rectangular piece of paper spiraling onto the floor.

"Aha!" he exclaimed bending over, and then moaning with pain and clutched at his back. I rushed over to help him.

"Here," he grunted, handing me the piece of paper.

I took it in my hands and looked at it. It took me a while to process what it was, but once I understood, I stood there transfixed.

It was a small photograph of the most amazing coloured building I had ever seen. It was like a huge rock of lilac candy, with circular doorways and mystical chunky engravings.

A beam of light caught part of the building's jagged roof, and it sparkled, very much like the purple cliffs on Crystal Bay in the sunset. A jade-green sea garden danced around the Amethyst Palace, and I closed my eyes for a minute and envisaged Llyr here, gliding through the waters outside his home.

"My mother took it back in the nineties. I brought her a disposable underwater camera when they first came out," George explained, taking a gulp from his mug.

I smiled at him and turned back to the photo.

I guess, like George, this was the closest I would ever get

to Llyr, Nephys, and the sea people's world. A photo and a bit of visualization to fill in the gaps. *Or was it?* As I gazed on at the picture something deep inside me told me that maybe one day, I may swim within those lilac walls. But then again, I have a big imagination ...

CPSIA information can be obtained
at www.ICGtesting.com
Printed in the USA
LVOW08s1833010617
536599LV00005B/715/P